GODS BEHAVING BADLY

First Published in Great Britain 2023 by Mirador Publishing

Copyright © 2023 by John McKie

First edition: 2023

A copy of this work is available through the British Library.

ISBN: 978-1-915953-46-9

Mirador Publishing
10 Greenbrook Terrace
Taunton
Somerset
TA1 1UT

Gods Behaving Badly

John McKie

Dedication

For my Mother and Father

Contents

Over the centuries and indeed over the millennia, there have been hundreds of gods across the world belonging to many different civilisations. Only a few of them are completely virtuous and most of them indulge in some form of bad behaviour, some more than others. They can murder, cheat, trick and otherwise take revenge on humans and deities alike.

Some use brute force in battle while others use ingenuity and guile. Many have magic powers which they use for good or ill. Many are shapeshifters who can transform themselves into anything living and inanimate. Zeus, King of the Greek gods of Mount Olympus makes extensive use of this skill, morphing into a cuckoo, a swan and a bull to name but a few.

In the Norse tradition, the trickster Loki turns himself variously in to a fly, a flea and a fish among his many disguises.

Some gods start out as mortals and later achieve the status of a deity. Some start out as benefactors to humanity but become cruel tyrants, while others, like the Monkey King achieve enlightenment out of a state of condemnation.

Similarities abound between the various world religions, signifying that they may share the same roots.

One of the most frequently recurring themes is that of a creation myth, where the world is created out of chaos or nothingness. This story even applies to the Big Bang theory of today, where order is created out of a void. It also occurs in the Biblical story of creation. But creation can also emerge from primordial chaos. The Ancient Greek writer Hesiod mentions this in his writings.

Another recurring story is that of a great flood, usually sent by a deity/deities as divine retribution for the sinfulness of humanity.

Also occurring frequently is the myth of older gods being deposed by younger ones, seen as more civilised than their primordial parents, although many are far from virtuous themselves. This is probably because, in life, the young always come to replace the old.

In the Greek myth of the 'Titanomachy', the Olympian gods defeat the older deities known as the Titans, a more primitive collection of deities. In so doing they bring order and balance to creation, despite their moral shortcomings.

Similarly, the Celtic gods defeat the malevolent forces of the Fomorians, a supernatural race whom they regarded as 'demonic pirates'.

Something that all mythologies have in common is a belief in life after death. For the Vikings only warriors killed in battle could reach paradise, called Valhalla, where they remained until called upon to join the battle of Ragnarok, which would end in the fall of the gods and their enemies too.

In Ancient Greek mythology the underworld took the form of Hades, ruled by the God of Death of the same name. The Greek and Roman versions of the afterlife are very similar. A hero or a warrior could make it to the paradise known to them both as Elysium. Virtuous ordinary people were also sent to a favourable afterlife. The domain of Tartarus represented purgatory, while the more sinful people resided in Hades.

To reach the Egyptian afterlife, a person's heart would be

weighed in the 'Hall of Truth'. It would be balanced against the feather of truth and only if one's heart was lighter than the feather would one be received into the afterlife, which was an Earthly paradise. If a person's heart was heavier than the feather, they would be devoured in the jaws of the monster Ammit and would cease to exist. In any case only the nobility and royalty could be transported to paradise.

As for the gods, many got away with their misdeeds, but others were expelled from heaven and were subjected to never ending punishment.

For many of the world's mythological deities, war was their domain. Many were fertility deities or both. Fertility here refers to sexuality and that of the harvest, meaning that the deities were called upon to encourage childbirth and bountiful harvests. When these were not forthcoming, this was seen as a sign of the gods' displeasure.

There are many other similarities between world religions, both monotheistic and polytheistic, but to list but a few establishes that there are indeed connections, suggesting a common origin for beliefs across the world. These include the misbehaviour of many deities, some of whom are punished, while others escape with impunity.

African Deities

A n a n s i   t h e   S p i d e r

Derived from the Twi language, spoken by the Akan people of southern and central Ghana, Anansi translates as 'spider'. The stories about him are known as the 'Anansesem', which means 'spider stories'. According to Mythology.net he is known as the 'king of stories, a trickster, a joker' and a general mischief maker who inspired anyone who wanted to do likewise. He is a god of the Akan people who are an ethnic group that includes the Asante tribe. As such he is the subject of many stories and is a purveyor of wisdom to the world.

Anansi's mother was the Earth goddess Asaase, and his father was the sky god and creator deity Nyame. This meant that Anansi was of the Earth as well as the heavens. His wife was called Aso, and best-known son was Ntikuma who played a role in 'the bringing of wisdom to the world' (Mythology.net).

He takes the form of a spider or a man with spider-like features or a mix of the two. He usually presents himself as a spider with the head of a man or as a man with eight legs.

In these tales he uses his wits to outsmart animals that are physically stronger than him. But he usually gets his just deserts in the end which is normal for a morality story. Anansi is clever and adaptable although he can be seen as greedy and unscrupulous because of his trickery.

The message of strategy is conveyed using the symbolism of a spider since these creatures are well known for their resourcefulness and always plan ahead. Their independence and self-reliance in weaving webs to catch their prey is a talent that Anansi shares with them, but in his case, it is his selfishness that is the theme of these stories.

In one tale, Nyame was the source of all stories and knowledge which he kept hidden in a box in the heavens. Anansi wanted this knowledge for himself. To get it 'He ascended to the heavens on a silken thread' (Mythology.net), not surprisingly because he was a spider, but Nyame was nonetheless impressed with his method of transportation. He challenged Nyame to name a price for the disclosure of all that he knew. However, the sky god did not want to give his secrets away.

Nyame did not refuse but set him a task which would be almost impossible to achieve. This was as the Mythology Book describes, 'to bring him a python, a leopard, a swarm of hornets and a fairy' notorious for her petulance. Apart from the fairy these were the most fearsome creatures the people knew of.

Under his breath, Anansi's father ridiculed the idea of his son achieving these tasks, thinking that he was bound to fail in his attempts to carry them out. But Anansi was more cunning than Nyame had thought and resolved to accomplish them using his trickery skills.

First Anansi located a python residing in a hole and challenged it to reveal the length of its body. On hearing this the python slid out of the hole and offered to rest on a tree branch so that Anansi could measure him. As he did this, the snake's body jolted a little so Anansi helpfully offered to restrain him, so that he could be properly measured. The python agreed but Anansi captured him in readiness to present him to Nyame. Thus, the python's own vanity allowed Anansi to capture him.

To successfully complete the other tasks, Anansi used trickery in all of them. He caught the leopard by tricking it into falling into a hole disguised with a covering of leaves. Once he had been trapped, the leopard appealed to Anansi to release him. The trickster responded by offering to spin a web which he would use to bring the leopard up out of the hole. But once he had spun this web, Anansi used it to capture the leopard in it and take him away, outwitting this sturdy creature.

According to the Mythology Book, 'To trap the hornets, Anansi trickled water onto their nest and began drumming on the ground with little sticks', tricking the hornets into believing that it was raining. Once this illusion had been established, Anansi offered them shelter in a gourd. The hornets took up the offer, but once they had entered the gourd, Anansi plugged its opening and captured the hornets. Their hive mentality gave them strength, but Anansi had successfully used it against them.

Anansi achieved his final task, that of capturing the fairy, by presenting her with a doll that caught her attention. The doll was covered in gum so when the fairy touched her, she became stuck and unable to release itself. This enabled Anansi to carry the fairy away and in so doing he completed all the tasks he had been set, which Nyame thought he would find impossible.

Nyame was much surprised that Anansi had carried out all the fiendishly difficult tasks he had set him. He kept his word and disclosed his wisdom to Anansi and honoured him with the title of 'God of All Stories and Fables' (Mythology Book). Anansi carefully stored all this information in a gourd, known as his calabash, and decided to hide it high up on a tall tree. As he climbed the tree, he repeatedly lost his footing and fell several times. At this point, Ntikuma, Anansi's son, who had trailed his father to the site where the tree was located, started to laugh at his mishaps and told him it might be easier if he carried the gourd in a different way, by attaching it to his waist. Although angered by his son's insolence, Anansi took heed of his advice and climbed the tree again in a way in which he was more likely to be successful. However, this time although he did not fall himself, he dropped the gourd and it shattered into many pieces.

At this point torrential rain started to fall and swept away the contents of the shattered gourd into a nearby river and eventually out to sea. This allowed all the people of the world to share the knowledge that Nyame had given Anansi. Because of this he lost his role as 'the God of all Stories and Fables' since the tales were known to everyone. Anansi consoled himself with the fact that what he had lost was now effectively worthless.

Another tale states that while Anansi was preparing his lunch, a turtle, encouraged by the smell of the food, knocked on the door, wanting to join him in eating the meal. Anansi was not keen to share the food but grudgingly admitted him. Anansi told him he needed to wash his hands before eating. Observing his hands, the turtle saw that this was a fair point and left briefly to cleanse them in a close-by stream. When he returned, Anansi was already eating. The turtle sat down to eat, but Anansi told him his hands were still dirty. The turtle duly went back to the water and washed them again. By the time he returned, Anansi had eaten all the food apart from a tiny morsel. The dejected turtle went home with his appetite unsatisfied. He kindly invited Anansi 'to join him for a meal sometime' (Verona Spence-Adofo).

It was not long before Anansi decided to take up the offer and went to visit the turtle for dinner. The turtle's home was a house at the bottom of a river. Anansi hungrily plunged in but, he found that, as a spider, he was so lightweight that he kept returning to the surface of the water. He decided to weigh himself down by putting stones in his pockets and dive in again. This time he was successful. Anansi hungrily sat down to eat, but the turtle asked him to take off his jacket before partaking in the meal, as it was not good manners to eat with your jacket on.

Anansi did as he was asked but found himself floating back to the surface of the river. Dejected and hungry, Anansi looked back into the water and saw the turtle enjoying his meal, having got his own back on Anansi.

Storytelling is an important part of African culture and as Spence-Adofo puts it: 'these are a means by which wisdom, social norms and the cohesion of society are imparted'. They were passed down orally from one generation to the next. By delving deeper into these child-like stories the underlying messages about Anansi's character can be understood, as we see the unfortunate results of his actions.

The fact that Anansi usually comes in for some form of comeuppance for his victories, is a way of teaching us to treat others as we would like to be treated ourselves. These simple stories convey what Spence-Adofo calls 'complex universal principles'.

Additionally, from Anansi we learn the need for planning ahead and calculating before making all decisions. Anansi shows us the need for strategy and perception of our situation.

In African culture, every aspect of nature is an embodiment of the creator god Nyame and as such it is treated with the utmost respect. It is not unusual in African folklore that as a trickster, Anansi straddles the human world and the spirit world and acts as a go-between for humanity and his father, the supreme god Nyame.

Stories about Anansi were passed down from one generation to the next by the Asante people of Ghana and are known throughout West Africa and the Caribbean. The stories have become so prevalent in popular culture 'that they have influenced plays, TV programmes and books' (Spence-Adofo). These include the Brer Rabbit fables, passed on by African Americans and the peoples of the Caribbean.

The adventures of Anansi have a purpose in moral instruction, to show that selfishness will not be rewarded. But the spider god is an expert in strategy and trickery, which he tries to use to his advantage. The fact that the eventual outcome is usually not good for Anansi is meant as a cautionary tale. We have much to learn from Anansi's abilities but also his greed which feature in the stories.

E s h u

The religion of the Yoruba people of West Africa, Nigeria, Benin, and Togo in particular, is known locally as the 'Ifa', in which people venerate spirits called Orisha, on a daily basis. As the Mythology Book explains, 'these include mortal heroes from the past who have been deified'. One individual who crops up in Yoruba legends many times is Eshu the trickster god, known in some places as Esu-Elegbara.

As Erik Davis puts it: Eshu is 'young, small and spry and has a ravishing sexual appetite'. Some of his escapades may seem innocent and amusing, but on occasion his actions can be harmful to humans.

Eshu is the Yoruba God of Chaos but contrastingly is also in charge of delivering justice on the people, and in keeping the balance of creation.

As well as being responsible for both mayhem and harmony, Eshu also has a role as a messenger between the people and their gods. To enact this, people are supposed to make sacrifice to Eshu. In return he brings 'divine gifts such as knowledge' to them (Mythology Book). He is omnipotent and can carry any message across the world in an instant.

Hermes is the European pre-Christian god most closely associated with Eshu, since they are both messenger gods who allow communication between the gods and the people. They are both known for their quick-wittedness and agility which makes them suitable for the job.

Eshu is also associated with the symbolism of the crossroads, where people's choices determine their future fortunes. He is known as a 'road-maker' because of his role in creating order in the world, as well as being a bringer of chaos.

The duality of Eshu's role is reflected in the Yoruban concepts of 'ori' and 'ese' meaning 'head' and 'legs'. While ori is, according to the Mythology Book, 'basically a person's potential and destiny', ese represents their hard work. Eshu's Yoruba worshipers see both these qualities as essential for success in life.

Eshu is a trickster, not just because he hoodwinks people and causes chaos and confusion, but also because he does not abide by the rules he himself has implemented. The fact that he has human failings makes him a more approachable god, in West African tradition. After tricking many suitors of the daughter of a Yoruba king, he took their place as her suitor. Her father was impressed by what Eshu had done and declared that he could sleep with any woman of his choosing and installed him as an intermediary between the people and the gods.

To the Fon tribe, who live adjacent to the Yoruba, he is known by the name of 'Legba'. For them too, he is omnipresent and speaks both the language of the gods and that of humans which allows him to act as an interpreter between the two parties. However, he is well known for his trickery when conveying messages, which makes communication unreliable. He is known to the Fon by the nickname 'Aflakete', meaning 'I have tricked you'.

The Orisha are deities of two kinds. One type is represented by the colour white, symbolising calm and gentleness, while the other is associated with the colours red and black, denoting, as the Mythology Book puts it, 'a more aggressive and mercurial nature'. Illustrations of Eshu typically show him wearing a black and red coloured hat.

According to Fon mythology he keeps the peace between the Orisha by the way he conveys information between them. One of his fellow Orishas once asked him 'Why don't you speak straightforwardly?' 'I never do,' he replied, 'I like to make people think' (Davis). He carries out many plots which run the risk of wreaking havoc in people's lives, but they also offer people the opportunity to act in a dynamic way, rather than remaining static.

Eshu is one of the foremost trickster deities in the world and is a leading West African Orisha. He is the most significant Orisha to those who do not worship them, because of his role as a communicator.

The gender-neutral creator god Olodumare delegated communication with the human population to these lesser gods, especially Eshu. The people did not make representations to Olodumare or build monuments in his name.

Legend has it that on one occasion, Olodumare, the supreme deity, called a meeting of all the Orishas to decide who should be his second-in-command. He declared that each must come carrying a huge sacrifice on his/her head (Davis). Keen to ingratiate himself, Eshu prepared to come bearing such a burden. But, according to Davis he consulted an oracle and realised that 'all he needed to bring was a bright red feather on his forehead'. When Olodumare saw this, he conferred on Eshu power over 'Ashe', a Yoruba word for a philosophical concept the tribespeople invoke to influence the course of events. He did this because Eshu was wise enough to come forward without a heavy burden, but also because of his ability as a messenger to impart information.

The reciprocal relationship between Eshu and the people means that the gods never go hungry for want of sacrifice. But Eshu tricks people into doing things which will incur the displeasure of the gods, so that they then feel the need to make sacrificial offerings, to keep on the right side of them. Yet as a skilled mediator and communicator, he moves between the realm of the gods and the people instantaneously, carrying messages between them.

Because he links the supernatural powers of the gods with the daily lives of the people, it is not surprising that he is associated with divination. But Eshu's powers of divination are somewhat ambiguous, since the information he gleans from the oracles is itself ambiguous, a quality for which they are well known.

Eshu's role in handing down justice means that he is prone to mete out punishment on the people, especially if he thinks they do not show him proper respect. According to an account in the Mythology Book, one such individual was a king who had never made any sacrifices to Eshu. Although the king had many wives, he showed a lack of interest in them, and one of these in particular took great offence at this. She decided to make a bargain with Eshu and pluck some hairs from the king's beard and use them to make a potion which she hoped would reinvigorate the King's passions.

Eshu disguised himself as a retainer to the King and visited the monarch's eldest son, who was heir to the throne but felt unjustly treated by his father. In the guise of the servant, Eshu told the king's son to bring his warriors that night to the royal palace since his father wanted to embark on a military campaign. Finally, Eshu visited the king in the guise of 'a trusted page' (Mythology Book) and told him that one of his wives was planning to kill him that night, hoping to replace him with his son as the new ruler. Eshu told the

King that he should take precautions to guard against this outcome.

That night the King stayed awake and when his wife who had conspired with Eshu crept into his chamber, to cut off a few of his whiskers to formulate the potion, the King assumed she was trying to kill him and grabbed the knife from her. The King's son, who was outside with his soldiers, heard the altercation and burst into the room. There he found his mother, apparently being threatened by her husband the King with the knife in his hand. The King's son assumed his father was trying to kill her.

At this very moment, the King, seeing that his son had arrived with a band of soldiers, thought that he was trying to usurp him. In the ensuing violence, the King, his wife and his son were all killed, and Eshu had got his revenge.

There is also a tale in the Mythology Book of two women who were 'the best of friends' and were almost inseparable. They wore identical clothing and took a pair of brothers as their husbands. They made a vow that they would be friends for life. To do this formally they approached a Babalawo (diviner), who cast sacred palm nuts to foretell the future and advised the two women to make a sacrifice to Eshu. But the women failed to do so, and Eshu decided, as the Mythology Book puts it, to 'teach them a lesson'.

He appeared to them while they were working in the fields digging the soil, wearing an extravagant hat which was white on one side and red on the other. One of the women remarked on the marvellous red hat the trickster was wearing. Her companion told her it was plainly a white one. They carried on with their work, but Eshu soon returned wearing the hat the other way round. The woman who had remarked on his red hat apologised to her friend and said that it was white. Her companion thought she was mocking her because she could now see that the hat was red. An altercation ensued, but they realised their friendship was more important. They took the Babalawo's advice and offered a sacrifice to Eshu. In return for this Eshu blessed their friendship, which lasted for the rest of their days.

While West African communities treated Eshu with great reverence, slaves taken forcibly from there to work in the Caribbean and the Americas had to worship their gods in secret or present them in the likeness of Christian saints. African traditions of 'song, dance and drum' (Davis) were disguised as celebrations of Christian festivals. At this time there were no written records of the Yoruba religion which was passed down the generations by word of mouth and represented by shrines and religious rites.

The various geographical groups (tribes) of African slaves developed the God Eshu in their own ways based on their various versions of him. His use of deception and retribution made him a popular deity amongst African slaves because he could be invoked to take revenge on the slave-owners.

Eshu's conflicted role as a bringer of both order and chaos, and the trickery which he often employed make him an ambiguous deity. He could convey messages and restore balance to the scheme of things, but he could also be a reckless mischief maker, which made him a hero of the enslaved plantation workers.

Oshun

Oshun brought all life to the world including humans, which the 16 male spirits, known as Orishas, had tried but failed to do without her. This is why she is venerated as Dani Rhys puts it as the 'giver of life and fertility'. If it was not for her interventions, the world would be devoid of life.

Oshun is a West African Orisha (deity) of the Yoruba faith who is first and foremost 'The River Goddess'. As well as this she is a patron of 'love and purity, prosperity, fertility and beauty' (Rhys).

For the people of the Yoruba region of West Africa, Oshun represents the empowerment of women and supports them in their daily lives, especially when they want to have children. Women faced with fertility problems petition her for relief. She is also a symbol of the fertility of the land and during periods of drought people pray to her to bring rain.

Although she ranks highest amongst the Orishas, Oshun has human-like fallibilities which will be addressed later in this chapter.

As the goddess of nourishing waters, such as rivers, she is associated with agricultural abundance and thus prosperity, having taught the people the skills of agriculture. She also instils the waters with healing properties. She is known, as

Ancient Origins describes, as a 'comforter of the poor, a mother to all orphans as well as a healer of the sick'. She also brought culture to the people, including 'music, singing and dancing' (Ancient Origins). As a goddess of love, she is associated with marriage, women with child and passion. She was also the epitome of beauty. Fine credentials indeed!

According to Joshua J Mark, 'she was possibly the most popular deity of the Yoruba', relevant to everyone, and this popularity continued amongst the slave populations of the 'New World'. These Yoruba slaves were nominally Christian but their own religion, known as Isese, persisted in their new locations. The word 'Isese' meant 'origin of our traditions' as the enslaved people managed to keep their culture alive.

In the Brazilian hybrid religion, known as Candomble, the Yoruba people adapted to merge their faith with Christianity, where Oshun took the name Oxum as well as other names based on the powers that she possessed. In the Caribbean version of the hybrid religion called Santería, as well as in voodoo practices, she took the name of Ochun and despite the nominal conversion of the diaspora, according to Mark, she 'remained a fertility goddess and a protector of women'.

The Yoruba religion itself dates back millennia. In many ancient world religions, love was the domain of a goddess. For the Yoruba people of West Africa this was Oshun who features amongst the great goddesses of the ancient world including Aphrodite, Freya and Venus.

Usually depicted as attractive, coy and youthful, she is sometimes shown holding a mirror, admiring her own good looks. She is usually dressed in gold and bedecked with jewellery, carrying a pot of honey which symbolises 'female fertility and male sexual pleasure' (Rhys) as well as being a sign of good luck. As a luxury condiment, it is associated with wealth and prosperity. The colour gold is not only a symbol of affluence, but along with yellow and amber represents the emotions of love and compassion as well as the attributes of light, courage, wisdom and sorcery. Oshun sometimes appears in the form of a mermaid which relates to her role as a water goddess.

In veneration of Oshun many African women wear pendants made from gold not only in the west of the continent but in the east as well. They hope that this will bring them what Rhys describes as 'fertility, femininity, sensuality and happiness'.

She is fabled to be a goddess with a plethora of husbands and casual lovers, the most significant being her husband Shango who presided of over storms, thunder and lightning. She was also the favourite Orisha of the supreme god Olodumare. He took pity on her when she appeared in the form of an injured peacock. In this guise she showed perseverance in bringing the news of the Orisha's repentance to Olodumare, after they had rebelled against him. She persuaded him not to unleash deluges on the world which he had been minded to do.

Oshun never participated in the various plots of the other 16 Orishas against Olodumare. She was the youngest of them as well as the only female. Sometimes described as the daughter of Yemaya, or Yemaya's younger sister according to other sources.

According to the Yoruba faith, known as Isese, after the supreme deity Olodumare had separated the land from the sea, he sent forth the 17 Orishas to the world to complete the work of creation.

The 16 male Orishas ignored Oshun's suggestions as to how to bring beauty and meaning to life, which meant that their efforts were unsuccessful. Seeing what they had done they were forced to apologise and allowed Oshun to instil 'love, fertility and beauty' (Mark) in the world, thus completing the work of creation.

Although she helped create and later save the world, she could also be destructive to those who were disrespectful to her. As a water goddess she could choose to withhold the rain, just as Olodumare had done, or send deluges to sweep away those whom she believed had wronged her or been ungrateful. Aside from this, Oshun is a benefactor to humanity.

For Oshun, both vultures and peacocks are sacred symbols of her power, since she had on occasions, transformed herself into both. These sacred birds represented, as Rhys puts it: Oshun's qualities of 'courage, perseverance and healing waters as well as life itself'.

Another of her associations is with the skunk, which represents independence and safeguarding. Otters, which symbolise liveliness and enjoyment of life, are also associated with the goddess, as well as butterflies and bees which are, according to Mark, 'both linked with fertility, happiness and change'.

The link with transformation has endless possibilities but is often associated with women's reproductive health as well as the spiritual and mental well-being of people in general.

Rhys explains that the Yoruba faith is celebrated with 'music and dancing as well as healing ceremonies'. Oshun is seen as a mother figure who protects and nurtures those who worship her and is seen as 'the Keeper of the Spiritual Balance' (Rhys).

As a very beautiful female deity, Oshun even won over the gender neutral Olodumare and became his favourite Orisha. A number of stories relate her various escapades.

According to one story, whilst out walking one day on the riverbank, Oshun was spotted by Ogun, who strongly desired her. He went in pursuit of her, and she fled into the river and was carried downstream. The goddess Yemaya, 'mother of the waters', saw that she was in difficulties in the water and rescued her. She gave Oshun jurisdiction over freshwater, so that she would always have a safe place of escape.

She has her own distinct personality and is fallible in the same way as humans, which means that people find her easier to relate to than a distant, infallible god. Oshun is reputed to have become jealous of her husband's lover Oyo, who was to become his third wife. Oyo asked her how to create Shango's favourite meal. Oshun set out to demonstrate to her how this would be done. Before she started, she wrapped a scarf around her head, concealing her ears. She added a type of mushroom to the delicacy which looked like a human ear. Shango ate the meal and greatly enjoyed it, so Oyo later tried to recreate it. Thinking that Oshun had cut off her own ears to make the meal, Oyo did the same to her own, to add to the offering. Shango was disgusted by this supposed delicacy and turned it away. As a result, Oshun and Shango laughed together at Oyo's expense.

With such human-like failings in a deity who was usually associated with good deeds and light, according to Yoruba tradition, this helps people forgive themselves for their own failings.

For centuries, many women have seen Oshun as their own personal deity and continue to do so. To many, Oshun is a source of self-empowerment who helps them achieve transformation and change in their lives. She inspires both men and women to greater self-awareness and to see the need in others for 'love, respect, and happiness' (Mark) as well as in themselves.

According to another story in Yoruba mythology, people migrating to seek out water sources settled on the banks of a river, only to discover to their great surprise that this territory belonged to Oshun. The goddess asked them to move their settlement farther up the river, since humans could not live near members of the spirit world. They deferred to her wishes and departed from their dwelling place of Osogbo, which became the sacred grove of Osun-Osogbo.

This sacred site in Nigeria has existed for many centuries. In the past there were many of these but today this is the only one surviving. According to Ancient Origins, the forest contains 'many sculptures and works of art, 40 shrines and two temples' dedicated to the water goddess. It was granted World Heritage Status in 2005 and continues to be a place of worship to this day.

The 12-day festival of Ibo-Oshun takes place at the sacred grove every August and is believed to have done so for many centuries. Since it was granted World Heritage Site in 2005, the additional publicity means that people from around the world are interested in the goddess and the qualities she brings to the world. The celebrations are attended by many people from across Nigeria and the world in general.

Shango

Originally a mortal king, Shango, also known as Chango or Xango, is, as Dani Rhys puts it: 'a god of thunder, lightning and war, worshipped by the Yoruba people of West Africa' and their diaspora in the Americas. He is seen by the Yoruba people as the most senior Orisha (spirit), which are known as Isese, and is regarded as an intermediary between the people and the somewhat distant supreme being Olodumare.

Nonetheless, he is a warlike individual known for his formidable power and belligerence. Shango's role as a bringer of thunder and lightning eventually led to his own demise as King of the Oyo Empire, which was, as described by Rhys 'the most powerful political group in Yorubaland'. The majority of his followers lived in what is now western Nigeria, but the region also took in Togo and Benin. The empire existed concurrently with the European medieval era and was a powerful force in the region until the arrival of European slave traders in the seventeenth century.

Shango was the Empire's fourth king, or Alaafin in the Yoruba language, which means 'Owner of the Palace'. The most significant of Shango's wives were Queens Oshu, Oba and Oya. According to Rhys, these three were also venerated as Orishas by the Yoruba.

For a society that placed great store on ancestor worship, it is not surprising that mortal people, like Shango became deified after death. Shango was probably the most powerful of these individuals.

He presided over many military victories and under his rule the Empire enjoyed great prosperity, according to Yoruba tradition. He ruled for seven years until his life ended in an apparent suicide, but this explanation was dismissed by his followers who said that he had instead become a god.

There are many myths concerning Shango, some of which have connections with historical fact. As well as being a great warrior, he was known to dabble in the magic arts and acted as a medicine man.

Legend has it that when Shango became entangled with the magic arts, in an angry outburst, he misused his powers by sending out lightning strikes to smite his enemies, accidentally killing some of his own wives and children in the process.

It is for this reason that he is thought to have ended his life. The story goes that when he went for an expedition on horseback, but did not come back, his servants sought him out and eventually came across his apparent suicide. There are differing accounts of the circumstances of his death, but it is generally believed that he was as the University of Miami website describes it 'found hanging from an Ayan tree with his horse close by'. His followers did not accept suicide as the explanation of his death, saying instead that he had become a god. His deification can be seen as a shrewd move by the House of Oyo to distract from his reputation as a despot.

Those who did not accept his elevation to the status of a god were believed to be vulnerable to lightning strikes on their homes. Such incidents increased the awe in which Shango was held, bringing about a popular cult of Shango as the most important of the Orishas. According to the University of Miami

'This cult was rich in symbolism and complex rituals'. In Yorubaland, a person whose house had been struck by lightning is expected to consult a priest, to find the best way of appeasing the deity.

Being an aggressive deity, Shango is often depicted wielding an axe. This double-headed implement is one of his most sacred attributes, which he is believed to use to dispense lightning bolts on people's homes. Small, hand carved images of Shango exist depicting the deity standing, or sometimes in a seated position, brandishing his axe as well as a sword. Sometimes he is portrayed with a cigar in his hand. These objects are important for the power imbued in them rather than for artistic merit.

Images of the god on horseback can also be found in Africa and the Americas. His association with horses is due to the importance of these animals in Yoruba warfare. In shamanistic cults like Shango's, horses are often seen as transporters of souls to the afterlife. He is also associated with the number five, which is considered sacred to him, and he is traditionally celebrated 'on the fifth day of each week' (Rhys).

Shango's priests dress and act effeminately when doing official business such as carrying out religious rites, which reflects the fact that Shango can adopt whichever gender he prefers. This is believed to make it easier for him to carry out his work.

There are three possible methods of becoming a devotee of Shango. One is to be born with a sign of Shango and it is also possible to receive a sign from him by consulting a diviner. The other way to receive a sign is by carrying out an exacting initiation.

Fire is used in the initiation rituals for the followers (sons) of Shango as well as a mesmerising beat of drums that send the candidate into a trance. The candidates are mostly male but can on occasion be female. They carry out rituals of purification by fire. This is an onerous task and sometimes they are asked to put their hand into the flames or even swallow fire.

Since he is a hot-headed god of war, this connection of heat with Shango is particularly significant and for this reason, Shango is associated with the colour red. His mother, Oblata, added her own colour, white, to cool him down. Priests will pour cooling water over shells and coconuts which they use as divining instruments as well as showering it over the heads of the initiates.

As the University of Miami website explains, 'initiation takes approximately one year and is a very expensive process' for which the priest will charge a hefty fee. Initiates make a pact with Shango to serve him and make sacrifice to him, in return for his help throughout their lives. Other Orishas have their own cult followings which all include ceremonies and customs of their own.

Yoruba slaves were transported to the Americas from the seventeenth to nineteenth centuries to work as slaves for plantation owners, taking with them their indigenous forms of worship.

The Yoruba religion spread from West Africa to Cuba and the 'New World' where it was conflated with the teachings of the Roman Catholic Church and the Yoruba Orishas became associated with the Catholic saints. The most significant of these is Shango. The process by which traditional beliefs became intertwined with the doctrines of the Christian Church is known as 'syncretism'. This took place over the centuries in the diaspora communities of the Americas, and still persists today.

In the syncretic religions Shango is conflated with the female Saint Barbara, patron saint of the military and others who risk their lives at work. The Cuban version of syncretic beliefs was called 'Santería', in which the god was known as Sango, while the Brazilian version was called Candomblé. At the time of the slave trade, Brazil was a Portuguese colony.

The word 'Shango' is synonymous between the name of the god and that of the syncretic religious practices that are followed in the former colonies of Trinidad and Tobago. This belief-system is similar to Santería and Candomblé, with Shango being the chief Orisha/Saint.

The stories of Shango as a glorious warrior were transmitted to the 'New World', especially Cuba. This was despite the fact that the Yoruba faith was subsumed into the Christian religion. It continued to develop his reputation as being a warlike god, concerned with freedom and adventure. Over time he came to be seen as a more human, fallible god.

As Rhys explains, one of the principal Orishas in Yorubaland is Oko, 'God of Farming and Agriculture'. It is not surprising then that the slave population working on the plantations were not keen to worship this god. Instead, they preferred to worship Shango, which was more appropriate given their situation.

Shango rose to fame amongst the enslaved plantation workers. He continued to play an important role in Yoruba religion (Isese) and especially in the syncretic religions of the 'New World', which persist to this day. His role as a god of aggression and belligerence suited the slave diaspora very well, because of their hostility to the slave owners, whom they hoped that Shango would smite on their behalf.

Asian & East Asian Deities

Brahma

According to early Hindu sources such as the Mahabharata, Brahma was the leader of a trinity of gods whose other members were Shiva and Vishnu.

Brahma is the source of all wisdom for both deities and humanity. As the creator of all things, he is credited not only with creating life and the universe, but also of every god in the Hindu tradition.

According to New World Encyclopedia, he 'represents the creative aspects of The Brahman which is the supreme cosmic spirit in Hinduism'. The two names originate with the Sanskrit root, 'bhr' which translates as 'to grow great and strong' but the two are distinct and separate beings. The Brahman is the source of all being, while Brahma merely represents the personification of The Brahman's power. He is the purveyor of all knowledge to deities and humans alike.

Brahma is frequently depicted as a four headed god. For this reason, he is sometimes referred to as 'Chaturanana' or 'Chaturmukha' meaning 'four headed' or Astakarna ('eight eared'). He is often shown with four faces each decorated with a white beard, indicating the longevity of his existence. He also has four arms each carrying symbolic items, sometimes including his bow Parivita and the sacred scriptures known as the four Vedas. In other illustrations he is depicted carrying no weapons of any sort. Instead, in one hand he holds a spoon which represents those used to anoint members of the Hindu faith, denoting their destiny. He also carries a cleansing vase and a rosary. He is most often depicted seated on a lotus flower, which represents The Earth. In most illustrations he is red in colour which represents fire or the power of the Sun.

His means of transportation was sometimes a peacock while on other occasions he travelled on a goose or a swan. This reflects his epithet 'Eka Hamsa', meaning 'One Swan'.

In Cambodia he is called 'Prah Prohm' and is often depicted flying through the air on a sacred goose, whose name was 'the Hamsa'. He is also represented in this way in Javanese art, in many illustrations. In Tibet he is known as 'Tshangs-pa' or Tshangs-pa dkar-po (White Brahma), and is often shown on horseback and carrying a sword.

Brahma had various wives, of whom Saraswati was the most important. It was Saraswati who brought forth for him the four Vedas (Holy books of Hinduism) and the Sanskrit language. She is also credited with bringing him the concepts of 'memory and victory' (Mark Cartwright) as well as the art of yoga. Brahma had several sons, including a group known as the 'Seven Sages', who helped him create the universe. These were sons of his mind (manas Patras), rather than his biological sons, which helps explain why Brahma is associated with thought and the ability to comprehend things. He also had four sons known as the 'Prajapati', meaning 'lords of all creatures', who were the ancestors of humanity, although in later Vedic texts these spirits become synonymous with the god himself.

One story of Brahma's origin is that he sprang forth from a lotus plant that grew out of Vishnu's navel. Another tale describes how originally the world consisted of nothing but a vast ocean, empty save for a magical egg. From this he hatched into the personified creator, while the remains of the egg were transformed into the universe. Sanskrit texts such as The Mundaka Upanishad explain how Brahma was the first Hindu deity to come into being and became the creator of the universe.

As Cartwright puts it, he 'created light and darkness, good and evil from his own person'. He created four types of beings: 'gods, demons, ancestors and men'. First, he created the demons from his own body, which he then abandoned and turned into night-time. In the same way he created the gods and then abandoned his own body which transformed into daytime. The gods are seen by the faithful as rulers of the day while the demons preside over the night. Next Brahma 'created ancestors and men again abandoning his body and turning it into dusk and dawn respectively' (Cartwright).

The first man he created was named Manu. Next, he brought all the creatures of the world to life, although some sources say his son Daksa, one of the Seven Sages, did this. Finally, Brahma deputed Shiva to become ruler of humanity but, later texts state that Brahma eventually became a servant of Shiva.

According to the ancient Hindu text, the Mahabharata, after creating men, Brahma created women, who were seen as the source of all evil in the world, rather like the Old Testament creation story. It was believed that Brahma did this to distract men whom he feared would otherwise become powerful enough to depose him.

In another version of the story, Brahma's first woman is 'death', an evil force but a necessary one to stop the world becoming overcrowded. She is described in old texts as dark in appearance and red eyed, wearing red clothing and adorned with jewellery.

Despite her foreboding appearance, she was very reluctant to take on the role of a deity of death, which Brahma had ascribed to her, and pleaded with him to relent. But Brahma was indifferent to her anguish and insisted she performed these duties.

In protest at being required to be the 'Goddess of Death', she performed various desperate acts including feats described by Cartwright as 'standing in water in silence for eight thousand years [and] standing on one toe on the top of the Himalayas for eight million years'. After she had done all this, Brahma still refused to budge, so Death, in tears, finally succumbed to his will. Her tears became diseases which afflicted the human population. Thus, Death reluctantly established the distinction between gods and mortals. Yet little did he know, eventually Brahma would be subject to divine condemnation himself.

A myth concerning his consort, Sarasvati, a goddess of art and education, explains why Brahma was relegated to a deity of lesser status. It concerns a sacrificial fire ceremony to be presided over by the most senior deity and led by a sage called Braharishi Bhrigu. The priest set out to ascertain which of the three members of the trinity of Brahma, Vishnu and Shiva was the greatest. When the priest found Brahma, the god was so captivated by Sarasvati's music making, that he ignored the priest's attentions. This made Bhrigu so enraged that he cursed Brahma never to be worshipped or invoked again. Although this destiny was not completely fulfilled, Brahma's lofty status was never the same again.

Another story goes that Brahma previously had five heads but one of them was cut off by Shiva who was enraged by Brahma's lusty regards for his own daughter, the goddess Sandhya, who would take on '100 beautiful forms' (New World Encyclopedia). She was affronted by Brahma's staring at her, so she moved in different directions to avoid his lustful attention. Brahma responded by giving himself five heads so that he could look at her in any direction she chose to go. Four of these heads each faced one of the four cardinal directions (points of the compass), while the fifth was above them, one which Brahma was destined to lose.

Ever since this time, Brahma has tried to atone for his sins by reciting the four Vedas (holy texts) with each of his remaining heads. According to the Puranas texts, Shiva not only cut off one of Brahma's heads, but decreed that he should be worshipped no more.

A different tale relates how Brahma visited Shiva with Vishnu and asked him the whereabouts of his 'beginning and his end'. The pair agreed that Vishnu would search for Shiva's end, while Brahma would search for his beginning. They both set forth in search of these but were unable to find what they were looking for. Vishnu approached Shiva respectfully and conceded in his task, while Brahma would not give up so easily.

While searching for Shiva's beginning, Brahma discovered a Kaitha flower and according to New World Encyclopedia, demanded of it that it should 'bear false witness that he had found Shiva's beginning'. When Brahma returned to Shiva's abode and reported the false claim to him, Shiva was so angered by Brahma's attitude that he put a curse on him. He also decreed that henceforth no one should worship Brahma.

The various myths about Brahma explain the decline in his popularity. While Shiva and Vishnu are still highly venerated today, Brahma very much takes a back seat. Although there are thousands of temples in India dedicated to the former two deities, only two temples dedicated to Brahma still exist. The best known of the two is at Pushkar in Rajistan, India and the other is at Kumbanad in Tamil Nadu state (formerly Madras).

He is worshipped to this day at an annual ceremony that takes place at Pushkar, which attracts pilgrims, and is also commemorated in Southeast Asia, especially Thailand and

Bali. Still an important figure in Hindu mythology, he is reputed to reside in Brahmapur city, a mythical place believed to be located on Mount Meru.

As the creator of the world, Brahma was possibly the greatest Hindu deity, but his own personal failings led to his fall from grace. Yet he did not lose out completely and has not been forgotten by the Hindu faithful.

Shiva

According to Mark Cartwright, Shiva is one of the most senior gods in the Hindu pantheon and is recognised as part of the Hindu trinity which also includes Vishnu and Brahma. He is a benevolent protector, yet conversely, he is also a master of evil spirits, thieves, villains and beggars. For the Shaivism sect he is the most important Hindu deity.

The name Shiva translates from the Sanskrit as 'auspicious one' and in the Tamil language means 'the supreme one'. According to legend, Shiva destroys and remakes the world every 2,160,000,000 years.

In the Hindu faith, deities go by various different names, depending on the specific stories about them, their associated functions and the manner in which they carry them out. Sometimes the same name is given to multiple deities, but where a name belongs to one god alone it is easier to identify their particular functions. Eight different versions of the Hindu text 'The Shiva Sahasra Nama' record a variety of names given to Shiva. Historians believe that various different versions of the identity of Shiva were adopted in different regions and were assimilated into one individual over time.

There are also various human incarnations of Shiva, which can be described as avatars. These include the eighth century philosopher Adi Shankara and Hanuman who is believed to be another of Shiva's 11 human avatars.

Shiva is a patron of people who practice yoga, known as Yogis and Brahmins, who are of high caste. He is also the guardian of the Vedas, which are Hindu sacred texts. Additionally, he is revered as a patron of householders.

Shiva is often found in the company of a band of spirits, called the Gana Gana. They are usually benign in nature but when their master is angry, they can carry out retribution. Shiva appointed his son Ganesha as their leader.

In one well known Sanskrit epic, the Mahabharata texts, Shiva is both invincible, mighty and ferocious as well as being imbued with integrity and wisdom who is reputed to be 'a bringer of delight'. As New World Encyclopedia explains he is associated with 'destruction and generation, eroticism and asceticism, sexuality and celibacy'.

One aspect of his personality, his asceticism, means abstinence from every kind of pleasurable indulgence, finding comfort in meditation instead. This is in stark contrast to his darker side, alluded to above. Shiva can thus be seen to have a dualistic personality.

Shiva's ambiguity as a figure of benevolence and destruction has led to him being attributed with a number of different names and characteristics. The name Rudra refers to the terrifying side of his personality. It translates from the Sanskrit root 'rud' which means to cry or to howl. Two other fearsome forms in which he manifests himself are that of Kala (time) and Mahakala (great time), 'the destroyer of all things', which Shiva adopts when bringing creation to an end. Another of his manifestations is Bhairavi (the terrible), who is also associated with destruction. In his benevolent guise he is given the name Sankara, meaning 'he who is beneficent and confers happiness'.

Shiva is worshipped in various South Asian societies and the stories told about him vary from one place to another, including Indian, Cambodian and Javanese. He has a supernatural third eye on his forehead which burns everything he gazes upon. He is usually represented as 'naked, with multiple arms and three horizontal stripes across his body' (Cartwright), sometimes carrying a trident. His hair is usually tied up in a top knot, and he wears a crown embossed with a skull that represents the head of Brahma, as well as the symbol of a crescent moon. This had earlier been lopped off by Shiva, because of Brahma's sinful acts. He also wears a necklace designed with a set of model heads, and a bracelet adorned with snake images. He holds a burning torch which he uses to destroy the world periodically before recreating it again and he also carries a drum which, as Cartwright puts it: 'makes the first sound in creation'.

In other examples of Shiva in art, he is shown with one leg raised and clasping a rosary in one of his many hands, a posture that represents meditation and quiet reflection. Sometimes he is portrayed riding on his sacred white bull, Nandi, and carries a silver bow (Pinaka). In some illustrations he is depicted wearing the hide of a tiger or elephant, which only the most senior Hindu ascetics, the Brahmarishis, were allowed to do. Shiva often has an ash-smeared appearance which may be related to the Hindu practice of cremation. For this he is given the title 'inhabitant of the creation ground'. He is often illustrated pressing down on the figure of a dwarf (Apasmara Purusha), with one foot, symbolically defeating illusion and the force that leads people onto the wrong path.

During the Vedic period (1500-600 BCE) in Hindu culture, sacrificial offerings were made to many deities, but later the concepts of 'yoga and asceticism became more important' (New World Encyclopedia). During this time images of Shiva seated in the yoga position became more popular. Yet Shiva is also portrayed as a family man with his wife Parvati and his two sons Ganesha and Skanda.

Parvati is identified as the 'Divine Mother' and the personification of divine energy. The couple also have a daughter, Kartikeya, who is popular in southern India, especially Tamil Nadu (formerly Madras), as well as in Northern India. In both regions she is known by a different name.

Shiva's wife Parvati is seen as the reincarnation of Shakti, whose father was the god Daksha. Her father so strongly disapproved of the marriage that he invited all the gods to a sacrificial rite except for Shiva. Shakti was so distraught at this slight to her husband that she leaped onto the sacrificial fire, which led to her reincarnation as Parvati. Shiva was so enraged by what Daksha had done and the consequences of it that he plucked hairs from his head which he transformed into two demons who brought chaos and confusion to the proceedings. He also summarily beheaded Daksha. The other gods at the ceremony pleaded with Shiva to put a stop to the mayhem, which he did. He also brought Daksha back to life, but this time he was cursed with the head of an animal, such as a ram or a goat. Once Shakti was reincarnated as Parvati, she became Shiva's wife for a second time, albeit in a new persona.

Parvati longed for a child, but Shiva had no such ambition. As the Mythology Book describes: Eventually when having a bath, she 'formed the dirt on her skin into a child, which came to life'. She asked the boy to guard the door while she was bathing, whereupon Shiva tried to gain entry. The boy refused to allow him in. The indignant Shiva asked him if he knew who he was talking to, but the boy replied that it was of no consequence, because his job was to protect his mother. 'Your mother?' cried the angry Shiva; 'that makes me your father'

(Mythology Book). The boy still refused to allow him entry and this made Shiva so enraged that he beheaded him. On hearing the disturbance, Parvati ran out of her bathroom to find to her horror that her son had been slain. She was so distraught that she threatened to transform herself into the Goddess of Destruction unless the child's life was restored.

The Mythology Book describes how Shiva ordered one of his servants to go out and get a new head for Ganesha, from 'the first creature he could find', which happened to be that of an elephant. Thus, Ganesha became known as 'the elephant-headed god'. Shiva then gave the boy the name Ganesha, meaning 'Lord of the People' or 'Lord of the Gana Gana'. Shiva acquired a second wife when Vishnu gave him one of his three wives, because they bickered so much.

Another popular tale concerns Shiva and his sacred bull, Nandi. One day Surabhi, known as 'the mother of all the world's cows', gave birth to a multitude of calves that were white in colour. They produced so much milk that Shiva's home was flooded. Enraged by this disruption to his meditation, Shiva struck down the cattle with his notorious fiery third eye. This burnt their skins and left them coloured brown. But Shiva was not through with his retribution and planned further violence. To placate him, and stop him taking more drastic action, the other gods gave Shiva the sacred bull Nandi. Shiva accepted the offer and took to riding the bull which came to be revered as the protector of all creatures.

Like most important gods, Shiva has many adventures which reflect the virtuous side of his personality, giving people an example to follow, as well as his darker side.

According to the Hindu religion, the sacred river Ganges spewed forth from Shiva's matted hair for which he is given the epithet 'Gandharva', meaning bearer of the River Ganges. The story behind this states that a sage called Bhagirathi sent the divine River Ganges to Earth to address a drought which was afflicting the people of India. It was foretold that the world did not have the capacity to survive such a deluge. Bhagirathi persuaded Shiva to intervene, who agreed to interrupt the descending waters and break their fall to Earth, by trapping the water in his matted locks and releasing it gradually into the world. Because of this the River Ganges is presented as flowing from Shiva's hair, in many illustrations.

Another tale concerns the vicious King of Serpents, Vasuki, who on one occasion unleashed his venom into the sea. Shiva helpfully transformed himself into a turtle and drank up all the poison, which left him with a blue scar on his throat, hence the epithet 'Blue Throat'.

Despite the prevalence of these mythical tales, for much of the Vedic era (c 1500-500 BCE), Shiva and Vishnu were relatively less important deities than they were during the Brahmanas period (c 900-700 BCE). By the time of the Puranic period, during the first millennium CE, both had a strong cult following and competed with each other for supremacy. Members of both cults portrayed their patron as the supreme being.

In the Hindu sect known as Shaivism, Shiva is worshipped by all the other gods including Brahma and Vishnu, as well as humanity and the creatures of the Earth. Even animals such as 'elephants, bees, spiders, snakes and cranes' (Cartwright) receive blessings at his many temples. Shiva will grant the wishes of those who are supplicant to him, allowing good to triumph over evil in their lives. Shiva enjoys great popularity in southern India where there are five major temples designated to him, based on his manifestations as each of the five elements: fire, ether, air, water and earth.

According to historian Gavin Flood, 'Shiva is a god of ambiguity and paradoxes' (New World Encyclopedia) who was a force for both good and ill. This leads to him being known under a variety of names and is reflected in the myths that elucidate his character.

Sun Wukong

Sun Wukong, known as 'the monkey king', was a trickster god who was renowned for his furious temper but is one of the best loved characters in Chinese mythology. According to a written account from 1592 CE, titled 'the Journey to the West', by Xiyouji, 'a stone egg was created at the union of Heaven and Earth, which emerged from a mountain of flowers and fruit' (Mythology Book) after countless ages of development.

From this egg a monkey was hatched whose name was Sun Wukong. At first his eyes were imbued with a blinding light, which reached the heavens and came upon the Jade Emperor, ruler of heaven, who was most perturbed. From the moment of his birth, Sun Wukong was able to walk and talk.

For a while, the monkey occupied himself by playing with his fellow monkeys who made the mountain their home. But he began to develop ambition and as the Mythology Book states, 'eventually declared himself "the monkey king"'. To prove his worthiness of such status he is reputed to have leaped through a waterfall and found a cave inhabited by an immortal. In so doing he became a demon.

His name translates as 'monkey awakened by the emptiness' which represents his journey from an ill-tempered monkey to what Mae Hamilton describes as a 'benevolent and enlightened being'. It has also been suggested that it means 'monkey who realises sunyata', which is an important part of Buddhist philosophy. He also features in Japanese culture as 'Son Goku'.

He was a highly skilled warrior who could take on 72 animal and object forms. His power was so great that he even jumped halfway across the world. Wukong was endowed with 'super-human strength' (Hamilton) with which he could manipulate wind, water and fire.

Since he was born of an egg made from rock, he had no blood relatives. He also had no wife or children. Before entering the Jade Emperor's court, as king of the monkeys and a demon, he did battle with many other demons, including 'the Dragon King', who was a sea monster. For his victories, he acquired much regalia including an eight-ton staff, which could increase in size enough to meet the skies or become as small as a needle.

As king of the monkeys, Sun Wukong was a mortal, and the time came when he was to be taken off to the underworld. Yet he defied his own fate and when the god of the dead, Yan Wang, transported him into hell, he as the Mythology Book puts it, expunged his name 'from the register of life and death', which made him immortal.

Yan Wang appealed to the Jade Emperor to help him, but impressed by Wukong's ingenuity, the Jade Emperor allowed Wukong 'to live in heaven with the other gods and gave him a position at court' (Mythology Book), hoping that that this would rein in his exploits. When Sun Wukong discovered that he had been given the lowly job of overseer of the stables, as the Mythology Book puts it: 'He flew into a rage and declared himself "the Great Sage", equal to the emperor himself'. He did this knowing that since he was a monkey, the other gods would always look down upon him.

Seeing how dissatisfied Wukong was with the post he had been given, the Jade Emperor offered him the role of 'Guardian of the Heavenly Peach Orchard' instead. At first Wukong was placated with this offer but, in a blatant snub, the emperor failed to invite him to a feast he was holding in honour of his wife, the 'Queen Mother of the West', at which all the other deities would be present.

Incensed by this rebuttal, Wukong gate-crashed the party and again rebelled against the emperor by stealing and eating the 'peaches of immortality', which he was supposed to be guarding, and making himself drunk on the immortals' wine.

The enraged Emperor 'called up 72 Generals, consisting of the most powerful Buddhist and Daoist gods and a 100,000 strong celestial army' (Jim R McClanahan). In response the Monkey King summoned up an army of demon kings and various animal spirits, including his fellow monkeys. Wukong himself grew three heads and six arms as well as multiplying the strength of his iron rod, and overcame the celestial army.

After the battle, Wukong and his army fled, with the Jade Emperor's nephew Lord Erlang in pursuit. Both being shapeshifters they battled through various animal transformations, but Wukong was finally defeated when as McClanahan describes, the god Laozi dropped a magical steel bracelet on his head, which incapacitated him long enough for Erlang's dog to take hold of his leg.

Attempts were made to execute Wukong for his crimes, but he seemed impervious to all of them, including fire, lightning and brutal weapons. He was imprisoned for 49 days in a mystical furnace, but when it was opened, in the expectation that Wukong had been reduced to ashes, he leaped out and caused mayhem in the heavens.

The Emperor asked The Buddha for help, who made a wager with Wukong that, if he was able to leap out of his hand, he would replace the Jade Emperor himself as ruler of heaven. The monkey leaped with one bound into the sky, high above the clouds until he came upon five pillars which he assumed were the boundaries of the cosmos. He wrote his name on one of them to prove that he had made this incredible journey and was confident that he had won the bet. But the Buddha explained to Wukong that as McClanahan puts it, 'the pillars were in fact the fingers of his hand. Before Wukong could do anything, the Buddha turned over his hand and slammed it into the Earth', creating a mountain under which Wukong was trapped for 500 years.

Five centuries later, during the Tang dynasty (618-907 CE) a Chinese monk called Xuan Zang travelled to India in search of sacred Buddhist texts. He was helped by the Goddess of Mercy, whose name was 'Guanyin' who provided him with several disciples to protect him, so that they could atone for past misdeeds. One of these was Sun Wukong who 'was freed from his mountain prison' (Mythology Book).

Before his enlightenment he appeared in the form of a monkey, unlike the gods who took human form. After being imprisoned for 500 years for his insolence to the Jade Emperor, ruler of heaven, he emerged as a warrior in full battle dress. As such he wore a golden chain-mail shirt and was armed with the feather of a phoenix. He wore boots made for walking on clouds as well as carrying his flexible staff.

Initially, Wukong was sceptical about helping the monk, being too aloof to be anyone's servant. But he soon came round to the idea, seeing that it would mean release from his imprisonment. Guanyin gave the monk power over Wukong, to keep him under control, by placing a band around Wukong's head that tightened whenever he recited a particular mantra (Mythology Book). As McClanahan describes, he also bestowed three magic hairs on the back of Wukong's neck which Wukong could transform into anything he chose, so long as his intention was to protect the monk.

On their travels they were joined by two other malign creatures who had been given the chance to redeem themselves, who were Zhu Bagie, the lascivious pig-demon and Sha Wujing, a water demon. These two were both former immortals who had been banished from heaven for various misdeeds. Later the party was joined by a serpent who had turned into an equine, namely the 'White Dragon Horse'. All these followers agreed to protect the monk wherever he went. Wukong's military prowess was particularly formidable. 'He defeated all manner of demons, ghosts and monsters along the way' (McClanahan).

The Buddha had set the monk Xuan Zang many challenges on his 17-year journey, designed to improve his spiritual development. He finally retrieved the texts from India and was endowed with Buddhahood (awakeness).

Sun Wukong had shown himself to be a reliable and trustworthy bodyguard, protecting the monk from many evil spirits. Through his loyalty and dedication to the teachings of the Tang dynasty (618-907 CE), he put an end to his trickery and bad temper and 'eventually achieved enlightenment' (Hamilton). As a reward, he was endowed with Buddhahood and was, as the Mythology Book describes, later given the title 'Victorious Fighting Buddha'. The Tang dynasty was a time when people in China generally practiced three religions at the same time. These were: Confucianism, Taoism and Buddhism.

The stories about Wukong rose to fame by word of mouth in the Song dynasty (960-1276 CE) and were eventually compiled in the form of a novel completed in the thirteenth century CE under the title 'The Story of How Tripitaka of the Great Tang Procures the Scriptures'. The full text was first published anonymously in the sixteenth century.

Sun Wukong took a formidable journey from being a demon to achieving Buddhahood, which is a godly state of enlightenment. Though he is not worshipped by Buddhists and Taoists today, in China, Taiwan, Malaysia and Singapore some people still see him as their own personal deity. He remains an important character in Chinese mythology and features in many TV series, movies, plays and more recently video games.

Susanoo

Susanoo is described by Gregory Wright as a 'tumultuous god of the seas and storms' in Japanese Shinto religion, who has a reputation as a mischievous and destructive trickster, so much so that he was considered unfit to reside in heaven. He has nonetheless a heroic side as demonstrated by his slaying of an eight-headed dragon. His reputation for being a trickster is demonstrated when he destroys his sister's property. As Wright puts it: 'A powerful and boisterous kami (divine spirit), his actions are as chaotic as his personality'.

Stories about him vary by tradition, and as 'the Great God Susanoo', the origin of his name is not clear. It has been proposed that it has its origins in the Japanese verb 'susabu', meaning to act violently or impetuously, or 'susamu' (to advance). Some even suggest that his name originated in Korea.

After visiting the underworld, in a failed attempt to bring back his wife Izanami, the god Izanagi, who along with his wife was central to the Shinto creation story, carried out a cleansing ritual to rid himself of impurities he had acquired there. It was during this process that he miraculously gave birth to the three children. Two of these were Amaterasu the Sun Goddess and Tsukuyomi, the Moon God, who were born from his eyes, while

Susanoo, the god of storms and seas, was born from his nose (Wright). Izanagi placed these three of his children at the top of the hierarchy of the heavens.

Susanoo is usually portrayed as having an unkempt appearance with unruly hair, wielding a sword. Like any storm or sea deity, Susanoo can be both benevolent and cruel, depending on what sort of weather he sends. Despite his somewhat malevolent nature, he is one of the great heroes of Japanese folklore especially for his killing of the dragon Orochi.

Susanoo was a wild and unpredictable god and Izanagi hoped making him the Guardian of Heaven would give him a responsibility that would temper his behaviour. But it did not take Izanagi long to realise that Susanoo was too temperamental to perform the role, or even to live in heaven at all. It is said that, because he had no mother, he wept so much that the Earth was flooded with his tears. As a result of his misbehaviour, Izanagi banished him from the heavens.

This was a punishment to which Susanoo submitted, but asked permission to return to heaven one more time to say goodbye to his sister Amaterasu, with whom he did not get along at all well. She was therefore suspicious of his intentions, so he set a challenge to prove his sincerity. This was that they would each take an object, belonging to the other and use them to create Kami (divine spirits). Whoever produced five male kami would be the winner. Amaterasu swallowed her brother's sword and spat out three female kami, while Susanoo took her 500-jewel necklace, ate the jewels before spitting them out, producing five male ones. Susanoo declared victory, but Amaterasu skilfully argued that since the necklace belonged to her, so did the men. The three female kami created by herself, she said, belonged to him. Using this ingenious argument, she won the contest and Susanoo flew into a rage.

He embarked on a campaign of destruction of his sister's

property, including her rice fields. He killed one of her horses and threw it into the place where she was doing her sacred weaving, killing one of her handmaids in the process. Amaterasu fled in grief to a cave, which left the world without light until the other gods managed to coax her out of it.

There was a meeting of eight hundred Kami to determine Susanoo's fate and they handed down the following punishments: Firstly, he was ordered to pay almost his entire fortune in reparations. Secondly, his beard was shaved off, and his finger and toenails removed. Finally, his banishment from heaven was made permanent.

It was believed by many chroniclers that he was sent to the underworld while others claim that he was consigned to the realm of the seas since he was the deity responsible for storms and rains. This was due to the islands' erratic weather patterns.

The story of his defeat of the dragon Orochi begins with him leaving heaven and descending to the Earth, arriving in Izumo Province. While he walked along the riverside, he was distracted by the noise of people weeping. He found an old farmer, his wife and daughter in tears and enquired of them the reason for their unhappiness.

They explained that a dragon had visited them several times, on each occasion taking one of their eight daughters. The one Susanoo had met, whose name was Kushinada-hime, was the last one remaining and they were expecting the imminent return of the dragon to take her away.

The dragon Orochi was a fearsome creature with eight heads. Susanoo promised the couple that when the dragon returned, he would slaughter it and save their last remaining daughter, in return for her hand in marriage, to which they agreed. Susanoo waited with them a short time whereupon the dragon appeared spitting fire.

While they were waiting, Susanoo had told the old couple to fill eight cups with a potent alcoholic drink called sake, and to leave them outside the entrances to their home. The dragon could not resist drinking up the beverages with each of his eight heads and became incapacitated by drunkenness.

At this point, as Cartwright puts it, 'Susanoo stepped forward from his hiding place and lopped off each of the serpent's heads with his sword'. After he had slain the dragon, he continued to attack it and while so doing he found an object buried in the creature's belly (or possibly his tail). It turned out to be the magical sword Kusanagi (Grass Cutter).

Instead of keeping it for himself, possessing a powerful sword of his own, he came to the decision to confer it on his sister Amaterasu, by way of apology for his earlier misdeeds. It is quite probable, however, that he did this in the forlorn hope of being readmitted to heaven. Legend has it that the sword was passed down by Amaterasu to the first imperial ruler of Japan, who was her grandson Ningi, and ever since the sword has been part of the Japanese Royal Family's regalia.

Susanoo's family lived happily, despite his many infidelities which produced a large number of children, many of whom went on to become powerful kami. Yet Kushinada-hime was always his most important wife.

Despite his great heroism in slaying the dragon and the fact that he made amends with his sister Amaterasu, according to some traditions Izanagi assigned Susanoo the unenviable role of guardian of the gateway to the underworld, known in Shinto as Yomi, upon his death in the mortal world. This is a role which he is believed by the faithful to carry out to this day.

Once he came to be seen as a god of the underworld, tales of his violent disposition became more frequent, and he was linked with disasters, violence and death. People began to associate him with plagues and all kinds of misfortune.

As the power of the Japanese Emperors grew, Susanoo took up the role of an opposing force to their rightful rule. Yet he was not always malevolent. He had a generous side which he manifested by bringing much needed rain to Japanese farmers.

There are shrines across Japan dedicated to Susanoo, of which the most important is 'Kumano Taisha', situated at Matsue in Shimane Prefecture.

In Greek mythology Zeus and Typhon were storm gods who slayed dragons, and in Norse mythology this role went to Thor who defeated the serpent Jormungand. Hindus associate this feat with the god Indra and the dragon Vritra. There are a number of other examples of dragon slaying deities, and it is a theme that occurs in most religions in Eurasia and has been a part of Christian and Islamic traditions.

Although his reputation as an unruly trickster led to him eventually being permanently banished from heaven, he did not always behave badly. He was renowned for his heroism in slaying Orichi, but he did this primarily in his own interests. Although he lived happily on Earth, it is believed by many that upon his death, he was consigned to the underworld, by his father Izanagi.

Tsukuyomi

Tsukuyomi is the Japanese Shinto God of the Moon. He is the brother as well as the 'estranged husband of the Sun Goddess Amaterasu' (Gregory Wright). A powerful and destructive deity, he is responsible for the creation of day and night through a curse placed on him for murdering the food deity Uke Mochi. Conversely, according to Wright he was previously regarded as 'a proud deity of order and beauty'.

'Tsukiji' translates as the word 'moon' or 'month'. The whole of his name means 'moon reading', which was an activity carried out by the Japanese nobility in order to keep track of time. He is sometimes referred to as 'Tsukuyomi-no-Mikoto', meaning 'the Great God Tsukuyomi'. He is also known as Tsukuyomi Otoko (Moon Reading Man).

As explained in the chapter on Susanoo, he was one of three children miraculously born to Izanagi, the creator god. These were Amaterasu, Susanoo, and Tsukuyomi. While the former two were born of Izanagi's eyes, Tsukuyomi was born of his nose.

Izanagi decided that together his three miraculous children should rule the heavens with Amaterasu being the most senior of the three. He installed Amaterasu and Tsukuyomi as the royal couple, with Amaterasu being the sovereign. Susanoo was appointed guardian of heaven, but it was not long before he was expelled from it by his father and made guardian of the gate to the underworld. Amaterasu and Tsukuyomi ruled together until the latter met his own downfall.

This was due to the extreme to which he took his strict adherence to etiquette, as seen in the following tale, for which he is best known.

On one occasion Uke Mochi, the Goddess of Food invited all her fellow kami to attend a banquet. Unable to attend herself, Amaterasu told her husband Tsukuyomi to go and represent them both. But when he saw how the food deity prepared the meal he was revolted. Mike Greenberg describes how the food goddess spat out 'venison, fish and rice' onto the tables and even 'pulled food out of her own body parts'.

To Tsukuyomi, 'a stickler for etiquette' (Yordan Zhelyazkov), this was such a great offence that he summarily killed her. According to Greenberg, once Uke Mochi was dead, the other gods gathered up the food they found emanating from her body and gave it to humans to allow them to cultivate the land.

But when word reached Amaterasu of her husband's crime, this was the last straw for their difficult and ill matched relationship, because now Tsukuyomi had distinguished himself as being evil as well. She forbade him to keep company with her ever again and expelled him permanently from heaven.

The breakup in their relationship is believed by followers of the Shinto religion to be represented by the fact that, as Greenberg describes 'The Sun and Moon appear at different times but follow a similar trajectory'. Like the Moon and the Sun, Tsukuyomi and Amaterasu can never meet, despite Tsukuyomi's endless quest to do so. This is how Tsukuyomi became the creator of day and night.

An eclipse is seen as a 'near miss', when he almost catches up with his wife, but is destined never to succeed.

For the human population, like The Moon, he represented tranquillity, calm and beauty, but Tsukuyomi is also a violent and aggressive god in Japanese mythology. He is a strict disciplinarian befitting 'the Moon's cold blueish light' (Zhelyazkov). Most of all he stands for the etiquette of the Japanese nobility, strictly observed during 'moon reading' ceremonies. Many nobles at the Imperial Court participated in this activity at which poetry was recited and celebrations went on well into the night. Whilst this was conducted in a peaceful way by the nobility, Tsukuyomi was prone to a violent temper which was to become the cause of his comeuppance.

Like his wife Amaterasu, Goddess of The Sun, he was proud of what he stood for, although they ruled over very different domains. While Tsukuyomi was by nature cool and pale, his wife was a harbinger of 'cheerfulness and light' (Timeless Myths).

Tsukuyomi's pride eventually led to him being expelled from heaven, yet he is forever trying to bring things back to the way they had been before his erroneous act.

Since he is stuck in his never-ending chase, Tsukuyomi most likely regards his decision to murder the food goddess as a mistake. Despite his crime, he is worshipped by adherents of the Shinto religion even today and is regarded as a life-giving bringer of rain and sustenance to the world.

While his character is not all bad, Tsukuyomi's dark side, as a representative of the night, is the dominant part of his personality. His wife Amaterasu, ruler of heaven, who expelled him forever from the celestial plane, is the most loved of all Shinto deities. But his endless quest to be with his wife reveals the ambiguity of his nature.

Due to the overwhelming negativity of his personality, he does not feature so much in Japanese mythology as many of his fellow Shinto deities, and was not a popular god, since as

Greenberg puts it: he 'broke the sacred laws to enforce his own view of propriety'.

Nonetheless, there are a number of shrines dedicated to him in Japan today, the most prominent one of them being at Matsumoto in Kyoto.

He exists today in Japanese folklore and is the subject of the video game 'Final Fantasy XVI' in which he appears as a female kami. This means that he is well known not just in Japan, but the world over.

Tsukuyomi's brother Susanoo too was far from popular. Both were banished from heaven, leaving Amaterasu to rule over the celestial realm single-handedly. This was unusual because she was female and a ruler. It was also not customary for a goddess to be a sun deity, most of whom were male in religions from across the world. It is common for a sun god to be male of great strength, reflecting the power of The Sun, while the paler light of the moon, with its cyclical nature, is more often represented by a female deity.

However, there are other male Moon gods, including, as Wright relates, the Egyptian Khonsu, Norse Mani, the Chinese Jie Lin and the Hindu Chandra. One other example where the gender roles are reversed is that of the Norse deities Sol and Mani who are also siblings representing The Sun and Moon, respectively.

Tsukuyomi was probably the highest ranking of these male Moon deities, being a king-consort of heaven.

Yet this distribution of power was so unusual that some scholars have historically mistaken him for a female, who attended Uke Mochi's feast as a deputy instead of the royal consort of Amaterasu. This theory is disproved by the earliest of Japanese sources on the matter which describe him as Tsukuyomi Otoko, meaning 'moon reading man', as alluded to earlier in this chapter.

While the Japanese imperial line claim to be descendants of Amaterasu, few people claim the heritage of Tsukuyomi. Although Amaterasu was the eldest of the three miraculously born siblings, it would have been customary for a son to be first in line to the throne, but Tsukuyomi's destiny made him what Timeless Myth calls: 'an undesirable ancestor'. Susanoo, meanwhile, as an erratic and mischievous trickster was completely unsuitable for the role he was given by Izanagi.

Tsukuyomi's dramatic fall from grace was a result of his preoccupation with etiquette. He took this to such an extreme that he murdered one of his fellow deities, which meant that he could no longer claim to represent it. He went from being a lunar deity of serenity and tranquillity to being a dark and destructive god, destined to pursue his wife for ever, as The Moon follows The Sun, without hope of ever catching her up.

Celtic Deities

Lugh

Lugh was chief of the Tuatha de Danann, a tribe of supernatural beings sometimes referred to as Irish gods. As their leader, he was given the title 'the shining one', who brings light and luminosity to the world and represents the light of the sun. He was also 'a Celtic god of Justice and Oath Keeping' (Gregory Wright) and patron of the nobility. Contrastingly to his association with light, Lugh was also a bloodthirsty warrior, who showed no pity to his enemies.

An almost identical Welsh deity is Lleu. Both their names relate to light, and according to Carl McColman and Kathryn Hinds, these gods were both regarded as 'gods of light', in terms of both sunshine and lightning strikes. Mythology about the two of them shows us that they were strong, skilful and full of youthful energy. While the two gods were practically the same individual, the stories about Lleu differ from those about Lugh, who also featured in English mythology as Lugus.

The meaning of his name is unclear. Many historians have argued that it is derived from the early European word 'leugh' meaning 'to bind by oath', which reflects Lugh's association with taking oaths and contractual obligations.

One of Lugh's dwelling places was Tara in County Meath,

while the other was at Moytura in County Sligo, a seat of Irish Kings and site of two major battles.

Almost invariably depicted as youthful, athletic and good looking, he carried an assortment of weapons which possessed magical powers. He was also accompanied by a retinue of animal familiars, most significantly a supernatural greyhound. His weapons included the spear of Assail, which was invincible in battle and could take the form of a lightning strike (Wright). It was reputedly so dangerous that it was kept in a cauldron of cooling water when not in use. The spear would respond to the command 'Ibur' by hitting its target and on the command 'Athibar' it would return to its master. He also possessed a sling shot with which he mortally wounded his grandfather, Balor of the Evil Eye. Additionally, he used the sword of his foster father Manannan, a weapon which compelled those faced with it to tell the truth. This sword was named 'Fragarach' (the answerer). He sometimes rode in a boat called 'Sguaba Tuinne' (The Wind Sweeper) which sailed with remarkable haste. He possessed a number of horses which he rode through the sea.

Due to the length of his trusty spear, he was known as 'Lampada', meaning 'of the long arm'. Alternatively, it has been suggested that this word translates as 'artful hands' because of his skills as a craftsman. As Wright describes, he was also known as Maunia meaning 'youthful warrior' and Lonnbeimnech – 'the fierce striker'. He was honoured for his association with justice, battle skills and as a man of many trades. Lugh was one of the most important members of the Celtic pantheon, as well as a warrior hero.

His father was believed to be Cian while his mother was Ethniu, daughter of Balor. He was brought up by a foster father Manannan and his foster mother, Tailtiu. Manannan was a sea god who taught Lugh his many skills. Alternatively, Mark Cartwright suggests that 'Goibniu the god of smiths and constructor of powerful weapons', including Lugh's invincible spear, may have been his father. Lugh had many wives including the daughter of a British king. He is usually assumed to have no children except his son, the warrior hero Cu Chulainn, whose mother was a mortal named Deictine. In some accounts, Lugh had a sister called Ebliu.

According to McColman & Hinds 'Lugh represented justice without mercy' and as such he lacks the ability to forgive. He showed no mercy to his enemies, such as the sons of Tuireann, who killed his father, and his wife's lover, Cermait. He is confident in the righteousness of his causes and assumes the way to resolve disputes between people is to go to war. Despite being a god of light, his darker side shows through in his warlike nature. He is known as a notorious trickster, especially before he took the throne, when he would, as Wright says 'lie, cheat and steal'. He was also known for inventing a number of Irish games such as horseracing, and feats of physical strength, as well as Fidchell, an Irish board game which preceded the invention of chess. He brought civilisation to Ireland, according to Irish mythology.

While the goddess Brigit offers motherly protection, Lugh acts with a duty to dispense justice. While Lugh offers strength and resistance to one's enemies, Brigit fills people with compassion, generosity and optimism.

This is why Lugh is a polar opposite to the goddess Brigit who epitomises mercy, a quality of which Lugh had no understanding. While Brigit tries to make peace with the Fomorians and even married one of them, Lugh goads them into battle.

While Brigit is the champion of those who do not know which way to turn, Lugh requires people to have some idea of how to procced but will multiply the reach of one's actions with his magical works.

Brigit's festival is celebrated at the arrival of spring, promising new life and growth, while Lugh's festival beacons the harvest and the promise of abundance. Brigit invites everyone to share in nature's abundance, but Lugh emphasises the need for hard work to achieve a reward.

The annual harvest festival known as the Lughnasad was celebrated across Ireland in Lugh's honour on August 1st, which included games, feats of strength and matchmaking as well as being a venue for the settlement of disputes (McColman & Hinds). These celebrations were carried out to try and ensure a plentiful harvest. The celebration survives to this day as Garland Sunday, a Christian Harvest Festival. Pilgrimages to hill tops were also made in his name, since his connection with light meant that he was associated with such places. For this reason, the modern festival is sometimes referred to as 'Mountain Sunday'.

In the First Battle of Mag Tuired, won by the Tuatha de Danann against the previous inhabitants of Ireland, the Fir Bolg, Lugh's father, Cian was killed by the sons of his great enemy, Tuireann. They twice tried to bury Cian, but on both occasions, as Wright puts it: The ground 'spat him up'. Lugh happened upon the event and asked the men who they were burying and when they told him that it was his father, Lugh vowed to seek revenge, using his skills as a trickster.

He invited Tuireann's three sons to a grand feast, an invitation which they gladly accepted. While they were enjoying the food and drink, Lugh asked them what a suitable punishment for the murder of their father would be. They replied that death would be the only suitable outcome, not realising they were talking to Cian's son and heir. Lugh immediately revealed his true identity and demanded they faced retribution. He set them a series of impossible tasks which led to their demise, and to justice for Lugh.

For 27 years the Tuatha de Danann were enslaved by a tribe called the Fomorians who took control of Ireland after the Fir Bolg had been defeated. Eventually Lugh provoked armed conflict by killing most of their tax collectors. In the resulting battle the Tuatha de paid a high cost in the lives of warriors, but the Fomorians were at last chased into the sea, where they drowned. This was the notorious second battle of Mag Tuired.

When Lugh paid a visit to the hall of the Tuatha de, in the early stages of the war, he was told by the doorman that only people with a skill could enter. Lugh told him that he was a skilled carpenter, to which the doorman replied that they already had one. Lugh went on to describe himself as skilled in many crafts, from a blacksmith to a physician. The doorkeeper replied that all these posts had already been taken. Lugh slyly asked whether they had a master of all these crafts to which he replied that they did not. The doorman consulted King Nuada who told him to let Lugh in. Amused but impressed by Lugh's impudence, the King asked him to prove his abilities in brute strength, strategy and the arts. Lugh outdid any of the Tuatha de in these tasks, and the King was so impressed that he not only gave Lugh the title of 'Master of All Crafts' but surrendered the throne to him. Lugh wasted no time in assembling and rallying his troops, for the battle against the Fomorians.

His rapid rise to power in the Tuatha de tribe was largely due to a prophecy that he would lead the tribe to victory over the Fomorians, and kill their leader, a giant called Balor of the Evil Eye, who happened to be his grandfather, but they were now sworn enemies.

Balor was most notorious for this 'evil eye' which could destroy anything it glanced upon. This meant that the Fomorians saw him as their most effective weapon. They placed him looking on to their opponents so that he could open his eye and destroy everything in his sight. It was usually covered with an eyelid so heavy that it took the strength of four men to lift it.

But Lugh launched a slingshot straight into Balor's eye, just as it was opening. The weapon penetrated his skull, killing him and leaving the eye gazing back on his own soldiers, annihilating them on sight.

Despite his aggressive nature, McColman & Hinds state that Lugh is cast in the role of 'a saviour of his people' defeating their enemies the Fomorians single-handedly by slaying the giant Balor. The Fomorians were a supernatural race or even 'demonic pirates' (Cartwright). Without him the Tuatha de Danann would most likely have been defeated. Lugh used his magical powers and skills in trickery to defeat his enemies, as well as brute force. While Lugh is a commanding and transformative force in his own right, he also brings the community together to defeat its enemies.

After the Tuatha de had been victorious, Bres, the King of the Fomorians, who had been taken prisoner, was brought before Lugh, and begged him for mercy. (Wright). Uncharacteristically, Lugh agreed on condition that Bres taught the Tuatha de how to cultivate the land, to which he reluctantly agreed. Nonetheless, Bres was later executed. The battle won; Lugh was finally empowered to rule over all Ireland. With the Formorians defeated, Lugh ruled over Ireland in a 40-year long reign of prosperity and peace.

This lasted until one of Lugh's many wives, Buach, had an affair with Cermait, whose father was The Dagda, partner of the ferocious Morrigan. In revenge, Lugh ordered the death of Cermait. When Cermait was killed, his three sons vowed to take revenge on Lugh and drowned him in a loch which came to be known as Loch Lughborta, because of its association with Lugh's demise.

With Lugh no longer there to protect them, it was not long

before he Tuatha de Danann were defeated, as his 40-year rule came to an end. Cermait's sons took power and 'divided up Ireland between themselves'. (Cartwright)

The main sources of information about the adventures of Lugh is the 'Cath Mag Tuired' (Battle of Mag Tuired) an 11th century Christian text which was a compilation of earlier sources. Such was the popularity of Lugh that early Christian writers tried to assimilate him into their own religion. But as Christianity gradually took the place of Irish mythology, Lugh's reputation became more tarnished, as people moved away from their traditional beliefs. Lugh was eventually consigned to the underworld, known as Sidh, with his fellow gods of pre-Christian tradition.

Lugh led his warriors to conquer their greatest enemy, the Fomorians, even though they were led by his own grandfather, whom he assassinated. As well as being a god of light, he used brute force to defeat his enemies. He killed people as a way of life, not just on the battlefield, but also because of more personal disputes.

M e d b

Medb is one of 'Irish mythology's most colourful characters' (Carl McColman & Kathryn Hinds), usually represented as a promiscuous woman who is manipulative and calculating. She takes most of the blame for one of the most notorious episodes in Irish folklore, 'The Cattle Raid of Cooley'. She is a fearsome warrior who according to McColman and Hinds has been described as 'seductive and cruel, and her beauty was said to be unmatched'.

Like The Morrigan, another pre-Christian Irish goddess, she has a title rather than a name – the word Medb means 'she who intoxicates'. This is related to the word 'mead', a popular alcoholic drink, which she encouraged people to imbibe. She is sometimes referred to as Meadhbh. In its anglicised form her name is 'Maeve'. In Shakespeare's Romeo and Juliet, there is a character called 'Queen Mab' who is thought to be based on the deity.

Queen Medb's parents were the Irish king Eochu Feidlech and his wife Cloithfinn. She had nine siblings, consisting of four brothers and five sisters.

Her father offered her first husband Conchobar Mac Nessa, King of Ulster her hand in marriage a union which ended in bitter acrimony. Her second husband, Eochaid Dala, became jealous of Aillil mac Mata, who was her lover and who became her third and most famous husband after she had Eochaid killed.

As Gregory Wright describes it: 'By Aillil mac Mata she had seven sons all called Maine', since she once heard a prophecy that her ex-husband Conchobar would be killed by someone of that name. She had one daughter, Findabair, who was reputed to be as scheming and good looking as her mother. She eventually had mac Mata assassinated because of his jealousy towards one of her lovers.

Medb was a historical woman who represented the goddess in human form, like the other Celtic deities. Although she is usually assumed to have been designated Queen by her father, it has been suggested that she ruled by popular mandate due to her divinity.

According to pre-Christian folklore, before acceding the throne as Queen of County Connacht, western Ireland, Medb lived in Tara, County Meath, which had a long tradition of being the seat of kings.

The large number of place names in Ulster and Ireland generally attest to her importance as a figure in Irish folklore. These include 'Baile Phite Meabha in County Antrim and Samil Phite Meabha in County Tyrone. There is also an earthwork built to commemorate her at 'Rath Maeve', 'the sacred site at Tara' (Dani Rhys). It is claimed that Medb in her mortal form was buried in a stone cairn on the summit of Knocknarea in County Sligo. Alternatively, it is said that she was buried at Rathcroghan in County Roscommon where a stone known as 'Misgaun Medb' marks the spot of her interment.

It has been claimed that there were a number of queens named Medb associated with the sacred site of Tara. Giving them the name Medb was supposed to elevate them to the status of goddesses.

On the occasion of her marriage, the true Medb offered the

king mead or wine. She did this on nine occasions because she was married nine times. After the drinking was done, the union was consummated as part of the initiation ceremony. The King's jurisdiction over Connaught was granted through his union with the goddess, symbolised by the sharing of the mead. The symbolic marriage of the two linked the human world (represented by the King) with the goddess who commands the fertility of the land. If she is displeased with him, she will make the land infertile, causing the harvest to fail, thus removing the King's legitimacy.

Medieval chroniclers gave her a bad reputation. They recorded that as Queen of Connacht she could be ruthless and aggressive, 'willing to expend the lives of many warriors to satisfy her own pride' (McColman & Hinds). But looking beyond her medieval characterisation a more complex individual emerges and she can be seen to represent sovereignty based on the fertility of the land, that legitimises the rule of the king. She shared the role of sovereignty goddess with other Irish deities such as The Macha and The Morrigan, as well as goddesses from other Celtic nations.

Sympathetic writers have more recently suggested that her reputation has been unfairly tarnished by medieval chroniclers, who cast aspersions on her because she was part of the pre-Christian religion. But her reputation for promiscuity and violent acts is attested by earlier sources.

According to Irish mythology, Medb would not allow any man to become King of Connaught who did not marry her first. This meant that a man was not worthy to become King without the authority of the goddess of the land. Medb's many marriages ended unhappily and represent the transitory nature of the King's rule while the land is constant. Her long list of nine husbands gave her the title 'the perpetual bride' (Dani Rhys) who legitimises the King's rule.

The legendary 'Battle of the Boyne' took place when Medb's father Eochaid deposed the King of Connacht, Tinni MacConrai, one of Medb's many husbands and replaced him with Medb herself. The deposed king Tinni stayed on as Medb's consort, and later made a comeback as co-ruler. However, things did not end well for the couple and her first ex-husband Conchobar eventually murdered Tinni, leaving Medb to search for a new husband.

After Tinni's death, Medb decided that her next husband should have certain qualities. Firstly, he must be, as Rhys puts it 'fearless without a cruel demeanour' and most importantly he must not be jealous of his wife for taking many lovers. She had a string of husbands, who were all Kings of Connacht by right of being married to Medb.

Another reason for her bad reputation was the story known in the old Irish language as 'Tain Bo Cuailnge (The Cattle Raid of Cooley), which is one of the most important myths concerning the goddess Medb. She has a notorious role in this story and takes most of the blame for what transpired.

She told her husband Aillil mac Mata in no uncertain terms that she was head of the household (McColman & Hinds) since she had more material possessions. He retorted that he is the owner of a prize bull that she could not match. Medb decided to take any equally fine bull for herself. The bull which she sought was owned by a man named Daire mac Fiachna in Ulster. She offered to pay him handsomely for the creature, but he would not let it go. Medb resolved to invade the territory and steal the bull. This led to a famous misadventure that causes much bloodshed in a hard-fought battle against the warrior Cu Chulainn and his forces.

A mysterious curse was inflicted on Cu Chulainn's army, most probably the work of Medb. All of the men, except Cu Chulainn himself, who was immune to the sorcery, were struck down. He took on Medb's warriors one by one and held them back single-handedly for three days before his men were restored to health.

Chulainn ridiculed and humiliated Medb and outwitted her tactics, so she vowed to take revenge and later had him killed. Her forces retreated to Connaught, taking the bull with them, but Medb was the winner, something to which she was well accustomed.

Her own death too, was a violent one, and some say she was killed by her nephew, Furbaide. This was due to Medb having killed one of her sisters who was pregnant at the time with Furbaide, from an affair with Conchobar. Furbaide survived and eventually killed Medb by throwing a lump of hard cheese at her.

From the point of view of medieval chroniclers, the goddess of sovereignty was also as McColman & Hinds state: 'A vindictive regional Queen' who caused all manner of violent events. She often fought battles using brute strength although she also had the ability to cause supernatural events.

Unlike the goddess Brigit, who was assimilated into the Christian religion as a saint, Medb was known as wanton and calculating. Like The Morrigan, she was 'an untameable goddess' (McColman & Hinds) who had no place in the Christian faith. This means that she is remembered for her misdeeds more than her role in sovereignty and the fertility of the land.

An important figure in Irish mythology, she is described by Rhys as a 'strong, powerful, ambitious and cunning woman', seen today as a feminist icon. She was ambitious and very strong willed. The fact that she had so many lovers indicates her desirability both in political terms and as a woman. Medb was stronger than most of her lovers, both physically and psychologically.

She married her nine husbands to use them as pawns in her political gameplay as she maintained her grip on power. She reigned for 60 years until she was killed by her nephew.

Her political and mystical fortitude, together with her appetite for power and her desire for men, mean that she continues to be a popular figure in Irish folklore.

The Dagda

The term 'The Dagda' is a title meaning 'Good God', 'The Big Father' or 'Great God'. In this context 'good' refers to his proficiency in many skills rather than his character. According to Mark Cartwright He was variously as a 'master craftsman, magician, warrior and ruler'.

While Lugh, another important Irish Celtic god, had a reputation as 'master of all skills', The Dagda was described as 'Master of All'. He was sometimes referred to as 'mighty one of perfect knowledge'. He was also known by various titles including 'Great Lord of Knowledge', 'The Striker' or 'Fertile One'. Despite these awe-inspiring titles, The Dagda was seen not so much as a fierce warrior as an obese figure of fun, but he did usually win his battles.

While Lugh was primarily associated with justice and protection, The Dagda was more interested in feasting and making love. However, he did go into battle when needed, using a heavy club which had supernatural powers. In fact, it was of such great weight that it required a large vehicle to transport it. With this The Dagda could kill up to nine people with one blow, but when the other end of the club was used, it restored life.

Gregory Wright describes The Dagda as a 'god of life and death' who, like his wife The Morrigan, had power over life and death. He was associated with fertility, both in terms of procreation and of the land. As a deity he possessed magic powers and was important to the Druids, whose religion arrived in Ireland later.

His mother is believed to be Ethniu, daughter of the monumental Fomorian Balor and his father is taken to be Elatha. This would make Lugh his brother.

His brothers are Nuada, King of the Gods and Ogma, a fearsome warrior. Sometimes The Dagda and these two brothers are regarded as a trinity, since they were similar in many ways. By some accounts, Nuada was King, while The Dagda was chief and Ogma was designated the role of champion.

He had plenty of children by many different lovers. The most significant of his offspring were Cermait, Aengus, Brigit and Midir. His most notable partners were his wife, the terrifying Morrigan, and Boann, Goddess of the River Boyne (Wright).

The Dagda became smitten with Boann, wife of Elcmar, a Tuatha de Danann judge. He sent her husband away so that he could more easily seduce her. Boann soon became pregnant with The Dagda's child. This was Aengus, described by Wright as 'a god of love and poetry' who was brought up by another of The Dagda's sons, Midir.

Once he was fully grown, Anengus tricked Elcmar into handing over his property at Bru na Boinne. He cunningly asked Elcmar to allow his father The Dagda and himself to live in his home for 'a day and a night'. This was a trick because the term 'a day and a night' was not necessarily to be taken literally and could be taken as meaning 'all days and all nights'. Thus, Elcmar unwittingly ceded his home to them for ever.

Some time passed before The Dagda shared out his land between his many children but left none to Aengus. Using the same ruse that had allowed him to trick Elcmar out of his property, Aengus tricked The Dagda into granting him his property at Bru na Boinne.

Despite this apparent gullibility, The Dagda's magical powers were reflected in the weapons he carried. As well as his club, he also possessed a cauldron that was big enough to feed an entire army and carried with him a harp that would, as Carl McColman and Kathryn Hinds put it: 'fly into his hand when he called for it'. He played his harp to control people by causing them to 'sleep, laugh or grieve' at will (Cartwright). With this collection of possessions, The Dagda was seen as a god who kept the world in order.

Somewhat surprisingly for such a venerated individual, The Dagda is generally portrayed as a giant with a protruding belly, a long unkempt beard, ill-fitting clothes and lacking in good manners. All these attributes contributed to his humorous appearance. Some historians have suggested that this was an invention of Christian chroniclers, who were the first people to make a written account of Irish mythology and did not want to portray him in a positive light. But even these accounts of The Dagda do not refute his wily nature.

As a paternalist god he is less stern and foreboding and much more of an amusing character who knows how to show generosity and love. Through his protruding belly, he represents the gift of prosperity and plenty. Not surprisingly his appetite is not easily quenched.

Another personality trait of the colossal god was his insatiable sexual appetite. Indeed, this was as great as his appetite for food. Although he was married to The Morrigan, he was not seen as morally degenerate for having many other lovers, but rather a representative 'of fertility and prosperity' (McColman & Hinds).

While Lugh represents skilfulness and ingenuity, The Dagda

takes pleasure in his entertaining reputation. Unlike Lugh's son Cu Chulainn, he readily accepts The Morrigan's advances and together they enjoy much power.

The first battle of Mag Tuired, also known as the first battle of Moytura, was fought by the invading Tuatha de Danann against the then inhabitants of Ireland, the Fir Bolg. Many of the Tuatha de's warriors had supernatural powers, especially The Dagda. With these attributes it is perhaps unsurprising that they won the battle. The Fir Bolg fled to Scotland and various remote islands.

Twenty-seven years later, just before the Second Battle of Mag Tuired, The Dagda first encounters The Morrigan while she is bathing in the Unshin River. It was not long before the two of them were making love, and The Morrigan made a prophecy that the Tuatha de would win the impending battle against the Fomorians, but many of their soldiers would meet their deaths.

As the battle was about to commence, Lugh sent The Dagda to infiltrate the enemy camp, disguised as an emissary. He asked for the battle to be postponed, to which they agreed. But they could not resist poking fun at such a comical messenger.

Etiquette required that he should not turn down any food that he was offered, and the Fomorians used this to their advantage. They prepared a huge meal for him, using his own magical cauldron, satisfied that it would be too much even for his great appetite. The meal consisted of vast amounts of porridge, broth and huge cuts of meat. This was ironic because the Formorians were not known for their generosity. The Dagda, undaunted by the meal proceeded to eat every scrap. After this he fell into a slumber and was ridiculed by the Fomorians as he slept. But The Dagda had the last laugh because as stated by McColman & Hinds, 'he seduced a Fomorian princess before leaving their camp'.

The Dagda's adventures in the battles of Mag Turied are recorded in the eleventh century text 'Cath Mag Turied' and a later, twelfth century volume called 'Lebor Gabala' meaning book of invasions. The site of the battles is situated in Connaught, northwest Ireland.

The Fomorians were known for their ferocity and were sometimes described as 'demonic pirates'. According to some sources they had only one arm, one leg and one eye but this made them no less formidable opponents (Cartwright).

Although Lugh took charge of the Tuatha de armies, The Dagda's involvement was crucial also, as he made extensive use of his magical powers.

During the second conflict, Balor, leader of the Fomorians, was killed but so was The Dagda's brother Nuada. The Dagda himself was fatally wounded when Balor's wife Caitilin took revenge and attacked him with a projectile weapon. He was carried back to his home at Bruna Boyne, on the banks of the River Boyne in County Meath, at a site where a number of neolithic earthworks existed. One of these mounds is called Newgrange and at the winter solstice it is 'aligned with the rising sun (Wright). This is where The Dagda was buried. People would make pilgrimages to these burial mounds, where they believed they could more easily make contact with him.

An alternative version of events is that he survived and reigned for 70 years, until he, as Cartwright describes, 'retreated to one of his underground palaces', most probably a metaphor for being cast aside by the onward march of Christianity.

Although not as significant as Lugh and Brigit, the god known as The Dagda has many counterparts in other civilisations. Many of these have similar attributes and behave in a similar way. These can be found, for example amongst the Celtic gods of Britain and France, as well as in the Norse legends (Odin) and Chronos, the Greek deity.

The Dagda and The Morrigan were worshipped especially fervently at the Samhain Harvest Festival, since, according to Cartwright: 'if the Dagda and the Morrigan came together at this time', it would bode well for agriculture in the coming year and so for the prosperity of the people. Nonetheless, it was considered appropriate to worship The Dagda at any time of year since he had the power to take or restore life.

A colourful character who at the same time possessed great supernatural powers, The Dagda was seen as the bringer of the harvest and of victory, but he indulged in feasting and promiscuity all the while. His behaviour was far from perfect, but he came to the aid of those in need, when he deemed it appropriate.

The Morrigan

Also known as Morrighan, Mor-Riogan and Morigu, 'The Morrigan' is not a name but rather a title meaning 'The Great Queen'. Various Irish place names are based on it, for example Fulacht na Mor Rioghna ('Cooking Pot of the Morrigan'), in County Tipperary.

While the 'mor' in her name means 'Great' in Celtic language, the latter part comes from the Latin 'regina' meaning 'queen'. At the time of the middle Irish era (900-1200 CE), the 'o' in her name was marked with an accent making the title 'Phantom Queen'. However, she is usually referred to by historians as 'Great Queen'.

According to Anne Williams, she was a 'goddess of death, destiny and battle', as well as procreation and the fertility of the land.

As Carl McColman & Kathryn Hinds put it, seen as 'a bringer of war and ill-tidings', she was a prophet who specialised in foretelling people's doom. According to Williams, to warriors in battle, she represented 'a terrifying omen of death'. As the god known as The Dagda discovered to his satisfaction, and the hero of Ulster, Ca Chulainn found out to his peril, she was also a goddess concerned with vigorous sexual desire. This was because she bestowed her favours on those whom she deemed worthy of them but scorned anyone who rejected her advances.

She was married to The Dagda, himself another warrior god, known as the father of the gods. It is recorded that The Morrigan's mother was Ernmas, 'the Great Mother God', but her father is unknown. Her only son is the malign spirit Mechi, who had three hearts, each containing a serpent. The identity of his father is not known.

Sometimes she is referred to as 'The Morrigana', the plural version of her title, because she appears as a trio of Great Queens, sometimes referred to as three sisters, instead of one individual. Some historians have argued that, as Mark Cartwright describes it: 'the trio of goddesses are simply different aspects of The Morrigan'.

These three sub-goddesses were also awe inspiring and comprised 'Badbh', the battle crow, who manifests in the battlefield, Nemain the inciter of frenzy and Macha who represented battle lust. This trio of goddesses had the power to act in their own right as well as in unison. In one tale, two of them, Neman and Badbh scream so loudly in the night-time at an army preparing for battle, 'that one hundred of them died of fright' (Williams). The shriek of The Morrigan herself was an omen of misfortune which put fear into the hearts of men.

As a spirited individual she was willing to engage in battle personally, but she more often goaded warriors to fight on her behalf. She did this by instilling fear. She would bring panic and confusion to retreating armies. Using these tactics, she was far more effective in the defeat of an army than hand to hand combat.

Yet she was not afraid to get blood on her hands. There is a mythological tale that she worked an army into frenzy by killing one of their enemies, and then pasted his blood onto soldiers on her own side.

She was a shapeshifter and appeared in many different manifestations, both human and animal. Known as 'the Washer of the Ford', she was often found in the guise of an old washer woman. The sight of her washing blooded clothing was a bad omen for any warrior because the garments represented his own clothing, after he had been killed in battle.

This was just one of the many ways she could instil fear in people's hearts. She was known to appear on the battlefield in the image of a raven looking for carrion. Sometimes she would as McColman & Hinds describe, appear as 'an eel, a heifer or a wolf' and others she would appear in the form of a seductive young woman or a warrior queen. This made people fearful of her visitations, whether these fears were well founded or not.

In addition to her other attributes, The Morrigan was something of a trickster, most famously when she tricked Cu Chulainn into blessing her during a conflict between the two of them.

Because later, Christian, accounts of her behaviour put the emphasis on her scariness, little of the wisdom attributed to her has survived. While the life and works of the goddess Brigit received more favourable accounts, reflecting her more benevolent nature, The Morrigan was treated with a sense of foreboding.

Her abilities of foresight give an insight into the deeper meaning of Celtic tradition. As a seer she would bestow her knowledge of things yet to come on favoured individuals such as heroes and kings. But she did so at a price, either material, or of sexual favours.

Since she is associated with prophecy and fate, she appears at the demise of various Irish leaders, often resting on their shoulder in the form of a raven.

With The Morrigan on their side, The Tuatha de tribe went into battle at Moytura on two occasions, each known as 'The Battles of Mag Tuired', which was another name for the location. In both cases, The Morrigan used her magic powers to repel the enemy. The Tuatha de won the first conflict, against the inhabitants of Ireland, the Fir Bolg, but in the second battle Fomorians, the ruling tribe in Ireland at the time, put up more of a fight than the Fir Bolg had done. As described in the chapter on The Dagda, before hostilities commenced The Dagda asked his wife The Morrigan to predict the outcome. She predicted their side would win, but many of their warriors would be slaughtered.

Sure enough, the battle soon became a bloodbath, with The Morrigan crying out to her men to be still more aggressive. This put fright into the Fomorians, who fled into the sea, where they perished.

In one story, called The Cattle Raid of Ragamain, the warrior hero Cu Chulainn 'attacks an old woman driving a heifer from his territory' (Williams). When the woman turns herself into a raven, he realises who he has taken on and expresses his regret. The old woman tells him that she will make a visitation at the warrior's death, by way of punishing him for his offence.

According to a seventh/eighth century myth, known as The Cattle Raid of Cooley, the territory of Cu Chulainn in Ulster was invaded by the forces of Queen Medb, with the intention of stealing a sacred bull. Every man in the province was cast down with a curse, save Cu Chulainn, who was immune to it, who was left to fight the enemy alone. During a lull in the fighting, an attractive young woman offered to become the hero's lover, but he spurned her affections. Once he had done so, he found himself under attack from all manner of animals from an eel to a wolf to a heifer. Cu Chulainn managed to see off these marauding creatures but was injured while doing so.

Soon afterwards, he met The Morrigan disguised as an injured old woman milking a cow. As Williams puts it: 'Her injuries matched the wounds the hero had inflicted on his animal opponents'. The Morrigan allowed him to drink from the milk three times. On each occasion he blessed her and one by one her three injuries disappeared. When she had regained full health, she revealed her true identity to him. She reminded the warrior of the hostility he had shown towards her and warned him that he would soon meet his death.

As Williams explains, it was in the battle with Queen Medb's forces that this prophecy was finally fulfilled. He was mortally wounded, but before he expired, he managed to prop himself up, tricking the enemy into believing he was still alive. It was not until the raven perched on his shoulder that they comprehended he had met his death.

According to some historians, the stories of the later Irish mythological figure, the 'Banshee', have a common origin with The Morrigan and shared with her an ominous shriek and a presence at the battlefield, in the aftermath of war. The Morrigan can be compared to the Valkyries of Norse and Germanic religions. These beings share her ability to foresee the future and her association with birds.

It has been argued that these characters were able to bring forth new life, through procreation and fertility, as well as to mete out death in combat. It was not unusual for mystical females to foresee or determine the destiny of men.

Around the time of the autumn equinox a 'festival of death' known as Samhain, was observed at the beginning of the new year. Not surprisingly, The Morrigan was the patron along with her lover, The Dagda. Yet these festivities were also associated with new life, because of The Morrigan's connection with procreation and agricultural fertility. In the same way there is a duality concerning The Dagda's role, since he wields a club which can kill with one end and restore life with the other. As well as his connection with death and battle, The Dagda too is associated with the abundance of nature.

Christianity eventually put an end to her veneration. She was last reported to be found 'shrieking at the battle of Clantarf in 1017' (McColman & Hinds), which took place around five centuries after Christianity had reached Irish shores.

While Brigit converted and took up holy orders, The Morrigan retreated to a cave at Rath Cruachan in the county of Connaught, northwest Ireland where she holed up intending to make a comeback in future. The site had been the seat of royalty in Connaught but was also reputed to be the gateway to the Otherworld, known as 'Hell's Gate'.

As noted, there is an element of duality in the character of The Morrigan. Although worshipped as a goddess who represented new life and agricultural fertility, she was also a purveyor of bloodshed and war. As a foreteller of misfortune, a visitation from The Morrigan was always scary, and when she appeared as a raven of death, no-one could escape their impending demise.

Classical Deities

Classical Deities – Introduction

Both Greek and Roman religions were polytheistic, meaning that they worshipped a number of different gods and goddesses. In total there were about 30 of these in each of the two civilisations. Twelve of these were the more senior ones, and are members of what was known as the 'pantheon'.

The gods of both these civilisations closely resemble each other especially in terms of their powers. The main difference is the different names given to them by the Romans and the Greeks. This is because the Romans derived their belief system from that of the Greeks.

These deities were seen as being endowed with human attributes, both good and bad, and represented exaggerated human characteristics. They interacted with both humans and other deities and were worshipped by people living in Greece and Rome from all walks of life, in temples dedicated to particular gods or goddesses.

Stories about them were passed down from one generation to the next, as well as inspiring literature, art and architecture.

These deities often behaved very extremely badly, but they also showed acts of kindness. Their cruelty meant that they were not good role models for humans to follow. Despite this they were widely worshipped and sometimes given sacrificial offerings, especially sheep and oxen.

While they displayed complex human characteristics, their stories always included an element of fantasy, along with a kernel of truth.

Ruling over the 12 strong Greek pantheon, atop Mount Olympus, was Zeus, King of the Gods, alongside his wife Hera, who was their Queen. These included Ares (God of War), Poseidon (God of the Sea) and Athena (Goddess of Wisdom), to name but a few. Their Roman equivalents were Mars, Neptune and Minerva.

It was during the 2nd century BCE that the Romans conquered the Greek civilisation and replaced the Greek deities with their own Roman equivalents.

There are many well-known stories about classical gods and goddesses, as well as those which may be less familiar, with mostly only minor differences between the Greek and Roman versions. These recount the often intrepid adventures of the members of the pantheon and others, which have enthralled readers and listeners over the centuries.

Aphrodite

As a symbol of desire and longing, and a goddess of love, Aphrodite had a great deal of influence in the mortal world as well as the realm of the gods. As one of the 12 senior deities believed by the faithful to live at the summit of Mount Olympus, she was worshipped widely in Greece and beyond. Known to the Romans as Venus, she was a patron of fecundity in humans and animals and the fertility of the land. According to Mark Cartwright, she was also a patron of 'commerce, politics and war'. In northern Greece, her main role was as a deity of city states, while her more general role as a war deity reflected the darker side of her personality. Aphrodite acted in conjunction with Ares the God of War in this respect, who was one of her many lovers.

Hesiod interpreted her name as coming from the word 'aphros' meaning 'sea foam' and therefore argued that her name meant 'born from sea foam'. Today this explanation is regarded as folklore. A number of other explanations have been put forward, but none of them with any great degree of validity.

Her most popular epithet was 'heavenly' (ourania), she was also known by other titles including 'Chryseis' meaning 'golden' and 'dia' (brilliant). (Thomas Apel & Avi Kapach) She was sometimes referred to as "Philomeleides", (smile loving) and "Skotia" which refers to her darker side.

Roses and other plants such as the apple tree which represented fertility had a symbolic association with Aphrodite. As Cartwright explains, so too did, creatures such as doves, swans and other birds, which were reputed to draw her chariot, as well as 'hares, goats, rams, dolphins and even tortoises' (Annette Gieseke). These were symbolic of the goddess, some representing fertility and others denoting the circumstances of her birth, according to the poet Hesiod.

According to Cartwright, Aphrodite was quite possibly 'derived from the Phoenician goddess Astarte or the Near Eastern goddess Inanna', sometime in the archaic period, before the eighth century BCE.

There are two different accounts of her birth. One of these is recorded by Hesiod. According to this legend the god Cronos castrated his father Uranus as a punishment for the cruelty he showed towards Gaia, who was Uranus's wife and Cronos's mother. Cronos cast Uranus's private parts into the sea which caused it to foam and bring forth the goddess Aphrodite as a fully grown adult.

As she stepped ashore, roses grew out of the sand and myrtle branches were provided by the Graces 'to hide her nakedness' (Annette Giesecke). This is supposed to have taken place on the island of Cythera or in Cyprus, which is why the goddess was give the title 'cyprian' or 'cypris' and is thought to have been based on a Cypriot goddess.

The other account of Aphrodite's origins is in the records of Homer. This states that she was the daughter of Zeus and the little-known Titan goddess Dione.

Thus, she is either a primordial goddess herself who was fathered by the creator Uranus, or alternatively she is a half-sibling to Zeus's many children.

Plato has suggested a version of events which reconciled both points of view. According to him there were two goddesses called Aphrodite, one of them being the goddess of male homosexual love (Heavenly Aphrodite) and the other of heterosexual love (Pandemic Aphrodite), meaning that her influence was ubiquitous.

Those assisted by Aphrodite in their amorous endeavours included Hippomenes, a hero who was infatuated by Atlanta (the Swift-Footed Huntress) and Jason whom she helped acquire the Golden Fleece. Another of these suitors was Paris, whom she assisted in seducing Helen, in return for a favour, an event which resulted in the Trojan War.

But in revenge at her rival lovers, Aphrodite caused Phaedra to fall in love with her stepson Hippolytus. She also led Clytemnestra, daughter of the King of Argos, who was considered to be something of a femme fatale, to murder her husband in his bath. She also caused the Cretan Queen Pasiphaë to be infatuated by a bull and the women of Lemnos to kill all their male relatives and slaves, because they failed to make sacrifice to her.

According to Apel & Kapach, the best-known epitaph to her birth from the sea 'is depicted on the base of the throne of the great statue of Zeus at Olympia'. She is often depicted alongside other deities, especially her son, Eros. Her birth out of the sea was a familiar topic in Ancient Greek art. She is often portrayed holding 'a flower, an apple, a sacred bird and a myrtle wreath'. (Cartwright) Some illustrations depict flying on the back of a swan or a goose. She often appears alluringly dressed, with a girdle around her chest imbued with magical powers of seduction. Sometimes she is portrayed in battle dress, clad in a helmet and brandishing a shield and a sword.

Aphrodite has been the subject of many artworks, usually depicted as exceptionally beautiful in appearance, especially during the Renaissance and Early Modern Period. The most famous example is the painting 'The birth of Venus' (1468) by Sandro Botticelli, Venus being the name given to her by the Romans. This artwork is now housed in the Uffizi Gallery in Florence.

Being a goddess of love Aphrodite was not just a purveyor of passion for both humans and the gods, but had as Annette Gieseke puts it; 'had various love affairs of her own'. She was forced by Zeus's wife Hera to marry Hephaestus, lame god of smiths and metallurgy, but found him unattractive and so sought to satisfy her sexual desire elsewhere. One of her most significant relationships was with Ares, God of War and she complemented his bloodthirsty battle prowess with tactical skills of her own. This affair was one of the most notorious of all the infidelities of the gods who inhabited Mount Olympus.

Her husband Hephaestus, a skilled craftsman, designed a golden bed to ensnare the lovers. When they lay on it, gold chains sprung forth and trapped the pair together. The Sun God Helios shone a bright light onto them so that all the deities of Mount Olympus could clearly see them. After their humiliation, they were eventually released. Ares took flight to Thrace and Aphrodite went back to Cyprus.

With Ares she gave birth to Eros, known to the Romans as Cupid, as well as Anteros and the other 'Erotes'. Her other children by Ares were 'Demius (fear), Phobus (panic) and Harmonia (harmony)' (Gieseke). She bore Hermes by her husband Hephaestus, despite rejecting his advances over a long period of time. She also had a son called Priapus, the fertility god, whose father was Dionysus, and had a progeny of lesser gods. Of her numerous mortal lovers, the best known one is Adonis. With them she had mortal children.

Adonis was the most handsome of men. She kept him in a box, guarded by Persephone, who also fell in love with him and took him for herself. Zeus adjudicated that the two should share him, each spending four months of every year with him, while for the remaining four months he was to remain alone. But as a mortal, Adonis died in a hunting incident, after which he became a scented flower. Aphrodite's grief was commemorated in 'The Adonis', an annual festival for women.

Adonis's death was not likely to have been an accident. There are disputed accounts of who was to blame. Some say it was the jealous Ares while others have suggested that it was due to the rage of Artemis or another of Adonis's enemies. Whatever the reason, it caused Aphrodite a great deal of distress.

According to Apel & Kapach 'the Ancient Greeks liked to blame females for their troubles'. This included their greatest calamity, the Trojan War. Hesiod states that this was in part due to the actions of Aphrodite. The story goes that, at the wedding of Peleus and Thetis, Eris, Goddess of Strife offered the prize of a golden apple marked with the words 'to the fairest' to whoever was chosen as the most beautiful goddess in the Ancient Greek pantheon (Apel & Kapach).

The three chosen contenders were Aphrodite, Athena and Hera. Zeus selected Paris, the Trojan Prince, to be the judge. To promote her candidacy, Hera, wife of Zeus offered Paris power over Asia and Europe. Athena, meanwhile, offered him military victory and wisdom. But it was Aphrodite's offer that won Paris over. She offered him the world's most beautiful mortal woman, generally acknowledged to be Helen of Sparta.

The goddess promised her to him, but she was already married to the Spartan King Menebos, so Paris abducted her, or she went willingly, whichever version you chose to believe. This led to the war between Troy and Sparta, known famously as the Trojan War, the most important battle in Greek mythology.

A much-worshipped member of the Greek pantheon, according to Apel & Kapach, Aphrodite's 'two most sacred sites were the islands of Cyprus and Cythera', near to where she is reputed to have been born out of the sea according to Hesiod, and the finest temples were constructed there in her name. They also existed across Greece and far across the Mediterranean including Italy and what is now eastern Turkey.

Festivals held in her honour were known as 'Aphrodisia' and these took place in Cyprus and throughout Greece, especially in Corinth and Athens.

Both men and women acted as her priests, depending on local traditions, and many sacrificial offerings were made to her, often of goats, especially by women on their wedding nights, hoping to be blessed with a successful consummation of their marriages.

The Romans came to regard the goddess as the mother by Anchises of their ancestor Aeneas who begat Romulus and Remus, the founders of Rome. This meant that the goddess they knew as Venus took on a special significance, and they built many statues in her name.

As both a goddess of sexual love and a war deity, Aphrodite had different sides to her personality. Being a goddess of sexual desire, she had a great influence over the human population. As a War Goddess she complemented the characteristics of her lover Ares, another war deity, whose capabilities were those of brute force, with her own tactical abilities. She was even held largely responsible for the Trojan War and was one of the most powerful of the 12 Olympians.

Ares

Known to the Romans as Mars, who was seen in a much more positive light, Ares was a God of War who was probably the least popular member of the Greek pantheon, since he was known for his often violent temper. Both gods and humans hated his savagery. According to Thomas Apel & Avi Kapach, he was widely acknowledged but not greatly admired. Described as 'gigantic and fierce' (THEOI) but also remarkably handsome, he is famous for his seduction of Aphrodite, who as well as being a goddess of sexual love was another war deity. Ares is well known for his failures as well as his successes, having done battle with Hercules and lost as well as incurring the wrath of Poseidon for the killing of his son, Halirrhothius. He was also overpowered by Athena who used her tactical abilities to match his brute force. His aggression and lack of self-control often landed him in trouble with the other Olympian gods.

Not just a god of war, Ares was also the purveyor of a host of other calamities such as plague, which did nothing to bolster his popularity with the people. Sophocles described him as 'the god unhonoured among the gods'. Despite his poor reputation with both the gods and the people, there were a number of temples dedicated to him in the Ancient Greek civilisation.

These were most often situated on the perimeter of towns, possibly due to him being seen as a protector who would not allow the people's enemies to enter them, or perhaps because he was so unruly that he was considered unsuitable for civilised urban life. There was an important temple in his name located in Athens and another at Olympia. In Thebes there was another which was designated for the worship of both Ares and his lover Aphrodite, who were often worshipped together.

He was known by various epitaphs such as 'man slaying', 'furious' and 'beast-like', as well as 'city sacking'. In Ancient Greek language his name was synonymous with war and was sometimes used with reference to other war deities such as Athena and Aphrodite. However, these two goddesses 'represented the strategic side of warfare' (Mark Cartwright), rather than belligerence and aggression, while Ares was a god who gloried in violence. He was considered as an outsider by most of the Greeks, since he came from Thrace, inhabited by a bellicose people whom they considered less civilised than themselves.

Ares's parents were Zeus and Hera, and he had a great many siblings due to Zeus's many sexual encounters. As Cartwright relates, these included Athena, Apollo, Artemis, Hermes, Dionysus and Hephaestus, lame god of the forge. Hebe (Cupbearer of the Gods) and Eileithyia (Goddess of Motherhood, Childhood and Midwifery) were also his sisters. Hercules, Minos and Perseus, were all mortal sons of Ares.

Although he never married, he had various children by several different partners, including Hippolyta, known as the Amazon Queen. The other burly female warriors known as the Amazons were also thought to be begotten by Ares.

As explained in the chapter on Aphrodite, with her he begat Deimos (terror and dread) and Phobos (fear), but also the more benign Harmonia, whose name is self-evident. The couple also begat Eros and Anteros who, according to Apel & Kapach were 'both winged gods of love and eroticism', as well as the Erotes, who played a similar role.

Ares was much feared by the Greeks as a lover of violence and participated in armed conflict accompanied by his sons Deimos, Phobos and his daughter Eris, Goddess of discord, hate and violence, who was often depicted alongside him as he drives his chariot into battle. Although frequently the subject of Greek art, illustrations of Ares as Mars were even more plentiful in the Roman era. He is usually depicted wearing full armour and a helmet, brandishing a sword and a spear in each hand. As such he looked no different from an ordinary soldier, but he was sometimes illustrated riding in a chariot driven by magical horses that breathe fire, which marked him out from other warriors. Many vases have been found which illustrate his battle with Hercules. These date from the sixth century BCE. By the time of the classical period (490-323 BCE) he was more often shown as clean-shaven, or even nude.

Sacred animals associated with Ares included 'the boar, the dog and the vulture' (Apel & Kapach). Also, mythological dragons were linked to Ares, especially the Colchian Dragon which guarded the Golden Fleece on his behalf.

Although usually greedy and ruthless, he won the affections of Aphrodite, Goddess of Love. He also came to the defence of his mother, Hera when she needed it, for example when his brother Hephaestus bound her to a magical chair. Also, when the jealous Hera became infuriated with Leto with whom Zeus fathered Apollo and Artemis, Ares drove the interloper away from anywhere where she planned to give birth.

Ares's handsomeness and bravery, for which he was well known, helped him find favour with Aphrodite, who became his lover. The god was banished from Mount Olympus for a time, because of this infamous affair.

Both Ares and Aphrodite took revenge on each other's rival lovers. When Ares had a sexual encounter with Eos, Goddess of Dawn, Aphrodite caused her to fall endlessly in love with someone else. When Aphrodite became smitten with the mortal Adonis, Ares transformed himself into a boar and savaged him to death, while Adonis was out hunting.

The best-known myth about Ares concerns his battle with Hercules. This took place because Ares's son Kyknos accosted people on their way to Delphi, to visit the Oracle. This enraged the god Apollo who dispatched Hercules to take his revenge. Kyknos was defeated and killed by Hercules which led his father Ares to join battle with Hercules himself, who, with the powers granted to him by Athena, was able to wound Ares and defeat him.

Another story about Ares relates how he was captured by twin giants, Ephialtes and Otus. The pair planned to kidnap Hera and Artemis, 'but first needed to remove Ares from the equation' (Apel & Kapach). So, they raided Mount Olympus, home of the Greek pantheon, captured Ares and incarcerated him in a cauldron, until he was eventually rescued by Hermes a year later. In any case the giants were unsuccessful in their endeavours.

In Homer's account of the Trojan War, Ares fought mostly for the Trojans, and according to Cartwright, 'he sometimes led them into battle along with Hector'. Yet he prevaricated about which side he was on and sometimes helped the Spartans instead. Indecisiveness as to what side he supported was something for which he was well-known, as he was more interested in doing battle than in what side he was on.

During the Trojan War Athena endowed Diomedes with supernatural abilities of great power enabling him to defeat Ares, using a spear. Homer compared Ares cries with those of 1000 men. At this point Zeus stepped in and decreed that the gods should take no further part in the battle. But on learning that the Trojans had killed his son, Acalyphas, Ares defied his father Zeus and intervened, only to be thwarted by Athena who used her magical powers to crush him with a heavy rock, which caused him serious injuries.

Though the Greek gods were famous for their misbehaviour, Ares was the one who most often got into trouble. He was tried for the murder of Poseidon's son Halilrrothuis in a case which disturbed the harmony of the gods. The trial was held at a site near where the incident allegedly took place. Ares was acquitted because it became clear that Halilrrothius had violated Ares's daughter Alcippe. Henceforth the site was called the Areopagus, meaning 'Hall of Ares', and became the venue for Athenian murder trials.

Militaristic culture meant that Ares was highly respected in Sparta (THEOI), where an early statue of him stood. Cult sites and temples could be found in Athens, Argos and other Greek cities. He had a particular cult following in his home city of Thrace. Many of the monuments built in his name no longer exist but his image is inscribed on many coins, illustrations and ornaments.

Only a few festivals are known to have been devoted to the worship of Ares in the Ancient Greek world. Not much is known about how this took place, but it is recorded that soldiers would sometimes make sacrifice to him, as they prepared for battle. One festival took place in Geronthrae in Laconia, in which women were not allowed to participate.

The Roman god Mars was a much more popular god of war and had a much higher status among the Roman gods than Ares had amongst his fellow Greek deities. He was similar in many ways, but like other Roman gods he is less human-like than his Greek counterpart.

The founders of Rome, Romulus and Remus, were reputed to

be sons of Mars. This meant the city had a sacred significance, as Athena did to the city of Athens. Both Athena and the two brothers were patrons of their respective capital cities. The month Martius (March) was named in Mars's honour.

Although Ares was an unpopular deity because of his thirst for battle, he commanded the fearful respect of the people, who also saw him as a protector from their enemies. He was worshipped out of necessity rather than enthusiasm, but nonetheless enjoyed high status amongst the Olympians.

Artemis

Artemis was one of the 12 senior Greek deities who resided on Mount Olympus. She was, according to Mark Cartwright, the 'Greek goddess of hunting, wild nature and chastity'. Despite her sworn virginity, for which she is best known, she was also a patron of fertility and childbirth. Greek mothers looked to her for a good birth experience. She was worshipped throughout Greece but especially at the temple dedicated to her at Ephesus which was particularly imposing and was one of the seven wonders of the ancient world.

Some scholars say that her name dates from the Mycenaean period (C 1750 – 1050 BCE) while others believe it has a foreign origin. In any case, not much is known about its etymological root.

She was known by many names and titles including Aidoios Parthenos (most revered virgin), Locheaira (she of the shooting arrows) and Agrotera (she of the hunt). In later antiquity she was sometimes called Phoebe by both the Greeks and the Romans.

Artemis was the daughter of Zeus and Leto, born either on the island of Delos or at Ephesus in what is in modern-day Turkey. The god Apollo was her twin brother. It is even suggested that she even assisted her mother with the birth of her twin, who was born after her. She had no husbands, lovers or children since she had taken a vow of chastity.

When she was a child, her father Zeus granted her list of wishes she had put to him. These included: 'that she should never marry' (Clark), that she be provided with an invincible silver bow so that she would be a match for her brother Apollo, himself a skilled archer, that she should be allowed to live the life of a huntress and that she should have an entourage of 60 nymphs to go out hunting with her who would attend to the hounds.

Her most significant attribute was her silver bow, with which she had an infallible aim, although she sometimes used other weapons, such as a spear.

Artemis is always depicted as a healthy young woman, wearing a knee length robe to allow her to run through the forests chasing wild beasts. She is usually portrayed in Ancient Greek art as a beautiful huntress carrying a bow and arrow or sometimes a spear, often accompanied by her hunting dogs and the animals she hunted, such as a deer or stag.

One of the finest surviving examples of her image is the renowned Francois Vase which dates from around 570 BCE. On one side she is depicted with a panther and a stag and on the other side she is shown accompanied by lions. In later versions she is pictured holding a torch.

She is often conflated with Eileithyia, who, like her, was also a goddess of childbirth. In later times, from the Hellenistic Period (323 BCE-32 BCE) onwards, she was closely associated with the Moon, and in particular with Selene, Goddess of the Moon. Meanwhile, her brother Apollo was associated with the Sun. As Avi Kapach puts it: While Apollo 'represented reason and order, Artemis symbolised the more untameable aspects of natural and human life'.

Although she was Queen of all animals, the most sacred of

these was the deer. She was often depicted riding in a chariot drawn by these animals. The boar and the bear were also important to her, with the boar in particular being an agent of her wrath. Some birds were also sacred to her, including guinea fowls and partridges. Plants had their place too such as Cypress and Palm trees.

She was also associated with boundaries and transition, which is why her temples were often located on the perimeter of cities or where dry land gives way to marshy areas. This association is also symbolic as Kapach describes: the transition of 'childhood to womanhood, virginity to marriage and marriage to parenthood'.

For young women and girls, she was a symbol of purity and chastity. Her zealous personality comes through in Homer's Iliad and other Greek texts. Although she is herself chaste and reclusive, she champions women and girls with her fierce temper, and shows a 'lack of mercy or sympathy' (Clark) especially to men. Her main weaknesses are her pride and lack of forgiveness. With her vow of chastity, she disliked marriage and the lack of freedom for women it incurs, despite being a goddess of fertility and childbirth. When she was not busy hunting, she was active defending women and girls. She was possibly the first feminist icon.

As one of the 12 major Olympian gods she had a great deal of influence over humanity and events on Earth. In addition to the powers held by all these gods she had an invincible skill with her bow and arrow, and the ability to morph into any animal she wished. She also had the powers of a healer but could inflict disease when she chose to.

As Kapach describes, 'she fiercely defended her virginity and her reputation as the greatest of hunters' and would inflict terror on those who offended her or her family.

This can be seen in stories about Artemis and Orion, who

was a hunting companion of Artemis. She had him killed for a number of possible reasons. Some accounts say he took advantage of her, or one of her chaste followers, others that he challenged her to a discus competition. An alternative story states that Eos, Goddess of Dawn became Orion's lover and Artemis killed him out of jealousy.

Another tale is that Apollo was worried that Orion was a threat to his sister's chastity. Knowing her immaculate skills with her bow and arrow, Apollo challenged her to hit a seemingly impossible target, way out at sea. Once she fired the arrow, she realised that the target was in fact Orion's head. When she realised that she had inadvertently shot her friend's head, she was filled with grief and begged her father Zeus to turn him into a constellation, known to this day by his name.

Another story of her vengeance concerns Calisto, one of her chaste followers who was seduced by Zeus, who made her pregnant. Artemis realised that Calisto had broken her vow of chastity and with Zeus in particular. The vengeful Artemis turned her into a bear. As such Calisto gave birth to a son, Arcus. Artemis went on to transform Calisto and her son into the stellar constellations of the Great Bear and the Little Bear, respectively.

Her cleverness is apparent in the story in which she encounters two giants known as the Aloadae brothers, Otus and Ephialtes, also mentioned in the chapter on Ares. They grew continuously and boasted that they would soon reach the summit of Mount Olympus, where they would abduct Hera and Artemis and make them their wives. Artemis realised that they had become so powerful that they could only be killed by each other.

She sought out the brothers while they were out hunting in the woods. Transforming herself into a stag, she ran between the two of them, causing them to throw their spears at her. She deftly avoided these and instead the two giants inadvertently shot each other dead.

Another tale of Artemis's vengeance concerns Niobe, the Theban Queen who had 12 children, six boys and six girls. She taunted Artemis's mother Leto who had only produced two children, claiming that with her 12 she was a more fertile mother. Artemis and Apollo responded by killing six of Niobe's children each. Apollo killed the six boys with his golden bow and arrows, while Artemis struck down the six girls with her silver bow. Niobe's boasting left her with no children at all. After all, she was a mortal, and her adversaries were gods.

Like Apollo, Artemis was an ally of the Trojans during the Trojan War, but her interventions were not very significant. Yet according to Homer's Iliad, the fighting broke out on Mount Olympus itself between Hera and Artemis, who, met with Hera's fury, sought refuge with her father Zeus.

There is a story that during this infamous war, Iphigenia, daughter of King Agamemnon of Mycenae, leader of the Greek army, had hunted down a deer in Artemis's sacred grove. As a consequence, Artemis becalmed the sea so that Agamemnon's fleet was unable to reach Troy. In return for a fair wind Artemis demanded that the King sacrifice his daughter, Iphigenia. Agamemnon was ready to comply with this demand, but at the last moment Artemis took pity on the King and his daughter and allowed him to sacrifice a deer instead. She also conferred priesthood on Iphigenia.

Artemis was worshipped especially ardently at the Temple of Ephesus since this was believed to have been her birthplace. The temple was almost twice the size of the Parthenon in Athens, and it is one of the seven wonders of the ancient world. According to Kapach, 'The ancients, from Herodotus to Plutarch, marvelled at its beauty and size'. Inside this temple stood a huge cedarwood statue representing the goddess, but the temple was eventually destroyed by the pro-Christian Roman Emperor, Theodosius in 401 CE.

Worshipped with particular fervour on the Island of Delos, she was also especially popular in Attica and in Lydia, which are now part of Turkey. Shrines in her name were constructed throughout Greece, especially in rural areas as she had no connection with urban life. The largest collection of such shrines can be found in Arcadia, but they were to be found in Athens too.

Due to her association with wild places, and her reputation as a 'bow-wielding maiden' (Danielle Mackay), she was matriarch of the band of female warriors, known as the Amazons. According to the chronicler Pausanias, the Amazons set up many shrines in her honour.

The Romans carried on the tradition of worship of this deity, whom to them was known as Diana. As Cartwright puts it: 'A second century CE marble statue of the goddess with [her] bow at the ready' and surrounded by her pack of hunting dogs baying for blood is now on display at the Vatican Museum in Rome. Her brother Apollo, unusually, was known by the same name to the Romans.

While Artemis was admired for her hunting skills and power over animals, she was worshipped by women and girls, to whom she represented an idealised 'freedom from society' (Mackay). Artemis's symbolism as a chaste maiden, who does not participate much in normal life and fights vehemently for what she believes in, has become especially relevant in recent years, as she embarks on her pursuit of justice.

Dionysus

Dionysus was the Ancient Greek God of Wine and High Spiritedness as well as of theatre, whose Roman equivalent is Bacchus. As Cartwright puts it: 'Cast as a bad guy on Mount Olympus, he was one of the most colourful characters amongst all the deities. Yet wine was so much a necessity of human life that Bacchus was just as important to the Greeks as was Demeter, Goddess of Grain and Harvest.

The origin of his name is unclear, but it is possible that 'nysus' is derived from Nymphs, known as Nysiads who were thought to be responsible for his upbringing on Mount Nysa. He was known by various epithets including Baccheios (reveller) and Eleutherias (liberator). His domains primarily included drunkenness (intoxication) and his followers were known to enter a state of Dionysian frenzy while carrying out his rites. According to Avi Kapach, Dionysus 'represented the most spontaneous and unrestrained aspects of human behaviour'.

Dionysus was most often described as the son of Zeus, King of the Gods and Semele, a Theban princess, who was unwittingly killed by Zeus, who was not keen to do Semele harm. However, Zeus's jealous wife Hera persuaded her to ask Zeus to show himself in all his glory. Being a mere mortal, this shocked her so much that she expired instantaneously. At the time she was pregnant with Dionysus whom Zeus took from her and nurtured in his thigh until he was ready to be born. This is why he was known as 'the twice born'. While he was reared by satyrs and nymphs, he received his education from a wise man called Silenus while residing on Mount Nysa where Hera's wrath could not reach him.

As he was growing up, Hera persisted in trying to destroy him. Legend has it that he was brought up by his Aunt Ino (Semele's sister) and her husband Athames, until Hera drove them into a homicidal frenzy in which they killed each other. There is some disagreement about what followed, but most sources agree that Dionysus's brother Hermes helped him to escape Hera's wrath. Hermes took Dionysus to the relative safety of Mount Nysa where the nymphs raised him. The location of this mountain is disputed. Some said it was in Thrace while others said that it was in Asia or North Africa.

The earliest known records of him date from as far back as the Bronze Age (circa 25000 BCE). Worship of Dionysus probably originated in the Near East rather than Greece itself, travelling via Thrace to Macedonia and into the Greek islands. Annette Giesecke recounts that he emerged at first as a god of 'sustaining fluids in plants as well as wine, milk and honey'. His popularity spread rapidly throughout Greece, and according to Giesecke he was seen by Greek citizens as 'the most democratic of gods'.

With all the powers of a major deity, by the time of the fifth and fourth centuries BCE Dionysus tends to be illustrated with long flowing hair and a copious beard, but later clean-shaven. He is generally shown wearing a fawn skin, holding forth a wine cup and carrying a staff wrapped with ivy and vine leaves which were symbolic of the god. A somewhat effeminate character, he is often represented riding a mule, in a reclining position. One of the best examples of this illustration of Dionysus can be found at the Parthenon (447-432 BCE). Many other images show him riding big cats, such as leopards, lions and panthers. Images of his face are embossed on ancient coinage from Crete, Thebes and Thasos. Because of his popularity, he is depicted in Greek art more than any other deity, often accompanied by Nymphs and Satyrs (half-goat, half-men) and later the maenads, a band of female spirits associated with him.

As he was always under the influence of an excess of wine, his character was the antithesis of his half-brother Apollo, who represented order and the rule of law.

According to Giesecke, unlike most other gods, Dionysus made no distinction between 'male and female, young or old, slave or free'. In his eyes, all were equal. This state of equality even put animals on a par with humans. Not surprisingly, as a god who believed in the equality of the sexes, Dionysus was especially popular with women, representing liberation from, as Giesecke puts it: 'the shuttle and the loom'.

Dionysus is believed to have discovered wine in the East, after a male lover of his, a satyr named Amphelus, met his death in a hunting expedition and was reincarnated as a grape vine. The Greek word for a grapevine was henceforth known as 'ampelos', from which the bereft Dionysus was the first to make wine. Another story goes that the vine existed long before Amphelus, but Dionysus was the inventor of the beverage, after watching a snake sucking the juice out of grapes.

Legend has it that 'Dionysus taught the Athenian Icarus how to make wine' (Kapach). Smitten with the effects of intoxication, Icarus taught the skill to his fellow Athenians, who became drunk and thinking they had been poisoned, went on to kill him.

On hearing the news, Icarus's daughter Epigone took her

own life. The distraught Dionysus, who was kind to those who loved him, made them both into constellations. Implicitly, this serves as a warning against drinking to excess.

Most sources concur that on coming of age, Dionysus was driven insane by Hera, which led him to roam around the world. By various accounts he visited Egypt, Syria and Mesopotamia.

Whilst on his travels, Dionysus hired a crew and went on a sea voyage, but the sailors were in fact Tyrrhenian pirates hoping for a hefty ransom. Seeing that he looked unusually handsome, they planned to take him to Asia for sale. But as Cartwright describes Dionysus 'transformed the ship's mast into a huge vine, while the sails dripped with wine' to the sound of eerie music, sung by a 'heavenly choir'. He summoned up spirits in the form of tigers and panthers, which panicked the sailors into jumping overboard and become dolphins for the rest of their days, apart from their helmsman, who had recognised the fact that he was in the presence of a deity and advised his men against the kidnap. Dionysus made landfall on Naxos, where he met and fell in love with his wife to be.

This was Ariadne, daughter of King Minos of Crete. As Kapach explains, 'they had many sons some of whom went on to become minor heroes and kings. Dionysus sired an abundance of children by other women, both mortal and immortal.

Ariadne assisted Theseus in slaying the minotaur, and then the couple eloped planning to get married in Athens. But for some unknown reason he abandoned her on the Island of Naxos. Hesiod states that Dionysus rescued her and took her to Mount Olympus, where he persuaded Zeus to make her immortal. According to other accounts she eventually died and was given a magisterial funeral by Dionysus. In any event, it is agreed by most sources that he transformed her crown into a stellar constellation, the Corona Borealis, in her honour.

Wherever he went he took his invention of wine, and this encouraged people to worship him. By drinking wine and making merry people achieved spiritual union with the god and released themselves from their daily routine. In earlier times the people would ascend the mountains catching wild creatures as they went and eating them raw, believing the blood of these animals to be an incarnation of Dionysus.

However, where his influence was met with resistance, the consequences were severe. In Naxos where King Lycurgus resisted him, he drove the king insane, leading him to murder his own son. Dionysus put a curse on the Thracians, 'that their land would be barren as long as Lycurgus was alive' (Kapach). There are various accounts of his demise, but it is suggested he died at the hands of his own people, after which Dionysus's curse was lifted. Dionysus also caused the women of Thebes to become insane, because people in that city did not accept his godly status. Next, he turned his attention to the city of Argos where again many people failed to recognise him as a deity. Here to, Dionysus drove the women of the city mad, this time so that they ate their own children.

Cartwright tells of another myth concerning Dionysus which is the famous tale of King Midas of Phrygia who one day found Silenus, who had been his tutor, inebriated in his garden. Silenus was Dionysus's favourite drinking companion. Midas gave him sustenance, before reuniting him with Dionysus. By way of reward the god offered Midas a gift of his choosing. Midas chose the gift of everything he touched turning into gold. But Midas soon realised this included food and drink and, parched and hungry, the King came close to death. At this point Dionysus released him from the enchantment by instructing him to cleanse himself in the Pactolus River.

Whilst there are a number of myths about his adventures, as a god of wine and merriment he was particularly popular with the Ancient Greeks. Homer called him "the joy of man" and Hesiod describes him as "much cheering'". He was worshipped throughout Greece and beyond and there are many temples dedicated to him. The island of Naxos was a particular stronghold for the worship of Dionysus.

Although his greatest cult following was on the island of Naxos, Dionysian Festivals were held in his name in many Greek towns and cities. These were occasions for drunkenness and debauchery, which the rulers of some city states tried to ban, only to be met with the wrath of Dionysus.

Ritual celebrations took place which allowed revellers to undergo a transcendental experience. The idea of leaving one's own person and being at one with the character they are playing, is thought to be the origin of Ancient Greek theatre.

As Greek culture developed, worship of the god was included in theatre performances, especially in Athens. For this reason, Dionysus also became patron god of theatre and art, for which more respectable festivals took place (Gieseke). At a theatre site in Athens a Dionysian temple existed where according to Kapach 'he was ritually honoured a few times a year'. It includes various paintings depicting his life story.

Dionysus and his Roman equivalent Bacchus were portrayed as wine loving hedonists who encouraged people into carousing and making merry. By worshiping him, they felt liberated from their daily routine through merriment and intoxication.

Eros

Eros, called Cupid by the Romans, was in the Ancient Greek world, as Annette Giesecke puts it, the 'personification of sexual desire'. His powers of infatuation not only applied to the human population; the gods were susceptible to it too. As a Greek god of eroticism, Eros is synonymous with this form of passion. According to Avi Kapach, he was known variously 'as "lovely", "beautiful" and "bittersweet"'. Armed with his famous bow and arrow to which everyone was vulnerable, he was notorious for being both capricious and cruel.

He was widely believed to be the son of the goddess of sexual love, Aphrodite, and her lover Ares. However, some sources say that he came into being before the creation of the world, in which he played an essential part. According to Hesiod he emerged from the primordial chaos along with Gaia (Earth) and Tartarus (Earth's depths). Another story goes that he was born out of an egg hatched by the primordial goddess Nyx (night). Other sources suggest that his mother was one of a number of minor goddesses, namely Eileithyia, Penia or Iris. With these varying accounts, he was either one of the earliest or one or the latest of the Greek gods.

His siblings included Deimos (fear), Phobos (panic) and Harmonia (harmony). By some accounts he also had a younger brother, Anteros, a more sinister character who took revenge for those whose love was unrequited. The Goddess Psyche would become Eros's wife according to a well-known myth.

Eros was usually represented from the sixth century BCE onwards as a handsome, winged adolescent, crowned with a wreath of roses, which represented his inevitable victory over his chosen targets. In early Greek art he is often portrayed carrying a lyre. It is not until the fourth century BCE that he is depicted carrying a bow and arrow. Images of him often appear on Greek pottery, where he can be seen attending marriage ceremonies and in pictures of romantic encounters. This includes the marriage of Paris and Helen of Troy.

Statues of Eros were constructed in many gymnasia (places of exercise) often along with statues of the god Hermes. Many others were built in the form of the deities described as 'Erotes', which represent the various aspects of love. The Erotes along with Eros himself make up a seven strong band of passion inducing deities. These statues were found in a temple of western Attica, which was constructed in the fourth century BCE to honour Aphrodite, where the main statue was an ivory carving of the goddess herself.

Eros also features as an illustration on the statue of Zeus at Olympia, which is one of the seven wonders of the ancient world. At the Parthenon in Athens there is an illustration of Eros with his mother Aphrodite. On a much smaller scale, Eros was also depicted in jewellery and gem carvings. Additionally, Eros and his wife Psyche are represented on many Ancient Greek terracotta figurines. It is not until the Hellenistic period (323-51 BCE) that he is portrayed as the chubby and troublesome child, recognisable as Cupid.

Because the passions he provoked could not be easily controlled, he was seen as a trickster who sometimes acted harmlessly albeit mischievously but at other times was quite vindictive, creating all sorts of difficulties for those he targeted. It is possibly because of this inconsistency of character that he is not a member of the pantheon of 12 senior Olympian deities, and as such was a lesser god.

Eros played a part in numerous mythological stories, with the role of making one individual fall in love with another. This applied to both gods and humans alike. Sometimes, however, he induced repulsion instead of desire.

Apollo, who ridiculed the powers of Eros, became smitten with the nymph Daphne, but Eros used his power in the opposite way to make Daphne find Apollo abhorrent. Medusa, the sorceress with snake infested hair, became infatuated with Jason, leader of the Argonauts, thanks to Eros who also caused Hades, the God of the Underworld, not known for a passionate disposition, to become infatuated with the goddess Persephone. Eros himself was pricked by his arrow and fell in love with the goddess Psyche. Aphrodite accidently pricked her own finger with her son's arrow and fell for the handsome mortal, Adonis.

Eros's power over mortals is exemplified by the story of how Hera wanted to help Jason retrieve the Golden Fleece from King Aeetes of Colchis. To do this, she sent Jason to meet with the King's daughter, who immediately fell in love with him, and helped him obtain the Fleece, thanks to the intervention of Eros.

Eros was the power responsible for Paris's passion for Helen, who won the right to marry her in return for a favour to the goddess Aphrodite. As the judge in a beauty competition, Paris declared that Aphrodite was the winner, since she offered him the hand in marriage of Helen, the most beautiful mortal woman in the world, in return for being so chosen. He carried Helen away in an elopement or abduction which was the cause of the Trojan War. This story shows the immense power that Eros had over his victims.

He often chose his targets at random, piercing their hearts with his magical arrow, which made them become intoxicated with sexual desire often with a subject of Eros's choosing.

Eros has little mythology in his own right but features in many myths about other deities and mortals. Homer describes how even Zeus fell victim to his power, when he fell in love with Hera, who was to become his wife.

According to one Greek poet:

'Neither can any mortal escape you, nor any man whose life lasts for a day'. (Kapach)

As for his own story of infatuation, this was with Psyche, an extremely beautiful mortal woman whose devotion and sacrifice for her husband Eros earned her the gift of immortality.

Aphrodite, Goddess of Beauty and Love was so envious of the interest taken in Psyche by men that she asked her son, Eros, who dispensed love and infatuation, to put a stop to it, by making her undesirable to men. Instead, Eros fell deeply in love with Psyche too.

Despite all the interest taken in her by so many men, Psyche remained unmarried. Her parents decided to consult the oracle to find out what the outcome of this situation would be. But Eros saw to it that the oracle would predict that she was to 'marry an ugly beast whose face she would never be allowed to see, [who would] wait for her at the top of a nearby mountain' (Greekmythology.com). Psyche's parents were understandably distraught to hear this news but decided that they had no option but to go along with it.

Once married, Psyche and Eros could only be together at night, when Psyche was unable to see her husband in the darkness. This was Eros, masquerading as the beast. Nonetheless he made Psyche very happy, and she confided in her sisters how upset she was at not being able to see his face. Knowing the identity of her husband, her envious sisters tricked her into believing that her husband was a monster, who was destined to kill her, if she did not kill him first herself.

With an oil lamp and a dagger in hand, Psyche was ready to carry out the murder. But when she saw her husband's face, she realised his true identity. In a moment of shock, she spilled a drop of oil on Eros's face. He awoke, startled, and 'told Psyche that she had betrayed him' (Greekmytholgy.com). He then flew away having told her that they would never meet again. Eros was subsequently imprisoned by his mother, the vengeful Aphrodite. Psyche pleaded with her to release him, so Aphrodite set her three apparently unachievable tasks to secure Eros's freedom.

Determined to succeed, Psyche carried out the first two tasks without great difficulty but had more trouble with the final one. This was that she should go to Hades and bring back the box containing the elixir of beauty to Aphrodite, who warned her not to look inside it. Psyche was unable to resist the temptation to look in the box, but when she opened it, instead of the elixir she released Morpheus, the God of Sleep and Dreams, and fell into a deep slumber.

When Eros heard this news, he went to Mount Olympus to persuade Zeus to awaken her. Zeus was so impressed by the couple's love for each other that not only did he do as Eros had asked, but according to Greekmythology.com, 'granted her immortality so that they could be together forever'.

Despite not being one of the most senior of gods, Eros had a cult following in Thespiae, a town in central Greece. He was also feted in Athens, where he shared a temple with Aphrodite. Many festivals in his name took place in these two cities. He was also popular in other places, especially Philadelphia in the Aegean region of Turkey. Cartwright describes how Eros was closely linked with the cult of his mother Aphrodite, Goddess of Love, throughout the Greek world. He was widely worshipped as a patron of passion and procreation. Festivals in his name regularly took place in cities such as Thespiae and Athens. The events in Thespiae included artistic and athletic competitions.

No one was immune to Eros's influence, be they mortal or immortal. He also had similar powers over the animal population. Despite his renown as a creator of the world, he did not have the status of the 12 Olympians, but had irresistible powers over them as well as everyone else.

H e r a

Hera was married to Zeus and as such was Queen of the Ancient Greek deities. Although she was never unfaithful to Zeus, she wreaked vengeance on her husband's many lovers, often killing them when she could. She did no physical harm to Zeus himself, even though he was the instigator of his affairs.

Her Roman equivalent was Juno, wife of Jupiter, King of the Olympians. But Juno was associated more with Hera's familial role than her vengeful nature. According to Mark Cartwright, 'Juno was one of the most important Roman deities along with Jupiter and Minerva'. She was the patron of Rome, and an annual festival was held there in the month of June, so named in honour of the goddess herself. In Roman times, this was the most providential time for a marriage.

Hera's name is based on the Greek word for a 'protectress'. She was also referred to by a number of epithets relating to her beauty such as 'Leukolenos' which refers to her pale skin and Boopis, meaning 'cow-eyed'.

As the faithful wife, she was, as Cartwright puts it the patron of 'marriage and family life and was known as a protector of women in childbirth'. But she was best known for her fury against her husband's illicit lovers and their children.

Hera was daughter to Chronos and Rhea, Titans who

deposed their parents, the primordial deities Uranus and Gaia. Hera had five siblings, who were her sisters Hestia and Demeter and her brothers Hades, Poseidon and Zeus. This made her Zeus's sister as well as his wife. With Zeus she was the mother of Ares (God of War) and Eileithyia (Childbirth). She also gave birth to Hephaestus (God of the Fire and the Forge). According to some versions of events she did this without a man, in retaliation for Zeus miraculously giving birth to Athena himself, conceived with Zeus's first wife, Metis. However, Hera threw Hephaestus down Mount Olympus because she considered him ugly. This left him permanently lame.

Some myths suggest that Hephaestus got his revenge on his mother by catching her in a throne with invisible chains strapped around it. When Hera sat on it, she was bound by the chains. She was eventually freed at the intervention of Dionysus, who plied Hephaestus with wine and persuaded him to release her.

Zeus's offspring with Hera were not the most significant of his children. Instead, this honour went to those he had fathered with his many lovers, both mortal and divine. These included Apollo and Artemis, whose mother was Leto, Dionysus who was born to Semele, and Hercules to whom Zeus's lover Alcmene was the mother.

It was foretold that Chronos would be overthrown by his children, just as he had deposed his own father Uranus. He therefore ate four of his children, with Zeus being the only one to escape this fate. Eventually Zeus forced Chronos to regurgitate the children, who sprang back to life and took their places amongst the Olympian Gods.

Hera herself is often depicted wearing a sleeveless robe and a cloak, usually sitting on a throne. In some illustrations she is shown crowned with a bridal veil covering her face and carries a royal sceptre. She is sometimes portrayed carrying a pomegranate, representing fertility. Other illustrations show her with the symbol of a peacock, representing pride, or a cuckoo, as which Zeus disguised himself when he first made advances towards her. She is often represented alongside Zeus 'in sacred marriage scenes (Avi Kapach).

Occasionally she was symbolised by inanimate objects such as a pillar in Argos and a plank in the island of Samos. From the earliest days in which she was worshipped she was associated with cattle, hence the epithet 'Cow-Eyed'. Thus, like the Egyptian goddess Hathor she was a goddess of motherhood whose appearance was compared to that of a cow. From the era known as the Hellenistic period (323–31 BCE) she was often portrayed, as Kapach describes, 'riding a chariot drawn by peacocks'.

Although it is obvious that she was both cunning and bold, Ancient Greek sources do not tell us much about Hera's character, which may be due to its inherent contradictions. Thus, she was the faithful wife who took revenge on her husband's lovers and the children he had by them.

Cartwright explains that one of Zeus's lovers was Leto, whose parents were Coeus and Phoebe. Hera was so furious with Leto when she had Zeus's child that she pushed her down Mount Olympus. Leto survived but Hera put a curse on any community that gave her shelter. Eventually she managed to escape to the barren island of Delos, where Hera prevented Eileithyia, Goddess of Childbirth, from visiting her and assisting her with the birth of her child. This meant that Leto's labour was extended for the whole of her pregnancy, making her experience much unnecessary pain. Eventually Leto gave birth to Apollo and Artemis who defeated a dragon sent by Hera to kill their mother.

When Zeus turned his lover Io into a cow, to disguise her from his wife, Hera enlisted the help of a 100-eyed monster called Argus to watch over the herd until Io revealed herself. However, Hercules, born to Zeus and Alcmene, came to the assistance of his father, by soothing the creature into a slumber with a song and then killing him.

Hera was so enraged by this that she set the monster's 100 eyes into the tail of a peacock, as they can be seen today. Hera persisted in persecuting Io and as Kapach describes, 'sent a giant fly to pester her'.

She tried to avenge Alcmene's relationship with Zeus by killing their son, Hercules, but he survived and went on to marry Megara, Princess of Thebes, and the couple had many children. Yet in the end Hera got her revenge by driving him mad so that he killed his wife and children. Full of remorse, Hercules consulted an oracle for the best way to try and make amends. The oracle instructed him to enter the service of Eurystheus, King of Mycenae, who was beholden to Hera. The King challenged Hercules with 12 seemingly impossible tasks, known as 'the 12 Labours of Hercules'. Eventually, Hercules succeeded in carrying out these tasks and thwarted Hera's attempts to kill him.

According to some myths, after death Hercules achieved the status of a god and eventually made peace with Hera, who gave her blessing to his marriage to her daughter Hebe.

When Zeus persuaded the Nymph Echo to distract Hera from his philandering by flattering her with false praise, Hera realised that this was just a trick, instigated by Zeus. She took her revenge on Echo, rather than Zeus himself, by cursing her to speak only the words just spoken by others, hence the meaning of the word 'echo' which exists to this day.

In another tale Hera again showed her vengeful nature. She and Zeus had an argument about who experiences greater pleasure from sex, males, or females. To settle the dispute, they asked a man, Tiresias, who had formerly been a woman, to adjudicate. Tiresias answered that it was women who got more satisfaction, which enraged Hera so much that she struck him blind. After Hera did this, Zeus could not reverse the spell but, according to New World Encyclopedia 'gave Tiresias the gift of prophecy'.

Hera showed her more helpful side when the hero Jason (of Golden Fleece fame) came to her aid unwittingly when she was disguised as a haggard old woman, who was in difficulties crossing a perilous river. For this she promised to be with him in his hour of need.

Two less fortunate souls were Ixion and Tityos, who both tried to seduce Hera. For this crime Ixion was trapped in an eternally spinning wheel in Hades, while Tityos was chained to a rock and visited once a day by a vulture, which would eat his liver, only for it to be magically restored for the next occasion.

At one point during her struggles with Zeus, she persuaded her siblings to try and depose him. While he was sleeping, 'they stole away his thunderbolts' (Kapach) and trussed him up. Her plans were thwarted when he was released by yet another of his lovers, the sea goddess Thetis (mother of Achilles). Furious at their insolence, Zeus made Hera and her siblings swear that they would never challenge his power again.

According to Homer, Hera was one of the main protagonists in the Trojan War, and plotted with other deities to defeat the armies of Troy. This was because she never forgave the Trojan Prince Paris for choosing Aphrodite as the best-looking goddess in a beauty contest of which he was the judge.

Although her own side was ultimately successful, Hera's interventions in the Trojan War proved futile, which evokes the perception of powerlessness of women in Ancient Greek society.

Nonetheless, she had an important role as Queen of the Gods. Despite Zeus having ultimate authority, Hera's temples were, as Kapach explains, amongst the earliest and 'most impressive of the Ancient Greek world'. One of these was constructed on the island of Samos circa 800 BCE, which is regarded by many as her birthplace. In the sixth century BCE, it was destroyed by fire and replaced with an even greater structure. Hera was the patron goddess of Argos, where a temple in her name was built during the seventh century BCE. She also had a temple at Olympia, dating from 600-650 BCE. Her temples were also situated outside Greece itself, for example in southern Italy.

The Cult of Hera was one of the most significant cultural practices of the early civilisations of Argos, Mycenae and Sparta (New World Encyclopedia). Samos was a cult centre for her worship from the second millennium BCE, known as the Mycenaean period. Her cult following continued into the Roman era.

Hera's cult festivals were known as Heraia, including sporting games for women held every four years at Olympia, which were the precursor of the Olympic Games of today. Another festival that took place in Argos involved a procession outside the city, ending in the sacrifice of 100 bulls. Similar celebrations took place in other cities such as Corinth and on the island of Samos. Hera was also the subject of a marriage ritual which took place in Euboea, known as the Great Daedala. This was due to her role as a benefactor of women in marriage, childbirth and motherhood.

Since she is the patron of marriage, it is not surprising that she took revenge on her husband's many sexual partners. Yet her reputation, described by New World Encyclopedia as that of a 'jealous schemer', may be a relatively late version of her story, as told by Homer. This reputation does not fit well with her role as Queen of the Gods.

Hermes

Hermes was 'one of the cleverest and most mischievous of all Greek gods' (Mark Cartwright). His Roman equivalent was Mercury, which is also the planet which travels with the greatest speed in its orbit around the sun. According to Annette Giesecke, Hermes was an Ancient Greek 'messenger god who meditated between heaven and Earth'. Stories about him first emerge in the Greek Bronze Age (1750-1050 BCE). He delivered messages from the gods to the human population. As an intermediary between the gods and humanity Hermes travelled effortlessly between Mount Olympus, the land of the living and the underworld as well.

He was not only a divine messenger but also a notorious trickster. 'Noted for his impish character and his (continual) search for amusement, he was one of the most colourful gods in Greek mythology' (Cartwright).

The name Hermes was given to him before the invention of the Greek alphabet. In the Greek language, his name is derived from the term 'herma', the word used to describe a boundary marker. Many of these were located on city limits with statues of the god atop them.

One of his most frequently used epithets was 'Argeiphontes' which denoted his destruction of the monster Argus. He was also described as 'Atlantiades', since he was the grandson of the Titan god Atlas, by his mother Maia. He was sometimes known as 'Cylllenian' since Mount Cyllene may well have been his birthplace, and he had a cult following in the vicinity.

As a god he had four main patronages. These were, according to Kapach, messengers and heralds, boundaries, travel and trade, shepherds and herdsmen in general. He also oversaw the 'mysteries', which were some of the most important Greek religious rites. In these roles he played an important role in the lives of the Greeks.

According to Annette Gieseke, his wide range of powers and sphere of influence also included luck, language and thieves. Additionally, he represented youthfulness. He took the role of protector of herdsmen and travellers as well as guide of the dead in their passage to the underworld. As well as a god of boundaries of property and city limits, he was also a patron of householders. The borders of property and the doorways leading into people's houses were often marked by effigies of the god. Furthermore, he brought culture to the world and invented the lyre as well as teaching humanity how to make fire.

Hermes is reputed to have been born in a cave on Mount Cyllene in Arcadia to Zeus and the nymph Maia. This is situated in the Peloponnese, which is part of the region of Arcadia. His mother Maia entered into a sexual relationship with Zeus in which she was not a willing partner and as Kapach puts it, retreated there to 'avoid the company of the other gods'.

He had an abundance of siblings resulting from Zeus's many sexual encounters, including the deities Apollo, Athena, Artemis and Dionysus and the mortals Hercules, Minos and Perseus, who were to become three of the heroes of Greek mythology.

Although he never married, he was thought to be the father of pastoral god Pan who was known for his pipe playing and was half-man half-goat. He was also the father of Autolycus the notorious thief. Hermes was known as a loner and unlike other gods was not accompanied by a large retinue of followers, although he was associated with various animal familiars including a rooster, a dog, a goat and a ram.

Hermes was an ambivalent character who intervened for good or ill, depending on his inclination. He valued cleverness above all other things, put his own interests above those of all others and primarily sought amusement for himself.

He was a trickster who stole from and deceived the other gods on many occasions. His traits were reflected by a Homeric hymn, written in his honour. According to this text, on the day of his birth, he sprang forth from his cradle and ventured outside of the cave which was his birthplace. He came upon a turtle whose shell he hollowed out and strung with reeds and animal sinews to create the original lyre, on which he started to play a tune (Gieseke).

Gieseke explains how 'on the same day he went to Pieria', where his half-brother Apollo kept a herd of cattle and stole 50 of them. He travelled far with the cattle, learning on the way how to make fire. He made them wear bark shoes to make it harder to trace their footprints. For this act, Hermes became known as a patron of thieves.

He eventually returned the cattle to Apollo when they were discovered by the Satyrs in an Arcadian cave. A hearing was convened, presided over by Zeus at which it was decided that Hermes could keep the cattle in return for the lyre. Apollo took to playing the instrument which was to become an important part of Greek culture. Apollo went on to become a highly proficient player, known, as 'the greatest of musicians.

But Hermes had not only stolen cattle. He also made off with

Poseidon's trident, Artemis's arrows and Aphrodite's girdle, all indispensable attributes for the gods concerned.

Well known by the other Olympians as a rogue and a liar, he preferred the company of ordinary mortals and shunned that of his fellow deities. Nonetheless he was not lacking in power over the other Olympians as well as humanity.

He did help the other gods and goddesses in their war against the giants, in which he succeeded in killing Hippolytus, one of the giants who invaded their home on Mount Olympus.

Hermes assists his great grandson Odysseus in his travails in the Trojan War. Homer's Odyssey relates how he used his quick wittedness to reunite him with his wife and son. Odysseus was a war hero who was held captive on the island of Crete by the sorceress Circe, who cast a spell on his crew transforming them into pigs. His grandfather Hermes gave him a magic herb which restored the sailors to their human form. Odysseus was imprisoned for a second time, on this occasion by 'the beautiful nymph Calypso, on the island of Ogygia' (Kapach). Hermes brought Calypso the news that Zeus had demanded Odysseus's immediate release. With Zeus on his side, Calypso had no option but to release him and his crew. The role played by Hermes in The Trojan War was not outstanding, but he interceded mostly on the side of the Greeks.

As stated in the chapter on Hera, he was renowned as the slayer of the monster Argus 'who guarded Zeus's lover Io when she was transformed into a cow' (Gieseke) by Zeus, who wanted to hide her amongst a herd of cattle. Hera told the monster to keep watch over the cattle until Io made herself known. Zeus called on Hermes for assistance, who used guile rather than brute force to defeat the monster, which is the means by which he usually won his victories. He gently lulled Argus to sleep and then killed him with his sword. This is why Hermes was given the title 'Argeiphontes', meaning 'killer of Argus', a feat for which he is well known.

He also freed Ares from imprisonment in a cauldron where he had been placed by two giants, Otus and Ephialtes. Furthermore, he was responsible for providing the god Perseus with the unbreakable sword with which he beheaded the Gorgon Medusa. On Hermes's behalf, the three graces led Perseus to the spot where he would find her.

In a more civilised fashion, as a god of language and rhetoric, he was the inventor of the Greek alphabet. To this day the study and interpretation of texts is known as 'hermeneutics'.

As well as creating fire, he invented knucklebones, which were animal bones used to serve as dice. As such he was worshipped by gamblers as a bringer of wealth and good luck. He was not only the inventor of the lyre, but also another musical instrument, the pan pipes, which he created for his son, Pan.

Whether working for good or ill, he carried a herald's staff known as the Kerykeion and according to Giesecke, wore 'a wide-brimmed traveller's hat and winged sandals' of his own invention, which carried him swiftly through the air.

In illustrations of the god, he was often shown wearing a leopard skin coat as well as his winged sandals. As Kapach explains, he was 'sometimes accompanied by a ram to represent his role as a god of shepherds'. Since he is also associated with youth, from the fifth century BCE he is usually depicted as a clean-shaven young man carrying a young child who was either Hercules or Achilles. However, some earlier inscriptions show him bearded. To represent his role as a god of trade he carries a purse. The most significant statue of him was located at the temple of Hera in Olympia and is now housed in an archaeological museum located there.

With his patronages encompassing so much of people's everyday lives, for many Greeks, 'Hermes represented the disorder and moral relativism' (Kapach) they found in them, and they venerated him because of this.

The god was especially popular in the Ancient Greek city states, especially Corinth and Argos, where temples were constructed in his name. His most important temple was on Mount Cyllene in Arcadia which was believed to be his birthplace.

As Kapach states: 'On the island of Samos, a festival took place in which everyone was permitted to steal'. This was to celebrate Hermes's patronage of thieves. He was believed to have a sanctuary on Crete where young men participated in rites in his name. There was also a regular festival held on the island where the roles of slaves and masters were temporarily reversed. This relates to Hermes's domain of crossing boundaries.

Hermes had two sides to his character, such as being the benefactor of both merchants and thieves, orators and gamblers. He participates in many Ancient Greek stories and features prominently in Homer's Odyssey. He can help or hinder, depending on his whims, but his primary concern is always for himself.

Poseidon

According to Avi Kapach, Poseidon whose Roman counterpart was Neptune, was 'one of the three chief Olympian deities, whose power was second only to that of Zeus himself'. As master of the seas and water sources, he was vacillating and unpredictable. When he was displeased, he was a bringer of storms and floods as well as earthquakes and other natural disasters, and his nature was as tempestuous as the sea itself. He had a reputation for acts of aggression which came unexpectedly, which reflects the nature of the sea, which can be calm and peaceful only to whip up a storm in moments.

Worshipped across the Ancient Greek civilisation, especially in seafaring communities such as the city states of Athens and Corinth, he was arguably the most destructive of all the Greek deities, but also had a positive side. As well as making the sea stormy, he could becalm it with a glance. Poseidon created new land by stirring the ocean floor with his trident, a tool used by many fishermen, but he also destroyed the land in a similar fashion. He was also a patron of horse taming and breeding and was believed to be the creator of the first horse.

As a patron of horses, he was described as 'Hippios' meaning 'horseman'. Because of his tendency to create earthquakes, he was sometimes referred to as Ennosigaios meaning 'Earth

Shaker'. Other epithets relate to his connection with the sea, for example 'Pelagius' meaning 'belonging to the sea'. He was even known as Phykios, suggesting that he was engulfed in seaweed.

His name Poseidon is likely to derive from two Greek words, the first of which is 'posis' meaning 'lord' or 'master'. The origin of the second part of his name is disputed but some have argued that it is based on the word 'dawon' meaning 'water'. This would give his name the meaning 'Lord of the Waters'.

Like many of the Ancient Greek gods, Poseidon emerged in the Mycenaean period. He had a cult following dating back to this period (late Bronze Age) which prospered from the fifteenth to the twelfth centuries BCE. He is believed to have been one of the most important deities to this civilisation which is not surprising since it has a close association with the sea.

Poseidon was the son of Titans Chronos and Rhea and fought on the side of his two brothers, Zeus and Hades and his sisters Athena and Hera, who became known as the Olympians, in the battle known as the Titanomachy. This was a battle against the Titans, who were represented by their own parents. The battle won; the three brothers drew lots to determine which dominion they would each rule over. Zeus took command of the skies and became King of the Olympians, while Hades took control of the underworld and Poseidon became master of the seas.

As well as residing on Mount Olympus, he dwelt in a grand underwater palace which included as Mark Cartwright describes it, a stable 'stocked with fine white horses. He also owned numerous herds of horses across the Greek civilisation. Nonetheless, Poseidon was not entirely satisfied by his lot and often took issue with Zeus's decisions. On one occasion he even plotted to overthrow him in a conspiracy involving his sisters, Athena and Hera.

As a punishment for his part in the failed coup, Zeus sent Poseidon to build the magnificent walls of Troy (Cartwright), a difficult task even for a god. When Laomedon King of Sparta refused to pay Poseidon for his work, the god unleashed a sea monster to ravage the city. According to Homer, it was for this reason that he sided with the Greeks in the Trojan War. The creature was eventually slain by Hercules, but when the king failed to recompense him too, Hercules sacked Troy and abducted the king's daughter, Hesione.

Poseidon was married to the nymph Amphitrite, who like her husband, was closely associated with the sea. While they were courting, she took flight to the Atlas Mountains. But the dolphin Delphinus persuaded her to return to Poseidon. Out of gratitude to the creature the god created the constellation Delphinus in his image, the name which is still used today.

With Amphitrite Poseidon had a son, Triton, who was known as a merman because he was the male equivalent of a mermaid. The couple also begat Rhode and Benthesikyme. However, Poseidon had many other children through his various illicit liaisons, with both mortal and immortal women. Amongst these were some of the best-known characters in Greek mythology. Because of Poseidon's sexual encounters with various mortal women, many people claimed the lineage of Poseidon, including the hero Theseus, despite the monstrous nature of some of his offspring, which are detailed as follows.

Poseidon had two children with the goddess Gaia whose names were Antaeus and Charybdis. While the former was a giant, the latter was a sea monster, who devoured ships at sea. He begat another monstrosity with the Goddess Medusa, who according to Greek tradition, according to Encyclopedia.com 'was once a beautiful woman' who allegedly seduced Poseidon in a temple dedicated to the goddess Athena, while some say that the encounter was at Poseidon's instigation.

Athena took revenge by transforming Medusa 'into hideous gorgon'(Encyclopedia.com), while she was pregnant with Poseidon's children. The two children of this union were Pegasus the winged horse and the monster called Chrysaor who begat more monsters of his own, including the monster of many heads known as the Hydra and the three-headed dog Cerberus. Medusa was eventually killed by the hero Perseus who cut off her head. Her two children with Poseidon were born out of the blood spilled by this action.

Poseidon's infatuation with Scylla, daughter of the minor deity Phorcys led his wife Amphitrite to transform her into a colossal monster which is described by Cartwright as having '12 feet and six heads'. Scylla was, like Poseidon, associated with the sea. She was a sea nymph who sent her own storms to engulf sailors and ate them just like the monster Charybdis.

Poseidon was also responsible for creating the monstrous beast known as the Minotaur. This came to pass when King Minos of Crete refused to give up for sacrifice the pedigree bull that the god had given him, thinking the bull was too fine to give away. In retribution, Poseidon cast a spell on the King's wife Pasiphae, making her become besotted with the bull, a union which resulted in her giving birth to the half-man half bull creature which lurked in the labyrinth of Knossos.

Poseidon himself is usually portrayed in Ancient Greek art as a mature, bearded man, clutching his trident with which as Cartwright describes, 'he would create earthquakes by striking the ground'. This is a tool frequently used by fishermen. He is often depicted riding a golden chariot drawn by creatures that were half horse, half serpent, known as Hippocamps, or sometimes golden-shod horses instead. In Greek art he is often shown in the company of dolphins, sea horses and tuna fish.

Possibly the best-known likeness of him is a two-metre-high

bronze statue originally situated in Artemisium. However, some images of Poseidon and Zeus are difficult to distinguish, and this statue could well represent the latter. This object was retrieved from a submerged ship, found in the 1920s CE and now stands imposingly in the National Archaeological Museum in Athens.

As a war leader, Homer's Iliad portrays Poseidon as a key figure on the side of the Greeks in the conflict known as the Trojan War. He gave them galvanising speeches and even led them into battle. Conversely according to Hesiod, he helped the Trojan hero Aeneus to escape from the wrath of Achilles.

After its defeat, Troy was left in ruins. Poseidon now turned his attention on the hero Odysseus as he returned from the battle. As Odysseus and his crew made their way home across the sea, Poseidon sent a storm which shipwrecked them off the island of Calypso where they found a secret hoard of food and drink. They helped themselves to this bounty, not realising that it belonged to the aggressive Cyclops Polyphemus, another of Poseidon's outlandish sons. When this giant tried to slaughter them, the seafarers tricked him into becoming inebriated and blinded him. In revenge for the blinding of Polyphemus, Poseidon forced Odysseus to sail aimlessly through the seas for a decade.

On the Parthenon frieze in Athens, he is illustrated participating in a contest with Athena over who should become patron of the city. This dates from 447-432 BCE. Poseidon offered the city a saltwater spring and a horse, but the people of Athens preferred Athena's offering of an olive tree and chose Athena as the city's patron. When Poseidon discovered this, he inundated much of the region of Attica with catastrophic floods.

A similar tale describes how Hera won the patronage of Argos, defeating the rival candidate who again was Poseidon.

He became so enraged that as Kapach puts it, he 'flooded much of the country' as he had done before in Attica.

Although the Greeks feared and respected Poseidon, his temples and shrines were located on the periphery of cities, since he was too unruly to be part of civilised urban life. Nonetheless, Poseidon was honoured by an annual festival and one of the winter months was given his name.

As a much-feared water god who controlled the weather at sea, he fathered a multitude of deities, mortals and monsters with his many different partners, and exacted revenge where he saw fit.

Zeus

Known as 'Lord of the Skies' and 'King of the Greek pantheon', the mythology around Zeus closely resembles that of his Roman equivalent, Jupiter. He dispensed thunder and lightning and generally controlled the weather. He ruled over the other gods and was known simply as 'the father'. Although Zeus's wife was the goddess Hera, he had many sexual encounters which the Ancient Greeks saw, according to the Mythology Book, 'as the origin of artistic expression and knowledge in the world'.

As a god of culture, he was a patron of music, drama, poetry and art, but he also had a voracious sexual appetite. 'One of Zeus's first affairs was with Mnemosyne, Titan goddess of memory' (Mythology Book). He had nine daughters by her, known as the muses, who acted as an inspiration to mortal artists, poets and musicians.

According to Annette Giesecke, he was also 'a civic god who was concerned with the establishment of cities and social order, as well as order within individual households'.

He was often portrayed holding a sceptre with which he meted out thunderbolts and was depicted in the company of his favourite creature, his faithful eagle. In the herbaceous kingdom he was represented by a royal oak.

Legend has it that Zeus was the son of the Titans Chronos and Rhea who were themselves the offspring of the primordial couple Uranus and Gaia. Chronos had seized power from his father Uranus. Fearing that his own children would do the same, Chronos ate the first five of them, who were Hestia, Demeter, Hera, Hades and Poseidon. In a bid to save her last child, Rhea hid Zeus away from his father on the island of Crete, where he was looked after by Rhea's mother, Gaia. To deceive Chronos in to believing that he had swallowed Zeus as well, Rhea gave her husband a stone wrapped in swaddling clothes, which he ate as he had done with Zeus's five siblings.

Zeus grew up safely in Crete, brought up by Gaia and her attendant nymphs. But once he had come of age, he went to seek his revenge on Chronos. Zeus defeated his father Chronos and forced him to regurgitate his five siblings. According to Apel 'To Demeter, Zeus gave dominion over agriculture, to Poseidon he gave power over the seas and to Hades he bestowed the underworld, while Hestia's realm was "the home and the hearth"'. Hera became Queen of the Olympians, as the wife of Zeus.

There are two main versions of how humanity and the world came into being. One of these states that there were four ages or creations. Ovid describes these as the Golden Age, The Silver Age, The Bronze Age and the Iron Age. Hesiod added 'the Heroic Age' to the list, which fell between the Bronze Age and the Iron Age. In each of these creations, Zeus played an important role.

Zeus was born of the Golden Age but brought it to a catastrophic end in the battle against the Titans known as the Titanomachy. Following on was the Silver Age in which he destroyed the mortal population for failing to worship him. The Bronze Age was created by Zeus himself, but the peoples of this world were such hot-headed warriors that they brought it to an end themselves. According to Apel, he also created the people of the Iron Age, which was the current one during the era of the Greek City States. This too had a reputation for conflict and moral degeneration. The heroes of the Heroic Age were created by Zeus, but most of these met their deaths in the Trojan War or other conflicts.

The second and better-known creation story involved Zeus's enemy Prometheus, who had previously been his ally. On one particular day, Zeus told Prometheus to form the first humans out of clay. It was Zeus's daughter Athena who brought them to life. All went well until Prometheus fell out with Zeus in a dispute about sacrificial offerings which meant that the people no longer provided the gods with sustenance. As Apel describes, in retaliation 'Zeus took fire away from the humans, but Prometheus stole it back for them'.

For his misdeeds, Zeus arranged Prometheus's cruel fate, to be chained to a rock and visited daily by a vulture that would eat out his liver, which was magically restored for the next day, just like Tityos, one of Hera's unsuccessful suitors.

In the pursuit of his own misdoings, Zeus would use his abilities as a shapeshifter to manifest himself as whatever he wished, living or inanimate. His trickery was an important part of his personality and influenced 'all his erotic exploits' (Mythology Book).

For his affair with Mnemosyne, he transformed himself into a fine-looking young shepherd, to seduce her. Many of his subsequent affairs would also involve shapeshifting including his courtship of his wife, Hera. At first, she showed no interest in him, so he conjured up a thunderstorm and appeared to her as a weather-worn fledgeling cuckoo. Hera took pity on the bird and held it close to her. It was at this point that Zeus resumed his normal appearance and seduced her.

In another of his affairs, this time with the Spartan Princess Leda, he manifested himself as a swan apparently trying to flee from an eagle giving chase, so that she would take pity on him. This story occurs in Renaissance art and literature and was later retold by William Butler Yeats in his well-known poem 'Leda and the Swan' (Apel).

Another shape-shifting story concerns King Acrisius of Argos who wanted to make sure his daughter Danae did not lose her virginity, after learning from an oracle that he would one day be killed by a son of hers. The king confined her in a cell, but Zeus transformed himself into a shower of gold, which showered into the prison through its skylight. As a result of their liaison, she gave birth to Perseus, who would later be inadvertently responsible for her father's death.

One of Zeus's other exploits concerns Europa, a Theban princess. The smitten Zeus disguised himself as a white bull and joined the throng of her father's cattle. Europa who was nearby, picking flowers, noticed what a fine specimen the bull was as well as how docile it seemed. She approached it to pet it, but it leapt up and carried her across the sea. They travelled as far as Crete, where Zeus finally revealed his true appearance. After having his way with her, by way of recompense, he appointed her the island's first Queen. With Zeus she begat Minas who would become Crete's first king.

Metis, Zeus's first cousin and also possibly his first wife, transformed her own appearance several times to outwit Zeus's advances until he eventually caught up with her. Even as this happened Zeus was worried by her reputation for shrewdness and cunning and because he knew from his oracle powers that she would one day give birth to a son who would match his abilities. Zeus feared being deposed by his children, just as he had overthrown his own father, Chronos.

So, when Metis was about to give birth, he challenged her to morph into a fly which he then swallowed up. Yet this did not bring Zeus victory, as the Titan god Prometheus wielded an axe to his head. But Athena, the Goddess of War and Wisdom, sprang forth from the wound in full battle dress and came to her father's defence. As the Mythology Book states 'She became one of the most important deities on Mount Olympus and the patron goddess of the powerful city state of Athens'.

Zeus killed another of his lovers, Semele, when she was pregnant with his child Dionysus, who was born out of Zeus's thigh, where the god had placed him when he killed his son's expectant mother.

In pursuit of Asteria, the Titan Goddess of Shooting Stars, Zeus took on the form of an eagle. Asteria transformed her own appearance into that of a quail, to escape Zeus's clutches, eventually plunging into the sea. As this happened, she was transformed into an island, which may be Delos or Sicily. This is where Asteria's younger sister Leto, another of Zeus's victims, fled in a bid to avoid his attentions. Here she gave birth to Apollo, God of the Sun, Poetry, Prophecy and Healing, and Artemis, Goddess of the Moon.

Despite his many vices, the Greeks did not consider Zeus to be a malign individual, and Plato even called him 'the best and most righteous of the gods'. He was also considered to be an oracle who could predict the future. Worshipped by the Greeks as their chief deity, he protected every city with the same zeal. However, the most significant festival dedicated to him took place once a year in Olympia. The Panhellenic games were a part of these celebrations, and a temple was established there in his honour where there stood a gold and ivory statue of him, crafted by the sculptor Phidias.

In the end Zeus was not to be outwitted by his jealous wife Hera and went on to father many children. The stories of Zeus's many forcible sexual encounters with females, both mortal and immortal, reflected the deeply misogynistic nature of Ancient Greek society and he was even seen as an icon to be emulated.

Egyptian and Middle Eastern Deities

G e b

As one of the most ancient Egyptian gods, Geb was originally a primordial deity who became an important member of the nine strong pantheon of Lower Egypt. Geb was an Earth God who, after seizing control of Egypt from his father Shu, eventually abdicated allowing his son Osiris to take his place as ruler of Egypt. Yet his influence reached over the Earth, the cosmos and the after world.

In early mythology, he ruled the cosmos in conjunction with the other senior gods, but this belief fell from favour at the onset of the monarchical system in Egypt, when he was believed to rule alone.

He was reputed to be the third Egyptian king, preceded by his father Shu, also a deity, and his grandfather Ra, King of the Gods, also known as Atum. The throne of Egypt was often referred to as 'the seat of Geb', while the pharaohs were described as the 'heirs of Geb'. They were regarded as his direct descendants, which gave them the divine right to rule.

His ascension to the throne is explained in a variety of ways. One of these is that he succeeded the Sun God Ra, who realised that someone more belligerent than himself was needed to defeat the evil serpent Apophis. A later tale tells of how he deposed his father Shu to claim the throne.

Geb was part of a complicated system of beliefs that developed in the Nile Delta (Lower Egypt), especially Heliopolis, from pre-historic times and lasted to 525BC. Dani Rhys tells us that residents of Heliopolis believed their city to be the birthplace of the gods and the location of creation. It was only towards the end of this period that Egyptian mythology was recorded in writing for posterity when it came under threat from foreign invaders.

Ancient Egyptian faith was based on practices and beliefs concerning the afterlife. This included 'texts providing moral guidance' (New World Encyclopedia) and rites which were supposed to ensure the safe passage of the deceased to eternal life.

Geb's importance is attested to by his role in the fertility of the land as an Earth God who was also linked to earthquakes, which were thought to represent his chortling laughter, as well as being responsible for rainfall patterns. Since he was an Earth god his domain included not only all living things but everything on the planet including all 'the stones, minerals and rocks' (Dani Rhys) of which the Earth is comprised. Thus, according to Rhys 'all things in the world were described as being 'on the back of Geb'.

Goods such as beer, bread and animal products were left with the deceased in burial chambers, as offerings in Geb's name, because of his association with the fertility of the land and its natural bounty.

He was associated with snakes and was often referred to as father of snakes, possibly because they live below the surface of the earth. The hieroglyph for 'snake' in ancient Egyptian, meant 'son of the Earth'. He was also renowned 'for his healing powers, especially regarding scorpion bites' (Meehan). Additionally, he had the status of being grandson of Ra, the all father of the gods, and in the fathering of five children, some of whom became important deities in their own right.

Over time he became associated with the underworld and featured in rituals concerning death and rebirth. This made him central to worshippers since rituals around funerary rites were a dominant part of ancient Egyptian religion.

Although some have suggested that it translates as 'earth' or 'ground' the origin of Geb's name may be lost in the mists of time, but according to Evan Meehan: 'its spelling and pronunciation have been subject to debate'. He has been described variously as Seb, Keb and Geb. The latter of these three names is almost invariably used today.

Over time the goose hieroglyph used to represent his name became interchangeable with that of the fertile lands of Lower Egypt, and thus plentiful crops and vegetation.

In tomb art and other artifacts Geb is usually depicted as a green-skinned man, representing growth and fertility. Some illustrations show him garlanded by plants or the hieroglyphs that represent them. He is often portrayed reclining and embracing his wife, Nut, the Sky Goddess.

As Meehan describes it, when shown in a standing position he is usually wearing 'the red crown of Lower Egypt or with the hieroglyph for a goose atop his head'. This sign in ancient Egyptian text represents his name. Geb is often depicted as a ram or sometimes with a snake coiled around his neck. In the 'Book of Death' he appears in the form of a crocodile, which characterises eternal life. Symbols related to Geb also include barley, representing the fertility of the land.

Geb's parents were the god Shu and the goddess Tefnut, who were the children of Ra, the 'all father' of the gods. With his wife Nut, who was also his sister, he had his five children, Osiris, Horus the Elder, Set, Isis and Nephthys.

Before this Geb and Nut were locked in a permanent embrace in which they remained until they were separated by

Ra, thus separating the Earth from the Sky. This was followed by the birth of their children. These events allowed for the creation of the living world. This story is told in more detail in the chapter on their daughter, Nephthys.

Before he ascended the throne of Egypt Geb was an unruly god to put it mildly, or a 'downright seditious one at worst' (Meehan). He once took on the disguise of a boar to eat 'the scared eye of Ra'. Ra was his grandfather and ruler of the gods. When his father Shu confronted him about this event, he protested his innocence, even though the eye's blood was seeping out of his skin.

The Eye of Ra was embodied as Ra's female counterpart who could annihilate most of her adversaries with just a glance, but unfortunately for her this did not include Geb.

According to a later story, which did not emerge until the 30th dynasty (380-343 BCE), Geb deposed his father and according to New World Encyclopedia, 'took his mother Tefnut as his primary consort'. This tale probably arose out of Greek mythology and in particular the story of Chronos, who overpowered and deposed his father, Uranus.

The myth says that after winning a significant battle with the malign serpent god Apophis, on returning home, Shu found his palace had been invaded by a band of renegades led by Geb. Shu quickly fled and Geb declared himself King of Egypt, following a nine-day storm which kept everyone in the palace confined there for the duration.

To legitimise his rule, Geb tried to emulate the achievements of his forefathers, Shu and Ra. When his attention was drawn to the fact that his predecessor Shu had worn a headdress made from a live cobra, Geb made great efforts to retrieve it. It was eventually found hidden in a wooden chest. However, it rose up and breathed fire at those followers of Geb who had located it, killing them and badly burning the interloper Geb in the process. He had to use the magical 'wig of Ra' to heal his injuries.

Geb was more successful in his later conquests, saving millions of settlers from the power of Apophis and making Egypt great again as it had been under the rule of his ancestors.

His time in power, despite its unruly beginnings, was, according to Rhys, an era of 'abundance, prosperity and order'. Nonetheless, he was an instigator of earthquakes, and was believed to be responsible for all manner of disasters that afflicted the Earth and the human population. Whether he was a cruel or a beneficial deity, depended on the circumstances.

Geb eventually stepped down and allowed his son, Osiris to take the throne of Egypt, but the reasons for this are unclear. Osiris ruled benevolently but was soon deposed by his malign brother Set. Meanwhile, Horus became the judge of the dead, who decided whether one could, as Rhys puts it: 'enjoy the afterlife or be lost forever in the jaws of "the monster Ammit"'.

His role in determining royal succession was partly due to his position in the lineage of Ra but also due to a mythological tale known as 'the contending of Horus and Set'. In this story Geb helped Osiris's son Horus (The Younger) take his righteous place as ruler of the Egyptians and banishes Set to the barren lands of Upper Egypt.

Despite his misbehaviour before he became King of Egypt and the despicable way he took power, Geb was a ruler who emulated the achievements of his father Shu and his Grandfather Ra and ruled with efficiency and stability. He was also responsible for agricultural abundance and allowed Egypt to remain a prosperous country.

Nephthys

Nephthys is usually portrayed as being of lower rank than her sister Isis but was to become one of the most important deities in ancient Egyptian mythology. She was a member of the Ennead of Heliopolis, a body which consisted of the nine most senior deities.

Nephthys is the name given to her by the Romans while the Egyptians called her 'Nebethwt', which means 'Lady of the Temple Enclosure' or 'Lady of the House'. In this context 'the house' does not refer to an earthly abode but was linked with the heavens. Temple enclosures would contain pylons which denoted her role as a protective deity, in this case guarding the temple premises, as she also protected the Sun God Ra.

Despite this positive aspect to her character, she came to be associated with death and decay and was 'associated with the setting sun, twilight and darkness' (Joshua J Mark). She was also believed to have magical powers, like her sister Isis. Once the deceased had been conquered by Set, described by David A Cintron as 'the force of death', Nephthys would guide them into the underworld. But if they survived to daybreak, Isis would carry them to the heavens. Although in appearance they were only distinguishable by signs on their heads indicating their names, the sisters can be seen as polar opposites.

Yet in her role as a goddess of the underworld, she helped the bereaved by bringing them news of how their loved ones were faring in the underworld, which earned her the epithet 'Friend of the Dead'.

Her 'nominal' husband was the god Set but their marriage was a troubled one. According to Evan Meehan 'Nephthys seemingly lived in fear of her husband' and their marriage produced no children.

As RH Wilkinson explains: 'She is sometimes represented as a kite', for example when searching with Isis for Osiris's body when he was murdered by Set, but she usually assumed a human appearance. She is one of the four deities represented in illustrations found in the tomb of Tutankhamun, because of her high rank amongst the deities and her role in the establishment of the world. To the Egyptians, their country was regarded as the whole of creation.

Originally there was nothing to the world except the primordial ocean and the darkness. Yet one day a mound called the 'ben-ben' arose from the waters on which the primordial god Atum stood. In some versions of events, it was the Sun God Ra who took this position. Feeling lonely, Atum/Ra conceived two children with his own shadow. These were Sha, God of the Air and Tefnut, Goddess of Moisture). As Mark describes it, 'the two deities left their father and went out to create the world'.

With his children gone, and fearing for their safety, Atum/Ra cast out his eye and sent it to go and look for them. When he found them, he realised that they had failed in their efforts to create the world. But he was so happy to see them again that he shed tears, which fell onto the fertile ground of the mound and from this sprang forth humanity. Since these beings had nowhere to live Sha and Tefnut conceived Geb (Earth) and Nut (sky). These two deities were born locked in a permanent embrace until Atum/Ra pushed Nut out of reach of Geb so that they could never meet again. This allowed for the separation of the Earth and the sky and led to the creation of the world.

Although the couple could never be together anymore, Nut was already pregnant with five children. These were Osiris, Isis, Seth, Nephthys and Horus (the elder). As Evan Meehan explains 'Nephthys was the youngest child of the gods Nut and Geb'. Despite his objections to the union that brought them about, Atum gave these five deities the task of maintaining order in the world, and in particular he gave Osiris, the first born, the role of ruling the world, which in this case meant Egypt.

Osiris married his sister Isis, and the marriage was a happy one. Together they taught humanity culture and art. They also taught them how to perform religious worship and showed them how to practise agriculture. Under their rule the world had effectively been paradise on Earth.

Nephthys was best known for the myth of Osiris in which she disguises herself as Isis to seduce Osiris, Isis's husband. To do so, Nephthys masqueraded as Isis so that he was unaware that he was sleeping with an interloper. This was not difficult for her to do since they looked almost exactly alike. It was vitally important that Osiris mistook Nephthys for his wife, since the punishments for adultery were very severe. One chronicler describes how male adulterers 'would be emasculated' and female ones 'would have their noses chopped off' (Meehan). Although Nephthys had no such excuse, she faced no action for the offence. The liaison between Osiris and Nephthys resulted in the birth of their son Anubis. Fearful of invoking Set's wrath, Nephthys discarded her child in the wilderness, and he was brought up instead by Isis.

When Osiris departed from his liaison with Nephthys, he left a flower with which he had been adorned. When Set returned to his wife Nephthys, he discovered the flower and which he recognised as belonging to his brother.

Set, the jealous husband, who was already resentful of Osiris's power, responded by murdering him. He did this by entrapping Osiris in a casket and throwing it into the river (see chapter on Set). Having done the deed, he seized the throne and took Nephthys as his consort. Under his rule there was much suffering in the world.

Meanwhile, 'Isis went in search for her husband Osiris and found him dead in the casket, [which was] lodged in a tree at Byblos' (Mark). Having found Osiris's body Isis returned home and set about preparing to bring him back to life using herbal potions. As this happened, Set was also looking for Osiris's body. Eventually he found it in the hiding place where Isis had left it.

Despite their differences Nephthys had agreed with Isis to stand guard over the body, but when he found her attending it, as Mark describes, Set 'chopped the body into pieces and cast them across the land and into the river'.

Nephthys offered to help Isis retrieve the pieces of Osiris's body. They managed to reassemble him with the exception of one vital part. Since he was incomplete, Osiris could not return to the realm of the gods but instead was consigned to the underworld where he would act as a merciful judge of the dead. Before he departed, Isis took the form of a bird of prey, just as Nephthys was wont to do, and circled above her husband's body, thereby conceiving their son Horus. She hid him in the marshes of the Nile Delta, where he was safe from Set's vengeance, 'just as she had done with his father's body' (Mark). Although she knew this, Nephthys kept the secret, showing fidelity to her sister.

On reaching adulthood, Horus set out to depose Set as king of the gods and take his place. The best-known version of this story is 'the contending of Horus and Set dating from the twentieth dynasty (1740-1077 BCE). This story is addressed in greater detail in the chapter on Set.

When Horus eventually managed to depose him, Set was exiled to the desert, while Nephthys kept her godly status as champion of female heads of household and later of all mature married women. Although she never matched the status of her sister Isis, she was still an important member of the Egyptian pantheon.

Nephthys was a well-known member of the pantheon long before the story known as 'the Osiris Myth'. In the Old Kingdom (2613-2181 BCE) she was venerated as the protector of the Sun God Ra while he travelled through the night in his chariot, alongside her husband Set, another protector god, who later gained notoriety in the Osiris story. During this journey Ra travelled through the day and night, bringing sunshine in the daylight hours. But at night as he travelled through the underworld, he was threatened by the serpent Apophis.

If this creature were to succeed in killing Ra, there would be no more daylight and the world would be permanently dark. The coming of dawn was in jeopardy every day as Apophis tried every night to murder the Sun god.

The threat from Apophis was so great that other deities joined the fight against him including Isis, Sekhmet and Bastet. The gods who defended Ra in this battle were known collectively as the 'Eyes of Ra', because they acted to protect him.

Nephthys was widely worshipped in the ancient Egyptian world, and many temples were devoted to her. This continued from the pre-dynastic period (6000-3150 BCE) until the Ptolemaic dynasty which was followed by Roman rule. Once Nephthys became associated with the dead, she was treated with even greater respect.

Sekhmet

Sekhmet was a vengeful incarnation of the goddess Hathor, created by the creator God Atum/ Ra, for the purpose of wreaking havoc on the world, as a form of divine retribution. Ferocious, but not all bad, she was one of ancient Egypt's most important leonine deities, (Richard H Wilkinson) meaning that she had lion-like characteristics. Some archaeologists have claimed that she was originally worshipped in Sudan which was inhabited by many lions at the time.

Since she was an important goddess, she appears in many illustrations. She is usually represented as a red coloured woman, representing blood, with the head of a lioness crowned with a solar disk. She often appears adorned with a serpent. Many statues of her were built during the reign of Anemopsis III, a number of them located at the temple of Mut. Here she is shown as Wilkinson describes, either seated or standing and carrying a papyrus sceptre, which is a symbol of her native Lower Egypt. She is sometimes represented as partially clothed or nude. Some statues portray her as a synthesis of Sekhmet and Mut, wearing a double crown. She was occasionally depicted in animal form rather than an anthropomorphic one.

The name 'Sekhmet' means 'the female powerful one' which related to both sides of her personality, aggressive and protective. She would inflict plagues and heal people at will and because of her propensity to mete out natural disasters she gained the epithet 'bringer of plagues' or 'lady of pestilence'. Known as the 'Lioness Goddess', other epithets for her included 'daughter of Ra', 'the one who is powerful', 'lady of slaughter' and 'mistress of dread'.

With her healing abilities and medicinal skills, she was associated with healers and physicians, and was sometimes referred to in this capacity as the 'Lady of Life' or 'The Gracious One'. Many of her priests were practising healers and doctors. She also had the power to solve at will any problem in the human world.

She was also a solar deity and a goddess of war. In her role as a goddess of war, Egyptian pharaohs would pray to her before going into battle, calling on her to give them the power to defeat their enemies.

As a protector of pharaohs, she is referred to as 'mother of the pharaohs. One of these in particular was so preoccupied with Sekhmet and her powers of protection that he created so many statues of her that a different one could be used to worship her every day of the year.

As a deity whose help was sought for the pharaohs on their journey into the afterlife, Egyptians would often place many statues of her in the tombs of the pharaohs when they laid them to rest. Rites were carried out to protect the deceased pharaoh as he went on his way.

Images of her were incorporated into the pharaohs' royal biers. The bier found in the tomb of Tutankhamun depicts the face of Sekhmet as well as symbols relating to her. Because of such representations Sekhmet was referred to as 'lady of the tomb'.

Her husband was said to be the god Ptah, patron of craftsmen and architects. She also had a son called Nefertem and a sister, Bastet who protected humans and cats, depicted with a feline face.

Her son Nefertem was represented by 'a beautiful lotus flower that rose [from] the waters at the time of creation' (World History EDU).

Because Bastet represented the opposite of Sekhmet's darker side, she was known as 'Lady of the East', representing sunrise, while Sekhmet was 'Lady of the West', symbolising sunset. Bastet was, as NAMMU puts it, a 'symbol of love and protection' and is seen by some as Sekhmet's alter ego, despite Sekhmet's more helpful side.

Greatly feared by the people, Sekhmet was renowned as one who would drink the blood of any human she wished to. This was one reason why she was associated by Egyptians with the colour red.

Whenever Ra or Sekhmet herself were displeased with the human population she would wreak havoc amongst them, but at other times would act as a benefactor to humanity.

Her motivations were far from clear because of the dichotomy of her character as both destroyer and protector.

In keeping with her fearsome qualities, Sekhmet was reputed to breathe fire, something many Egyptian kings wished to be associated with. Indeed, Wilkinson states that: 'The hot desert winds were said to be the breath of Sekhmet'. Kings and pharaohs were also keen to associate themselves with her power to inflict or repel plagues. This was because they wished to be worshipped themselves as well as the gods.

She was one of a number of deities who represented the power of Ra's eye, known as the 'Eyes of Ra'. Others were Hathor, Horus, Wadjet, Mut and Bastet. Sekhmet was generally seen as the brutal and belligerent manifestation of Ra's eye.

According to Wilkinson, legend has it that 'when Ra became old, his [human] subjects began to plot against him' to remove him from power. He called a council of the gods to decide what to do about this. They advised him to send Sekhmet, 'the Eye of Ra', to the Earth, to carry out retribution. This 'led to the near destruction of humanity' (Wilkinson).

Ra unleashed Sekhmet, 'the destroyer of rebellion', on the world. The story goes that Sekhmet left the land of Egypt in a pool of blood (World History Edu). Ra became worried that she would go so far that there were no humans left there. He told the people to put red dye in the River Nile so that Sekhmet would mistake it for blood. Since she was a particularly bloodthirsty individual, she immersed herself in the river and drank it up, making herself drunk. She then returned to Ra's side having curtailed her mission to destroy humanity, just as Ra had planned.

An annual festival was held early in the year to mark the end of Sekhmet's reign of terror over the world. This included heavy drinking and merriment which lasted through the night. Yet, this was done in part to invoke Sekhmet's mercy from plagues and disasters, too.

Her cult following was centred in Memphis but was also prevalent throughout the delta region and she was worshipped in other areas too, into the Greco-Roman period. Sekhmetic priests held services from the time of the Old Kingdom (ca.2700-2200 BCE) and in later times this worship was associated with 'the magical aspects of medicine' (Wilkinson), such as prayers for the sick. The rites of Sekhmet were performed by priests to combat epidemics and to protect people from her rages and those of her attendants. Especially feared were the 'seven arrows of Sekhmet' which were purveyors of ill-fortune.

The Egyptians were most superstitious at the end of the year and amulets of Sekhmet were exchanged on New Year's Day to appease the goddess. When disaster struck, people redoubled their efforts to make supplication to Sekhmet.

One day in 2006 a German/Egyptian archaeological team discovered 17 life-size sculptures of Sekhmet at the site of the temple of Amenhotep III in Luxor. They had discovered several other examples the day before. Many other statues were constructed in temples on the western and eastern shores of Thebes (NAMMU). These included life size examples, and a few were even double life sized. They were crafted out of black granite and are believed to have been more significant than other statues manufactured in Egypt at the time, both of pharaohs and other deities. These were created at a time when numerous plagues and other disasters are known to have befallen the Egyptians. It is thought that these statues were built with the intention of making offerings to Sekhmet, to encourage her to relent in her attacks on humanity.

It is important to note the significance of the female power which Sekhmet characterises, whether this was an intentional part of the story or not. Such examples of 'strong, capable and intelligent women' (NAMMU) are somewhat lacking in recorded history, unlike those of their male counterparts.

As well as being a bringer of epidemics and other calamities, Sekhmet was also a healer, when she was so minded. She could be a protector against pestilence and disease as well as a protector of the pharaohs when they went into battle or embarked on their journey to the afterlife. This is why so many illustrations of her, and other memorabilia are found in Egyptian tombs.

Set

Sometimes called Seth or Sutekh, Set was a desert god who according to Richard H Wilkinson, came to represent 'chaos and disturbance in the world', having originally been a benevolent deity. He dates from the Pre-Dynastic Period (prehistorical) and continued to be popular in the Early Dynastic period (ca 3100-2686 BCE). In his heyday many kings were keen to be associated with him, but he eventually fell from favour.

He was one of the first five deities created by the union of Geb (Earth) and Nut (Sky) who were brought into existence by the primordial god Atum/Ra as he created the universe. Geb and Nut had four other children: Osiris, Horus, Isis and Nephthys. Set's wife was his sister Nephthys, and their marriage took place while they were still in the womb. Set developed a particular antithesis for his brother Osiris with whom he vied for the throne of Egypt. With his various consorts, but apparently not with Nephthys, Set had many children, of whom the most significant were possibly Neith, Antcheret and Taweret (the hippopotamus goddess).

Evidence shows that during the Early Dynastic Period he was known for his goodwill to gods and humans, but by the time of the New Kingdom (ca. 1550-1070 BCE) he was seen as a god of darkness, sometimes depicted as a red, dog-like animal 'with cloven feet and a forked tail' (Joshua J Mark). Set's name is often identifiable in hieroglyphics as a man with the head of an aardvark or ant eater, but it is conjectured that he was a mythical beast, not identifiable as any one animal.

As a benefactor people invoked him to bring them luck in their love lives, and his name was carved on amulets for this purpose. He protected the Sun God Ra on his journey through the night, combatting the serpent Apophis to make sure the sun rose every morning. He was also seen as a benefactor of the dead who looked after them in the afterlife.

Although the precise translation of his name has not been positively identified, it is usually taken to mean either 'great of strength' or 'pillar of stability' and he carried a sceptre which was said to weigh as much as 4,500 LB (2000 KG).

Fragments of text attest to the rescue by Set of the goddess Astarte from the destructive sea god Yam, who commanded that she be given up to him as a tribute (Wilkinson). Many ordinary people also invoked Set to bring them relief from adverse situations.

But during the New Kingdom era, a myth emerged in which he murdered his brother Osiris, who stood for peace and prosperity, in a bid to replace him as ruler of the world, meaning the kingdom of Egypt. He was still called upon for protection by royalty and the public, mostly to spare them from his own wrath.

In his latter persona as a god of destruction, he was as Wilkinson puts it, an ill-tempered god who 'personified anger, rage and violence'. In particular he represented conflict and discord. Legend has it that he burst out of his mother's womb instead of being born in the normal way. His mythical relationships were usually aggressive and ferocious.

As he became vindictive, Nephthys abandoned him and

became a follower of Horus as did his daughter Taweret and the warrior goddesses Astarte (from Syria) as well as Anat who came from Phoenicia, all of whom had also been his consorts.

From the time of the New Kingdom, described as a malevolent character, he was responsible for unhappy events in the world such as crimes, sickness and warfare. He was also thought to be a bringer of storms and bad weather, on the sea as well as the land.

In his capacity as a dark deity, he was associated with other malign gods such as 'the great chaos serpent Apophis' (Wilkinson), against whom he had originally fought. He was later linked by the Greeks with their own evil god Typhon.

Despite all this, Set was not all bad. He put his powers to good use when he was so inclined. Sometimes he would hold back droughts and their subsequent famines, acting in these cases as a benefactor of the people.

Later Set came to be associated with the enemies of Egypt, including the Assyrians, as ruler of the deserts and neighbouring lands. His loss in battle to Horus was celebrated with the ceremonial sacrifice of a hippopotamus, and his birthday was thought to be a particularly inauspicious day.

During the first millennium BCE, representations of Set disappeared altogether from texts and illustrations save those where he was as Wilkinson describes 'depicted as an ass with a knife in its head, to render it harmless'.

The 'Osiris Myth' first arises in the fifth dynasty (2448-2345 BCE), but did not become popular until much later. According to this story, before Osiris ruled over Egypt, the people had been barbaric and unruly. Osiris gave them civilisation and taught them agriculture. He bestowed Isis's gifts of compassion and equality on humanity, and ruled over a paradise on Earth where everyone, male and female, was equal under his rule.

Set became more and more dissatisfied with Osiris's power

and success. This came to a head when Nephthys, enamoured with Osiris's good looks, seduced him in the guise of Isis. Osiris believed he was sleeping with his own wife. Together they had a son named Anubis. The jealous Set resolved to murder his brother Osiris and replace him as king.

To do this he had an ornate chest constructed which fitted Osiris's measurements exactly. He threw a party and offered the case to whoever could best fit in it. Of course, this was Osiris, but when he lay down in the case, Set slammed the door shut and fastened it. Next, he took it to the River Nile and threw it in the water. This remainder of this story is covered in the chapter on Nephthys, who came to the aid of her sister Isis in her attempts to resurrect Osiris.

After Set was eventually defeated and banished, Horus was designated as king by the gods and ruled in much the same way as his father Osiris had done.

Documents from the twentieth dynasty recount two much earlier stories of Horus and Set, known as the 'Contending of Horus and Set'. In one story the two gods fought a battle to determine who would rule over Egypt and in the other there was a legal battle in which the gods deliberated over which of them should become King, despite Set's wrongdoing. A unanimous decision was required, and all were agreed that Horus should take the throne, except for Ra. He was not convinced Horus was suitable for the job, because of his lack of experience. The deliberations rolled on and 80 years passed while Set continued to rule in his haphazard way.

As Mark explains, Isis intervened 'for the sake of the people'. She morphed into the form of a young woman and sat crying at Set's gate. On passing by her Set enquired of her what was the matter. The woman explained that her husband had been murdered by his own brother, who had stolen all of his property, denying her rightful inheritance. Set was outraged at what he heard and vowed to bring justice to the woman. She then revealed her true identity and to the presence of the gods listening to their conversation.

At last Ra was convinced that Horus would make a better king than Set, and he was driven out of the fertile lands of the Nile valley and banished to the deserts to the south, known as Upper Egypt. Horus took the throne and ruled benevolently over the people and took Isis as his consort.

An older version of the story is that the gods could not agree on who should become king and asked the goddess Neith to adjudicate. Neith is a goddess from earlier times who was at the height of her popularity during the Predynastic period. She was chosen for this task because she was renowned for her wisdom. She decided to grant Horus rule over Egypt but gave the barren lands and foreign territories to Set. By way of consolation, she gave Set two foreign goddesses, Astarte and Anat, to be his consorts.

Set eventually perished at the hands of his great enemy, Anubis, son of Nephthys and Osiris who assassinated the malign god in the most brutal manner.

According to an inscription called the Shabaka stone, Horus was eventually granted rule over the whole of Egypt, by his grandfather Geb.

Despite his malign reputation, Set was invoked by many people as Egyptian civilisation took its course. His cult centres tended to be based in Upper Egypt over which he held sway, counterbalancing the benign rule of Horus in Lower Egypt. Statues of Set were looked after by his priests, and no ordinary people could venture close to them. The priests carried out daily rituals and curated the temples, of which members of the public seeking to petition the god were only permitted to enter the outer enclosures.

As their culture came under threat from foreign invaders,

the Egyptians meticulously recorded their beliefs in writing for posterity.

The mythology concerning Set was eventually incorporated into Christianity by comparing him to the devil, who also morphed from a character associated with light to one associated with darkness. Thus, Set's popular image became one of a red-haired beast. As Mark puts it, 'Like Satan he was cast out from the land of the gods for rebelling against harmonious rule'. He was, as such, opposed to the Egyptian concept of Maat, meaning truth.

Set, originally a benefactor to humanity, whom people would pray to for good luck, became a fearsome god who was only petitioned for leniency in inflicting plagues, droughts and famines on the world. Despite the long period for which he was worshipped, he eventually became completely discredited.

Mesoamerican and North American Deities

Chalchiuhtlicue

The name of this goddess means 'she who wears the jade skirt'. She was seen as the personification of youth, beauty and zeal.

Chalchiuhtlicue is amongst the most senior deities of the Aztec civilisation (1110-1521 CE). She is also the patron of marriage, and protector of women in labour, new-borns and aider of the sick.

As such she was invoked by the midwife in a form of baptism where the child's head was sprinkled with water. Midwives were of great importance since childbirth was often fatal for the new-born and for the mother.

Yet her main role was that of a rain deity. She was also a goddess of rivers, lakes and oceans. Chalchiuhtlicue is the wife or sister of Tlaloc, God of Rain, or alternatively, she can be seen as a female incarnation of Tlaloc himself, since both were deities associated with rainfall. By some accounts, she is Tlaloc's mother rather than his sister or his wife. Chalchiuhtlicue is also linked with Tlaloc's subordinates, known as the Tlaloques, who are either his brothers or his sons. In some stories she is married to Huehueteotl Xiuhtecuhtli, the god of fire.

According to some versions of events, Chalchiuhtlicue and Tlaloc had no parents but were created as a married couple after the world had been made. These two water deities were fashioned by the four creator gods, Tezcatlipoca, Xipe Totec, Quetzalcoatl and Huitzilopochtli.

She is reputed to live in the mountains, but the various Aztec communities linked her with different ones. This is because, according to Aztec mythology, all rivers come from hill-top sources.

Chalchiuhtlicue appears in many illustrations found in colonial era books, known as codices. Here she is clad in a blue-green skirt, hence her name 'She of the Jade Skirt'. Sometimes water is shown flowing out of this garment with new-born children floating in it. She is often depicted in a kneeling position and her face painted with black stripes, wearing a tasselled headdress. Many statues of the goddess were fashioned from jade or other stones with a greenish hue. On occasion her costume is marked with identical emblems to those of Tlaloc.

According to some sources she ruled over the fourth of five ages, known as the Fourth Sun. Rule over the fifth and final age, which was believed to be the current one, was contested by Tezcatlipoca and Huitzilopochtli. The first four ages were created and later destroyed by various deities who were dissatisfied with what they had created and brought it to an invariably catastrophic end. The First Age was created and ruled over by Tezcatlipoca. The second era was the work of Quetzalcoatl and the third of Tlaloc.

In the Fourth Age, Chalchiuhtlicue created and presided over a world that was for the most part a watery one, inhabited by many schools of fish, although it was inhabited by humans as well. She was generally a benevolent ruler, who showed great kindness to her people. It was during this age that the people started to cultivate the land with their staple crop of corn (maize). This era lasted for 676 years before she destroyed it.

This came about when the envious Tezcatlipoca accused her

of 'faking her feelings' (Evan Meehan) for them to win their favour. Chalchiuhtlicue was so distraught about this accusation that according to Meehan she 'cried tears of blood for 52 years' engulfing the entire world, which according to some versions of mythology, left all the people turned into fish, except for the virtuous ones for whom she built a bridge that allowed them to ascend into the heavens.

Thus, it is said that she created and later put an end to the 'Age of the Fourth Sun', by causing a deluge, in a myth that somewhat resembles the biblical one.

The Spanish treatise the 'Codex Ramirez' recounts that the volume of her tears was so great that the heavens caved in. Tezcatlipoca and Quetzalcoatl were forced to intervene by turning themselves into two trees of such great height that they propped up the heavens back into the sky where they should rightfully be.

After this came the Age of the Fifth Sun, which Tezcatlipoca and Quetzalcoatl were instructed to create by their parents Ometecuhtli and Omecihuatl who are sometimes regarded as the same individual, with both male and female aspects.

Spanish chronicler Fray Drago Duran (1537-1588) observed that Chalchiuhtlicue was worshipped by all the Aztec people as a water deity who could act both in the interests of humanity and against them. This was during what they believed was the fifth and current Age.

When she was in a good mood, she was the bringer of rains which filled irrigation channels allowing for a healthy crop of the Aztecs' staple cereal, corn. In this, she acted with the help of the corn god Ixonen. Since water was a scarce resource for the Aztecs, they were very much beholden to her. She did not simply regulate the water; she instilled it with healing properties, which befits her role as a healer of the sick.

When she was displeased with the human population, she

worked together with the vicious serpent goddess Chicomecoatl to bring drought, crop failure and famine. Additionally, she would sometimes create whirlpools at sea which endangered the lives of mariners. She also whipped up storms which made it difficult for seafarers to safely navigate the oceans. Furthermore, she was also thought to have a hand in drownings and other fatal incidents involving water.

Chalchiuhtlicue was one of a group of deities that held patronage over water and the fertility of the land. Throughout the month of February, all of these were worshipped in a number of ceremonies called Atlcahualo where religious rites were carried out. These usually took place on mountaintops and often included the sacrifice of children, whose tears were thought to be auspicious for plentiful rain.

This ceremonial month was the sixth month of the Aztec calendar, known to the people as Etzalcualizti This took place in the rainy season when their crops were starting to ripen. The celebrations took place beside or on lagoons and people would cast offerings into the waters. This included corn, 'the blood of quails and resins made of copal and latex'. (Maestri).

There were periods of both fasting and of banqueting throughout the year and priests would even sacrifice themselves to the gods. Along with them prisoners of war and women and children were also given up in sacrifice. One reason for the Aztec practice of human sacrifice was that they assumed their deities needed sustenance even though they were immortal. But it was mostly because the people feared them and relied on their goodwill to survive.

Of the 20 major festivals held during the Aztec calendar, five were dedicated to the two major water deities, Tlaloc and Chalchiuhtlicue As these celebrations took place, priests would dive into a lake and mimic the activity and noise of frogs, to encourage the gods to bring forth rain.

All this was because the Aztec people relied on Tlaloc and Chalchiuhtlicue to save them from dying of thirst and starvation, so they lived in fear of and worshipped them with great reverence.

But ownership of the Fifth Age, which followed Chalchiuhtlicue's destruction of the fourth, was disputed between Tezcatlipoca and Huitzilopochtli. The latter of these two brothers led the Aztecs to the city where their great imperial capital city would be built. The location was revealed in a dream which was shared by a number of the high priests. This premonition described to them what they would find at the site where they were instructed to build the city, Tenochtitlan. This was a lake where they would find an eagle perched on a cactus, eating a snake.

As Meehan describes: 'Today the lake at Tenochtitlan is mostly drained and all that remains is a marshy area, located on the outskirts of Mexico City'. Yet archaeological evidence has shown that a construction called the 'Pyramid of the Moon' was built there between 200-600 CE. This is thought to have been dedicated to Chalchiuhtlicue. It was here that during the mid-nineteenth century archaeologists discovered this 20 ton monolith buried underground which is believed to be carved in the likeness of Chalchiuhtlicue. Another pyramid, was also found buried there, known as the 'Pyramid of the Sun', which was dedicated to Tlaloc.

When rainfall was plentiful, the Aztecs had Chalchiuhtlicue to thank for it, but when it was scarce, this was put down to her displeasure. Nonetheless, Chalchiuhtlicue was regarded as a benevolent deity of fertility of the land and of family life, who provided for the people in their time of need.

Huitzilopochtli

Huitzilopochtli was one of the most important deities of the Aztecs (Mexica People), whose name means 'Hummingbird to the Left'. Modern historians point out, that, according to Aztec cartography, the left represents the southerly direction. Since all warriors were to become reincarnated as hummingbirds, this is likely to mean 'Reincarnated Warrior God from the South'.

He first appears in Aztec mythology as a minor deity associated with hunting, but after the establishment of the capital city Tenochtitlan he gained the status of a major god. As well as being a god of war and sacrifice he was also a god of the Sun. According to Mark Cartwright, he was also the patron of 'fallen warriors and women who died in childbirth'. While these women would form his celestial entourage, the fallen warriors would be transformed into hummingbirds four years after their death.

Although he was a great warrior himself, he was not believed to be invincible. According to Aztec mythology, he would eventually be defeated, and the Aztec empire would fall. Despite his eventual fallibility, he was regarded as a warrior of great power, suitably so for a God of War. By some accounts he was originally a historical person, possibly a priest, who became a deity after his death.

There are two different accounts of his parentage. The first is that Huitzilopochtli's mother was the goddess Coatlicue whose name means 'she of the serpent skirt' (Nicoletta Maestri). Her daughter Coyolxauhqui, primordial earth goddess and her four hundred brothers were fearful when they heard she was pregnant by a strange means and hatched a plot to kill her. This was due to Huitzilopochtli having no father, as his mother was impregnated by a ball of hummingbird feathers, which appeared miraculously to her. This is taken to mean that she became pregnant by an unknown warrior, since warriors were associated with the birds. The story has been compared with the Christian story of an immaculate conception.

This multitude of brothers decapitated their mother, Coatlicue. But as they did so Huitzilopochtli sprang forth from her womb, fully armed and ready for battle. In another tale Huitzilopochtli saved his mother from his murderous siblings.

It is not clear whether Coyolxauhqui was involved in the plot or not, but he killed her anyway by decapitating her and casting her body down a hillside. As Mark Cartwright relates, he also 'slung her head into the sky where it became the moon'. He then turned his attention to his 400 brothers, whom he also slaughtered, transforming them into stars.

The struggle between Huitzilopochtli and his sister was enacted every day, with the rising and falling of the sun and the moon. The first half of each day represented Huitzilopochtli's journey across the skies as a God of the Sun, attended by the souls of fallen warriors who would later be transformed into hummingbirds. In the later part of the day, from noon onwards, he was accompanied by the souls of the women who had died in childbirth. During the hours of darkness, he travelled with his retinue through the underworld, before returning to the skies at dawn.

The Aztecs commemorated these events every morning when the sun triumphed over the moon and the stars.

The second version of his birth is that his mother and father were the male and female manifestations of the primordial creator god, known as Omecihuatl and Ometecuhtli, respectively. The couple had four children, the last of which was Huitzilopochtli. His three brothers were, as described by Evan Meehan: 'Xipe Totec, God of Agriculture, Goldsmiths and Rebirth, Tezcatlipoca, omnipresent god of the Night Skies and knower of all thoughts [and Quetzalcoatl], God of the Wind, provider of harvests and inventor of books and calendars'.

Yet unlike his brothers, Huitzilopochtli was born as a skeleton with no flesh. Thus he remained for 600 years. After this time elapsed, he and his brothers set about creating the world and the laws by which it was governed.

Whichever story you choose to believe, he is usually depicted with a dark face marked with yellow and blue stripes and a black mask. Generally, he is shown fully armed carrying a sword in the form of a snake and what is known as a 'smoking mirror', made of volcanic glass, with wisps of smoke emerging from it. Paintings of the god show him as Maestri puts it: with 'the head of a hummingbird attached to the back of his head', or in the form of a helmet. He was often illustrated carrying a shield decorated with eagle feathers, which feature in images of the gods of the Aztec pantheon and only Aztec royalty and nobility were permitted to wear.

Whatever the case, the body of his effigy at Templo Mayor was adorned with hummingbird feathers. It was covered with cloth and jewels. Huitzilopochtli is usually symbolised 'either by a humming-bird or by an eagle sitting on a cactus with a snake in its talons' (Cartwright), representing the site where Tenochtitlan was to be established.

Sculptures of him were usually made of wood which have not survived, but the Templo Mayor is Huitzilopochtli's most important shrine built in the shape of the island where he was born, Coatepec (Snake Island). The temple steps were painted red to symbolise blood spilled in war.

It was discovered in 1978 during electrical works at the site, which is located at, as Maestri describes, 'the centre of a crossing of four causeways that connected the island to the shore'.

This temple was built for the dual purpose of worshiping Huitzilopochtli and Tlaloc, the God of Rain. It was one of the first buildings to be constructed in the new capital city, Tenochtitlan.

The month of December, known as Panquetzaliztli, was dedicated to the worship of Huitzilopochtli and during this time people garlanded their homes and worshipped him with singing and dancing as well as sacrifice. A huge effigy of the god, made of dough was assembled, and carried through the streets and eaten on arrival at the temple known as Templo Mayor and the god was also impersonated by a priest during the festivities.

Three other annual festivals were celebrated at least in part in Tezcatlipoca's name. The most significant of these was the 'offering of flowers' (Tlaxochimacho) which spanned 19 days in July and August. According to Maestri, this was dedicated to 'war, sacrifice celestial creativity and divine paternalism'. Human sacrifice was offered up to honour the dead and the god himself.

As described in the chapter on Chalchiuhtlicue, Huitzilopochtli's most important myth is that he instructed the Aztecs where to build their capital city, for which he was known as 'the portentous one'. He selected a site on an island in the middle of Lake Texcoco where he told them they would find an eagle perched on a cactus, eating a snake (Meehan).

The message was conveyed to the high priests in a dream which they shared.

Whilst on this journey, the Aztecs carried a large icon of Huitzilopochtli which whispered directions to them to find the right location for their city. The god promised them prosperity if they worshipped him in a suitable way.

It took the Aztecs nearly 300 years of travelling to reach the spot. From time to time, they built a temple dedicated to Huitzilopochtli en route, which they hoped would bring them luck in finding the prophesised destination. The people left their home at Aztlan around 1065 CE and led a nomadic lifestyle as they went in search of the sacred location in which they were to build their capital. It was another 270 years before they came upon the site that Huitzilopochtli had described to them, and at long last they reached their destination. This was the island on a lake where they found the eagle perched on a cactus and eating a snake, which is just what Huitzilopochtli had predicted. The imagery of the snake being devoured by an eagle appears on the modern-day flag of Mexico, and it continues to be an important part of the cultural heritage of that country.

While he was one of the most senior members of the Aztec pantheon, it has been argued that the Spanish invaders overstated his importance. This was something they tended to do with Aztec gods who could be considered to have European counterparts, in this case Mars the Roman God of War.

The role of supreme deity was disputed between Huitzilopochtli and Tezcatlipoca but in the Aztec capital city Tenochtitlan Huitzilopochtli held sway. This was because he told the Aztec people where to build what was to become the capital of their empire, Tenochtitlan. He was the foremost god of war and sacrifices were made to him after every battle, be it won or lost. Considered powerful enough to require human sacrifice, he was much feared by the Aztec people. The sacrifices were usually taken from foreign prisoners of war but sometimes women and children were also selected.

As the primary God of War, Huitzilopochtli was involved in the defeat of many neighbouring peoples, but his people acknowledged that he would eventually be defeated in the fall of their empire.

During the reign of Montezuma I (1440-1469), a temple dedicated to Huitzilopochtli was razed to the ground which was seen as a portent of ominous times ahead. When the people tried to use water to extinguish the fire, it simply made things worse.

It was under Montezuma II, who reigned from (1502/3-1520) that the Spanish took up arms against the Aztecs for the first time, led by the conquistador Pedro de Alvarado', on the day of Toxcatl, an annual festival in honour of Huitzilopochtli. This led to the downfall of their civilisation.

Tezcatlipoca

The name of this Aztec god means 'smoking mirror', which is a reference to obsidian mirrors, constructed out of volcanic glass, which are emblematic of him and signify the smoke resulting from war and sacrifice. As Nicoletta Maestri explains: 'He was associated with the sky, the Earth, kingship, and war'. As a feline spirit he was important to Aztec shamans, priests and kings.

He was sometimes referred to as 'Ilhuicahua Tlalticpaque' meaning 'Possessor of the Sky and Earth' or Yohualli Ehecatl which translates as 'Night Wind'. He was also referred to in a negative way as 'Sower of Discord'.

He was a paternalistic deity who is reputed to have had a hand in the creation of the world and all that is in it, known to the Aztecs as 'soul of the world'. He was a patron of VIPs, such as 'nobles, leaders, warriors and merchants' (God of the Month). He could bestow or take away riches at will, and could inflict famine if he wished to do so. These powers made him probably the most important Aztec god and regular festivals, fasts and prayers were held in his name, since understandably the people wished to please him.

To displease Tezcatlipoca meant downfall for the prosperous, while venerating him could allow a person to achieve great things. But Tezcatlipoca was friend to no-one, he simply bestowed or withheld favours at will.

Legend has it that Tezcatlipoca was the progeny of the creator god, Ometeotl (male) or Omecihuatl in female form. His siblings included, Quetzalcoatl (plumed serpent), Xipe Totec and either Tlaloc (Rain God) or Huitzilopochtli (God of War). He was married to four wives, named Xocchiquetzal, Xilonen, Atlatonan and Huixocihuatl.

In art, Tezcatlipoca is generally depicted with no left foot, which he lost in combat with the monstrous sea creature Tlatelolco.

Tezcatlipoca is also easily identifiable in parchment or papyrus volumes of the time since his face is usually daubed with black stripes. He was usually portrayed with as Maestri describes it, 'an obsidian mirror on his chest', which allowed him to see all human acts and read people's thoughts. He often carried an obsidian knife as well.

His statue in the Aztec capital Tenochtitlan was constructed from Obsidian. He was shown wearing opulent clothes with gold and silver earrings. The statue was adorned with a gold ornament embossed with spirals representing smoke, which symbolised the supplications of the devout population.

In his left hand he clutched a shield, while in his right hand he brandished four spears and a dart, which was lifted up in readiness to be hurled forth in retribution. In a more gruesome fashion, as a dispenser of justice, he sat on a cloth decorated with skulls and shin bones.

This statue dates from the early Classic period, around 1325 CE. The creation of images of him was particularly prolific during the Late Postclassic period, when he gained his place as the most important Aztec god. This occurred around the time of the fifteenth to sixteenth century, before the Spanish invasion of 1521 CE, after which the statue at Tenochtitlan was destroyed by the 'Conquistadors'. Images of the god also occurred in Mesoamerica beyond the Aztec empire during this era, which could be evidence of a wider cult following.

Certain animals were symbolic of Tezcatlipoca. One Aztec Emperor, Xocoyotzin held a large collection of animals in his palace, such that it resembled a zoo. Some scholars think that the animals were believed to be Tezcatlipoca's representative on Earth. The god himself was symbolised by a variety of creatures including, as listed by God of the Month, 'a coyote, a lobster, monkey, a turkey and a vulture'. In his most regal animal manifestation, he was a jaguar, the most formidable creature in Mesoamerica.

Aztec kings too were regarded as Tezcatlipoca's Earthly representatives, which gave them great power, but they had to carry out certain rituals to prove their legitimacy.

Being omnipresent, Tezcatlipoca had no particular home but inhabited, as God of the Month explains, 'the Earth, the heavens and the underworld all at the same time'. He could see what ever happened in all of these domains, and his vengeance was much feared by the people. As well as being omnipresent he was omnipotent.

The fortunes of ordinary people depended on luck. To be born under the birth sign of Ce Ocelotl promised bad luck, and men who did so were likely to become slaves, prisoners of war or womanisers, while their female counterparts could well be destined to commit adultery or face a life fraught with difficulties.

Contrastingly, to be born under the sign Ce Miquiztli' was a good omen for dedicated worshippers of Tezcatlipoca, but for those who did not worship him, the sign would also mean bad luck.

The powerful and wealthy born under this sign needed to keep on the right side of the deity to prevent their privileges and riches being taken away from them, and to bring them good fortune. Likewise, by worshipping him the ordinary people had the chance to prosper.

The 13-day calendar period known as 'Ce Miquiztli' was an auspicious episode when slave owners would release their captives, wash them and clothe them in fine robes. Moreover, they would present them with gifts. This was a time when the slaves were considered to be children of Tezcatlipoca. Anyone who mistreated a slave at this time would be cursed with bad luck, lose their fortune and be struck down with ill health. This punishment was the work of Tezcatlipoca himself. Alternatively, any slave who managed to escape from their owner and become prosperous would have Tezcatlipoca to thank for their good fortune.

Aztec tradition has it that 'the world as we know it was created at the beginning of an age called the Fifth Sun' (God of the Month). This was preceded by four previous ages or Suns. All these ages ended in a tumultuous way. The fourth age ended when everything in it was destroyed in a catastrophic flood. According to one tale, after this happened all that existed was a vast ocean, which was inhabited by a huge creature called Tlazolteol, an Earth Goddess covered with a multiplicity of eyes. She also had a plethora of mouths which she used to satisfy her ravenous appetite.

It is said that Tezcatlipoca and his brothers were tasked by their parent Ometeoti with the creation of the new era of the Fifth Sun, so they transformed themselves into snakes and went in search of the Earth Goddess in order to kill her.

Although defeated, Tlazolteol managed to bite off one of Tezcatlipoca's feet. But once conquered, the top half of the monster became the Earth, while her upsided bottom half became the heavens. Her back formed the mountains, and the rivers ran down her sides. Thus, the creature was killed for the good of humanity, who nonetheless thought it wise to make human sacrifices to her.

The brothers worked together to create the physical world, but as Maestri describes 'they later became fierce enemies. According to some tales, Tezcatlipoca, was sometimes referred to as Black Tezcatlipoca and his brother Quetzalcoatl as White Tezcatlipoca. They vied with each other for power over their creation. Huitzilopochtli was known as Blue Tezcatlipoca and Xipe Totec was referred to as Red Tezcatlipoca.

While they had alternated as rulers over previous ages, Quetzalcoatl was in charge as the solar deity of the fifth sun. He was a peaceful and benign ruler of the mythical city of Tollan. Legend has it that he was deposed by Tezcatlipoca who lowered himself to the Earth on a thread fashioned out of spiders' webs. He then took revenge on the Toltec people who had dutifully worshipped his brother.

In another story, to topple his brother, Tezcatlipoca disguised himself as an old man and tricked his brother, now an elderly priest, into taking an alcoholic drink, which he assured the cleric would reinvigorate him. Once he had consumed the drink, it was too late; he had been duped by his brother into breaking his religious oath of abstinence from alcohol and became intoxicated, leading as God of the Month puts it, to his 'downfall and exile'.

With Quetzalcoatl out of the way, a ritual ceremony took place annually during the festive month of Toxcatl which took place during May, at the height of the dry season. This was the One Drought sacrifice in which a young man, chosen for his handsomeness and unblemished body and described as the Ixipltla, was selected to be the god's representative on Earth for one year. The man would be chosen from amongst prisoners of war that the Aztecs had taken in their campaigns abroad.

While he was treated as the embodiment of Tezcatlipoca, he

was always accompanied by eight page boys, who would wander the streets of the Aztec capital Tenochtitlan with him, playing mournful tunes on the flute. Ceremonies and banquets were held in his honour and everyone he met 'would prostrate themselves before him' (God of the Month). He also became a scholar in music and religion.

Twenty days before the culmination of the Tezcatlipoca festivities he was married to four women, representing the goddesses who were Tezcatlipoca's wives. They 'entertained him with singing and dancing' (Maestri) as they strolled through the city streets. As the celebrations reached their climax, he would slowly climb the steps of a temple, playing on four flutes as he went, each symbolising one of the four cardinal (compass) directions. He would break one of these at a time as he ascended. When he reached the summit, he was seized by the high priests and given in human sacrifice to Tezcatlipoca in the most gruesome manner.

As soon as the execution had taken place the next victim was chosen from amongst the foreign prisoners and the next year of celebrations began.

Although being chosen as the Ixipltla was seen as a great honour, it was not really worth all the adoration since it ended in such a bad way.

The deity himself could do anything that pleased him, since no one, human or immortal, could stop him. He was believed to have the power to pull down the sky and destroy the world if he wished to do so. Along with his powers over the distribution of wealth, this made him perhaps the most feared Aztec deity.

Nanabozho

A creator demi-god of the Algonquian peoples of eastern Canada and the east coast of the USA, Nanabozho is known by many different names, including Nenabozho, Manabozho and Minabozho.

As James White puts it Nanabozho is the personification of life itself in its 'various phases and conditions'. This means there are many facets of his personality which are sometimes contradictory. He helps people survive the 'want, misfortune and death' (White) that they experience in their lives.

According to tribal tradition, Nanabozho is the eldest of four brothers, begotten by a primordial being and an earthly mother. The names of his three brothers were Chipiapoos, whom he dearly loved, Wasobo and Chakekenepok. Nanabozho's role was to be a friend of humanity. The less fortunate Chipiapoos was awarded the job of warder of the dead. Wabooso 'Maker of White' followed the sunlight to the northerly regions and took the form of the 'Great Hare'. Lastly, Chakekenepok, named after flint or another rocky substance, started off as the personification of winter, but was later to bring about his mother's violent death.

Having come of age, Nanabozho was still carrying a great deal of resentment towards his brother for his mother's death and resolved to avenge this by killing Chakekenepok. The two brothers soon came to blows and Chakekenepok eventually turned and fled, but Nanabozho chased him across the world, finally killing him by striking him with a deer-horn, fracturing many parts of his body and tearing out his entrails. These became vines while the fragments of Chakekenepok's body turned into two large rocks and the flintstone that is found in the area of his death.

Nanabozho and his brother Chipiapoos lived together a long way from human habitation. They were known for their physical and mental prowess, and Nanabozho for the magical powers he possessed. The manitous, evil spirits who resided in the air, earth and water, were envious of their power and tried to kill them. Nanabozho himself was immune to the effects of their dark arts, and being all-knowing, was aware of the manitous' schemes and was able to avoid them.

However, Chipiapoos was without Nanabozho's magical powers and was more susceptible to the plotting of the manitous. Nanabozho warned him to stay with him or at home at all times so that he could protect him. But despite his brother's warnings, Chipiapoos did venture out of their lodge and travelled to one of the great lakes, probably Lake Michigan. The manitous took this opportunity to break the ice, causing Chipiapoos to sink to the bottom of the lake where they concealed his body.

When Nanabozho returned home and found his brother missing, he surmised his fate and became inconsolable. He sought him everywhere on Earth, but his endeavours were in vain.

Next his feelings turned to anger, and he waged a relentless war against the manitous sending many of them to their deaths in 'the abyss of the world'(White). After this he declared a truce so that he could mourn his brother in peace. It is said that this period of mourning lasted six years.

During this lull in the combat, four manitous who were not party to Chipiapoos's death, nor inexperienced or lacking in wisdom, sought to make peace with Nanabozho. They constructed a lodge of condolence near where he was living, and prepared a feast to welcome him, as well as bringing peace pipes, and as White puts it, 'silently and ceremoniously' approached him. The four peacemakers brought with them a bag made from the entire skin of an otter, a beaver, or some other type of animal, which contained powerful magic potions. When they reached his abode, they chanted their good wishes to him ceremoniously and asked him to accompany them to their lodge.

Nanabozho was moved by their supplications and agreed to accompany them to the place where they lived.

As White explains, when he entered the lodge 'the manitous offered him a cup of purification medicine [to start] his initialisation into the Mide' (Grand Medicine Lodge). On drinking from this cup, Nanabozho was overwhelmed by feelings of peace and tranquillity.

Once the initialisation had been completed, Nanabozho joined the assembled company in dancing and singing and they all smoked peace pipes together. After the ceremony was over, Nanabozho thanked his hosts for initiating him into the mysteries of the Grand Medicine Lodge.

In a further show of goodwill, the manitous brought Chipiapoos back to life, yet owing to his metamorphosis (White), he was reincarnated as ruler of the dead, and as such was forbidden to enter the lodge.

Having learned the secrets of grand medicine, Nanabozho initiated all men and women into all of its mysteries. He gave each of them a medicine bag containing curative potions and luck charms. He enjoined on them the need to keep carrying out the rituals of grand medicine in this and future generations, explaining to them that observing these practices would ensure good health, abundance in fishing and hunting and what White describes as 'complete victory over their enemies'.

According to indigenous mythological tales, Nanabozho made many journeys to the Earth where he destroyed many monsters of land and sea who would threaten the wellbeing of humankind. His abode is located in the frozen lands to the north, where he resides on a great floating island of ice. It was believed that if he set foot on land the world and all its inhabitants would be destroyed by fire (White).

Nanabozho is said to have created four venerable beings in human form, each of which he placed at one of the four cardinal directions (points of the compass) to allow the human race to flourish. East provides 'light and starts the sun on its daily journey through the sky, South provides warmth and the refreshing dews' (White) that encourage the growth of tobacco plants and other crops and shrubs that bear fruit, West provides cooling and life-giving showers and lastly the North provides snow and ice which causes some animals to hibernate, which makes them easier to hunt. The custodian of the southern point of the compass is assisted by lesser beings, also created by Nanabozho, who are bird-like in their appearance. Their voices are the thunder, and their eyes are the lightning, so offerings are made to them when these phenomena occur, to placate their perceived anger.

According to another version of the Algonquin creation story, in the beginning, the world consisted of 'a vast expanse of water' (White), which had existed for all time. On it there floated a raft, populated by various animals in need of dry land. The leader of these animals was the 'Great Hare'. Being unable to find any land on which to alight, they asked a beaver to dive to the bottom of the water and bring back some soil. A handful was all they needed to create dry land, but the beaver made his excuses and said that he had already tried to reach the bottom but was unable to do so. They urged him so strongly to try again and he agreed. After a long time, he re-emerged motionless and nearly dead. They checked his paws and tail for signs of soil but were unable to find any.

Next, they persuaded an otter to carry out the same task. He too returned unsuccessful, and the animals on the raft despaired of ever finding dry land.

Finally, they asked a muskrat to fetch them some soil from under the water, although he was a weaker species than the beaver or the otter. They told him that if he brought back any soil, he would become the ruler of the world. He dived in and eventually resurfaced, floating dead on the water, but in his claws the raft-bound animals found traces of soil. This was all they needed, and it gradually increased until it grew to the size of a mountain. The Great Hare instructed the fox to use his powers to enlarge it still further. The fox agreed but only to create a sufficient area of land for him to carry out his hunting activities. The Hare looked over his work and found it wanting. Since that time, he ceased to trust any other animal, and took to travelling over the Earth ceaselessly to make the land for ever grow in size. The rumblings the Algonquin hear in the caves confirm to them that the Hare is still carrying out this task. He is honoured by them, and they credit him with the creation of the land.

Once all the animals had established their niche for feeding and hunting, the first of them to die were reincarnated as humans by the Hare, who gave each type of them a different language or dialect.

Thus, both the Great Hare and Nanabozho are revered by Algonquian tribespeople as creators of the Earth and all that lives in it. While the Great Hare is ingenious and adaptable, Nanabozho is a creator god who ruthlessly destroys his enemies.

Red Horn

Although he had nine earthly brothers, Red Horn was one of five spirits brought into being by the creator, who sent them to Earth to defend humanity. While he was here, he battled against giants and water spirits as well as other foes who threatened the wellbeing of humanity. The five spirits were sent to Earth by the creator one at a time, to come to the aid of humanity. One by one they botched the job and were recalled by the creator.

Red Horn was the penultimate of these five spirits and was nearly successful, but was killed in a fight with an enemy of humanity. He too was recalled, while the fifth spirit called Hare was successful in defeating humanity's enemies but accidentally invoked death. To mitigate this, he set up what was known as 'the Grand Medicine Lodge' whose members would live forever.

Red Horn was previously named 'He Who Gets Hit With Deer Lungs'. This is explained by a story of an occasion when he and his brothers were going deer hunting, when he gorged himself on venison instead of helping his brothers. One of these, named Kumi, rebuked him and threw deer lungs at him (which was a delicacy in indigenous culture). When his other brothers saw him with the deer's entrails smeared on him, they laughed and gave him the name 'He Who Gets Hit With Deer Lungs'. It was only later after winning a contest with his brothers that he declared he should in future be known as Red Horn.

The peoples of the Mississippi area created beautifully designed artefacts connected with their religious rituals, including the cult of Red Horn. A cave painting found in Missouri has been identified as an image of Red Horn because it includes his trademark human head earrings. Many similar earrings have been found in the area which people wore as a mark of respect and to emulate Red Horn. It has also been argued that the so-called 'Bird Man' images in Mississippi represent Red Horn because they are often portrayed wearing human head earrings. Most of these items are believed to have been fashioned in Cahokia, near St Louis, Mississippi, which is where Red Horn in his human form is thought to originate.

In this area many smoking pipes have been found fashioned into effigies of Red Horn the largest of which is called 'Big Boy'. Such artefacts have also been found from Oklahoma to Georgia in the southern USA. Rituals included human sacrifice and at one site 250 people, mostly young women, were killed for this purpose. According to Julie Zimmermann Holt, the scale of this was 'unmatched anywhere north of Mexico'.

Rituals were associated with myths and in one of these, known collectively as 'the Red Horn Cycle', he and his nine brothers compete in a race, which Deer Lungs won by taking the form of an arrow which flew across the world, quicker than any of his competitors could travel. This won him the right to marry the chief's daughter, but he allowed his elder brother Kunu to take this prize instead. On winning the race, he announced that he would henceforth be known as Red Horn.

The story goes that one day, a messenger arrived from another village declaring that the Great Chief was organising a race, of which the winner would be allowed to marry his daughter, named 'Yellow Robe'. Red Horn's brother Kunu had seen the girl, and she was very beautiful. He thought she had given him a hint of a smile. The messenger encouraged the brothers to meet the challenge and go with him to where the race was taking place. When the brothers arrived at the village, the locals were amused to see that He Who Gets Hit With Deer Lungs had joined them. Kunu told him that in his ill-fitting clothes he was an embarrassment and should return home. But his other brothers said he should be allowed to stay as a spectator.

The chief told them to run around the world in pursuit of the setting sun. When he declared that whoever won would have the right to marry his daughter, Yellow Robe looked at Kunu and smiled. Yet one of the brothers, whose name was Turtle, notorious for his rule breaking, was already moving ahead before the race was due to start.

Try as they might, the others could not keep up with Turtle and they spotted him on the mountain ahead of him, taunting them by shaking his pipe. They reached the top of the hill as fast as they could only to find that Turtle was already atop the next one. They raced up three more mountains, but each time they found Turtle had already reached the peak of the next one.

Kunu's suspicions were aroused as he did not think Turtle was quick enough to be so far ahead. On top of the fourth hill, they found a turtle. It turned out that Turtle himself had not been climbing the mountains at all, but had run along the valley floors instead, and what they mistook for him were in fact ordinary turtles, sent there by their cheating brother as decoys.

It was at this time that the youngest of the brothers, He Who Gets Hit With Deer Lungs, joined the race, which he won by turning himself into an arrow which flew around the world faster than any of his competitors. Meanwhile, Turtle had been so convinced of his impending victory that he had stopped for a drink. The outcome of the race was close, but it was clear that the youngest brother had won.

Nevertheless, Turtle insisted that he had won and tried to claim his 'prize' by forcibly taking hold of the chief's daughter. When this came to Kunu's attention, he lost patience with Turtle and clobbered him with his club, which forced Turtle to concede, but he claimed he had only done so for the sake of his younger brother.

Kunu walked back to the village with Yellow Robe, and they laughed and teased each other as they went. He was falling deeper in love with her and she too with him. But they agreed with sadness that she must be betrothed to the winner of the race.

When they arrived Kunu congratulated his brother on his achievement, who declared that he was too young to marry and argued that since Kunu was the one who loved Yellow Robe, he should be the one who married her.

After winning the race He Who Gets Hit With Deer Lungs creates 'living, miniature human heads' on his earlobes and made 'his hair into a long red braid' (EN Academic), known in the language of the Lake Winnebago community in Missouri as a 'he' meaning 'horn'. For this reason, he acquired the names Red Horn and He Who Wears Human Heads as Earrings.

In a later story from the Red Horn Cycle an orphaned girl who, as EN Academic describes it, habitually 'wore a white beaver skin wrap' was coerced by her grandmother to woo Red Horn, who together with his men was preparing to do battle away from the village. A group of women including the orphaned girl went to present the warriors with moccasins. It is she who presented Red Horn with his pair, which he accepted gratefully.

Red Horn and his men went off to fight their battle and when they were victorious, they played a hoax on the villagers, by sending a messenger to report that Red Horn and one of his friends had been slain. The orphan girl's grandmother cut off her granddaughter's hair according to tradition, as if they were already married.

The pranksters returned and made merry after their victory, dancing for four days. Many young men encouraged Red Horn to court their sisters, but he was only interested in 'The One Who Always Wears a White Beaver Skin Wrap' and he asked the villagers where she lived. That night Red Horn went to her home and joined her as she slept. 'Her grandmother threw a blanket over them both, to symbolise their union' (EN Academic).

In another episode Red Horn and his brothers enter into various contests with a race of giants known as 'man eaters' which had killed many humans. In one of these games Red Horn competed with a giantess whom he distracted and amused by causing the human heads on his earrings to, as Zimmermann Holt puts it, 'wink and stick out their tongues' at her. This caused her to laugh and lose the game and she became Red Horn's second wife. Yet in the end the giants overcome the brothers and kill them all.

Meanwhile Red Horn's two wives had both become pregnant by him and each gave birth to red haired sons like their father. The girl with the beaver skin wrap produced a son with human heads hanging from his earlobes, like his father, while the giantess's son had human faces on his chest in place of nipples.

Once fully grown, the two sons raided the giants' village and took the heads of Red Horn and his brothers and ran. They shot the giants with their arrows as they fled, and when they had run out of arrows, they dispensed most of the remaining giants by using their bows as cudgels. Red Horn and his brothers were all found alive in the Grand Medicine Lodge a day later.

Red Horn was a great warrior hero and defender of humanity who got into a great many escapades. Although he was sent to Earth by the creator, he did have human fallibilities, such as when he and his men tricked the villagers into believing that he had died in battle, which was a somewhat cruel prank.

Norse Deities

Freya

Known for her beauty and as a patron of love, fertility, magic and wealth, Freya had a reputation for being able to foretell the future. As a fertility goddess, she was important to the everyday lives of the people and played a role in the cycle of life. As well as these associations she was also known for her love of material possessions.

She was one of the most important members of the Vanir tribe of Norse deities who according to Thomas Apel was known as 'a gentle ruler and a fierce warrior'. She was also the most important female in the Norse pantheon and features in many Norse legends in which she was renowned as an object of sexual desire.

Despite her honourable talents, she indulged in many infidelities with mortal men as well as gods. She even had sexual relations with a group of elves, in return for a magical necklace they had fashioned.

The root of the English 'Friday' is based on Freya's name. Her name translates as 'the lady', from the Old Norse language, from which the Germanic word 'frau' is derived, used to describe a married woman. Another acronym attributed to her was 'Gefyn' meaning giver, because or her 'role as a goddess of plenty' (Emma Groeneveld). In some accounts she is given the name 'syr' possibly meaning 'protector' or 'shielder'.

Freya was married to Odr, synonymous with Odin, and together they had two daughters, Hnoss and Gersemi, both names meaning 'treasure'. As Apel describes, her father Njord was associated with maritime activities such as 'sailing and fishing as well as wealth and crop fertility'. Like his daughter, Njord was a member of the Vanir tribe. The identity of her mother is not clear but by some accounts it was Nerthus, a Germanic deity of peace and plenty. The similarly named Freyr was a brother of Freya who represented wealth, good weather and male fecundity.

Odin, whose name can be translated as 'furious and passionate', spent much of his time away travelling in the nine realms which made up the Norse cosmos, leaving his lonely wife to shed golden tears. He did this to evade those who would do him harm.

Many historians have tried to portray Freya as more promiscuous than Odin's wife Frigg, but there is little evidence to support this. It is more likely that Freya and Odr are synonymous with Frigg and Odin. Communities with different cultures, languages and traditions told varying stories about the Norse gods and goddesses. There was no one authoritative version of events and different mythological accounts existed in different places at the same time.

Freya resided in the palace of Sessrumnir, where half of the warriors who had died in battle shared her home. The others went to Odin's realm known as 'Valhalla'. As such she was as a death deity, or according to Emma Groeneveld 'a divine patron of battle'.

Although she had the status of a warrior, Freya was not known to carry weapons. Instead, she carried with her an assortment of items with magical powers. These included a cloak made from falcon feathers that allowed anyone who wore it to fly. She would lend this cloak to those who agreed to use it as she wished them to.

Freya habitually wore a gold necklace with magical powers, known as the Brisingamen, manufactured by a band of dwarves. This was her 'most prized possession'(Apel).

She would traverse the cosmos in a bejewelled chariot drawn by two cats. With her she carried 'Hildisvini', a sacred sow who represented her role as goddess of fertility, who was her 'familiar'.

She played a leading role as a goddess from the Vanir tribe and was seen as a 'volva', meaning one who practices the art of sedir. These were women who used their power to foretell and change future events, to protect their friends and condemn their enemies to oblivion. They were not only venerated, but often scorned, which lent ambiguity to their social standing.

Freya had a gentler nature than any of her fellow Norse deities. While Thor used force to get his way and Loki used trickery, Freya achieved what she wanted to with femininity and guile. Despite this she did not always put her own interests first and was known to help people in difficult situations. She was concerned with all aspects of sexuality except for childbirth in which she showed no interest.

Like most other Norse deities, information about her childhood is sparse. Once she had reached adulthood, there is more information available. Most sources agree that she participated in the war between the Aesir and Vanir tribes of deities. When the dispute was eventually resolved, Freya kept the peace among the gods.

She was also responsible for the cycles of fertility in the human world, which allowed life to continue. This made her so popular with the people that all women of high social status were named after her.

Freya's generosity becomes clear in the text known as 'the Poetic Edda' a Norse scripture which was compiled over 300 years between 800–1100 CE. One example of this is what happened when one of her servants needed to prove his ancestry to win a bet. Freya agreed to help the man, named Ottar. She took him to visit a seer, a woman whose name was Hyndla. When it became clear that the woman did not want to help, Freya threatened her with death. This persuaded Hyndla to give Ottar an account of his genealogy.

Fearing that the servant would not remember all this complex information, Freya demanded that the seer allow Ottar to drink from 'the beer of memory' which allowed Ottar to retain all the information she had given him.

More because of her eroticism than her generosity, Freya was a highly desirable woman, of particular interest to the giants. According to Sturluson's Poetic Edda, Freya's hand in marriage was as Groeneveld puts it: the price 'the other gods had to try to avoid paying'.

On one occasion a giant offered to construct an unassailable fortress (Apel) for the gods, which would protect them against his fellow giants, but only if he was allowed to marry Freya. This story is discussed in more detail in the chapter on Loki.

A fourteenth century text written by Christian priests describes her eroticism in vivid detail, and with great disapproval. The other gods too are deemed to be disreputable in this account. The story refers to her as Odin's concubine with whom he was much smitten. Freya, one day, came upon four elves crafting the magical gold necklace called the Brisingamen in their subterranean abode. She asked them to give it to her, but they would only do so in return for sexual favours, to which she agreed.

Her encounter with the elves was discovered by Loki who went directly to Odin and reported it to him. Odin told Loki to steal the necklace, which he did by transforming himself into a flea and entering Freya's bedroom. He bit her on the cheek, which caused her to turn over, giving him the opportunity to seize the necklace. Loki gave it to Odin on his return to the Great Hall of the Gods.

Freya told Odin about the theft, without realising that he knew how she came by it. He told her he knew of her infidelity with the elves. Odin offered to return the necklace to her but only if she carried out a quite peculiar task. She was required to create two kings each ruling over 20 lesser kings to fight a never-ending battle. When killed in the conflict, they would return to life to continue the fight.

This battle is reputed to have lasted hundreds of years before the Christian King of Norway, Olaf Tryggvason brought it to an end in the eleventh century CE.

Although Freya was a very popular goddess who features in many Norse tales, there is no evidence that she had a cult following. Yet the names of many localities in Northern Europe are linked to her name, such as 'Froi hov', meaning temple of Freya and Frovi (Freya's shrine).

As a patron of beauty, love and plenty, Freya used her power to benefit humanity and was a generous force in the world. The only negative aspect to her personality is her many illicit affairs while being the wife of Odin. But she was more than just a pleasure seeker. She was a goddess of great power who introduced the art of Sedir to her fellow deities, which allowed them to predict and change the course of future events.

L o k i

'Notorious for being impulsive with a quick and often malicious tongue and a cunning nature' (Emma Groeneveld), Loki was known for indulging in the sheer enjoyment of his trickery. Although he often created hazards for his fellow deities, he would sometimes come to their assistance.

Belonging to the Aesir tribe, he was one of the four ruling deities along with Thor, Odin and Freya. Although Odin was a trickster too these three deities devoted themselves to stability in the relations between the gods while Loki's bad behaviour meant that his own allegiances were called into question. It was even foretold that in the battle at the end of the world, Ragnarok, he would side with the Jotnar, a band of giants, who were the enemies of the gods. In fact, as Thomas Apel puts it 'he was neither for or against the gods'. Like trickster gods of other religions, he had both benevolent and malevolent intentions.

In the old Germanic language, his name is believed to represent the word for 'knot, loop or tangle'. This is thought to be because his trickery is likened to that of a spider catching its prey. It is also likely that Loki was known as 'the knot' because of his tendency to act as a 'knot' in the relationships of the gods, which would otherwise be a 'straight thread' (McCoy).

This was a fatal flaw in Loki that would ultimately lead to the demise of the gods.

Although he had no cult following or specific role in the Norse religion, he was one of the three most senior deities including Thor and Odin. No records of any worship of the deity have been uncovered as part of the historical record. This is probably because as McCoy describes 'his character is the antithesis of traditional Norse values of honour and loyalty'. The followers of the Norse religion were not sure whether Loki was a god, a giant or some other kind of being.

Loki was the son of the giant Farbauti, known only for the meaning of his name which was 'cruel striker'. His mother was also a Jotnar whose name was Laufey or possibly Nal.

He had two brothers, both Jotnar, named Helblindi and Byleistir, but he also counted Odin his brother, which linked him with the Aesir.

His wife was a goddess called Sigyn, known principally for being the mother of Loki's son, Nari/Narfi. Loki also had three children by his mistress Angrboda, another Jotnar, who all turned out to be enemies of the gods. Their progeny were: the Serpent of Midgard, the great wolf Fenrir and Hel, the ruler of the underworld. However, it is believed that Hel was brought into the narrative during the Christian era.

Curiously, Loki gave birth himself, while disguised as a mare, to the eight-legged horse Sleipnir, begotten of the giant stallion Svadilfaridi, who was to become 'Odin's favourite mount' (Thomas Apel).

Loki was notorious for, in Apel's words, his 'wit and wile'. He used these qualities to win his battles, rather than physical strength, and was therefore not normally depicted carrying any weapons. He was not known for wearing any particular attire, except his winged shoes which as Apel recounts, allowed him to run 'through the air and over water'.

He was the most prolific shapeshifter amongst the gods and on occasions turned himself not just into a mare, but also a fly and even a flea, as well as various other creatures, including those associated with water, such as a salmon and a seal. Also, from time to time he disguised himself in different human forms such as that of a young maiden or an old woman called Thokk, who was notorious for refusing to weep at the death of Baldur, for which Loki was responsible.

Loki appears in the Norse legends later than most of the other characters, and early texts such as the Grimnismal make no mention of him.

Loki does feature in Snorri Sturluson's Prose Edda, an Icelandic text written in the thirteenth century from a Christian point of view. He also appears in a few pre-Christian Skaldic verses, and the Poetic Edda dating from 1270 CE, again from a Christian perspective, which was an inevitably biased point of view.

According to Christian sources, in a rash moment, Loki mischievously cuts off the beautiful hair of Siff, wife of Thor. This makes Thor so angry that as Mary Litchfield puts it: 'He threatens to crush every bone in his body'.

The fearful Loki tries to make amends by replacing her golden locks. To do this he visits the subterranean home of the black elves, where he finds amongst them 'the sons of Ivaldi' who Apel states were renowned as 'the greatest of all craftsmen'.

Loki persuades them to make not only a new set of hair for Sif, but also two other gifts, which were the ship Skidbladnir, which could be folded up like a napkin and put in a pocket and the spear Gungnir, which could never miss its mark. These he planned to give to Freya and Odin, respectively. But before he could do this, Loki's mischievous nature let him down again. He sought out two dwarf brothers Brokrr and Sindri, who were also master craftsmen. Loki offered them his head, if they could create better gifts for the gods than those made by the Sons of Ivaldi.

The two dwarves were keen to accept the wager, insulted by this belittling of their skills. They soon made ready the golden maned boar Gullinbursti that shone brightly in the darkness, and travelled faster than a horse. Next, they set to work on the ring Draupnir which had magical properties and the invincible hammer Mjolnir which was also endowed with magical powers. It could grow or shrink to any size and will, according to Litchfield, 'always return to the hand that that flings it'.

Once all the gifts had been created, Loki returned to the court of the gods in Asgard with the two dwarf brothers with whom he had made the wager, and Thiassi, one of the sons of Ivaldi. Loki presented the gods with the two sets of gifts, made by the elves and the dwarves. These included the items that Brokrr and Sindri had created. These were the boar which he gave to Freya, the ring to Odin and the hammer Mjolnir to Thor, with which Thor was to become famously associated.

'The gods agreed that the hammer was the finest gift of all' (Apel), so Loki's adversaries had won the bet and could have Loki's head. But Loki used his cunning to get out of trouble, saying the dwarves could have his head but not his neck. They had to settle for sewing up Loki's lips, a condition which he later escaped from.

As well as making trouble, Loki sometimes came to the assistance of his fellow gods, when they were in difficulties. This happened when a giant, disguised as a master builder, offered to build an impregnable wall for the gods' palace at Asgard, to protect them against his fellow giants. He asked in return the right to marry Freya, with whom, like many, he was much enamoured.

The gods discussed the proposal, which was vehemently

opposed by Freya and were about to dismiss the idea when Loki suggested a cunning plan. He said that the gods should agree to the wager, on condition that the giant performed the insurmountable task of finishing construction of the wall 'by the first day of summer'. The gods surmised that the giant would lose the bet, but the wall would be built anyway.

The giant agreed to the conditions so long as he was able to use his stallion to help with the task. The gods did not foresee any problem with this and agreed. But the horse shifted huge quantities of masonry and completed most of the wall by itself. As the wall neared completion, the gods became increasingly worried that they would lose their bet and tried to think of a way to sabotage the builder's plans, rather than give Freya up to him.

For this purpose, Loki, the most prolific shapeshifter of the Norse deities, transformed himself into a mare and gained the attentions of the stallion who then lost interest in working for his master and took up the company of the mare instead.

The giant gave up his disguise as a master builder and railed against the Aesir gods, who called upon Thor the God of Thunder to protect them. Thor quickly dispensed with the giant by killing him with a hammer blow.

The problem of the wager had been resolved, and the wall was largely complete, but while in the form of the mare, Loki had given birth to the eight-legged foal.

In another story found in the Poetic Edda, Loki shows the better side of his personality. Thor told him one morning that his hammer had gone missing. In an act of generosity that was suspiciously out of character, Loki offered to find the hammer and return it to him. He donned Freya's magic falcon-feathered cloak which enabled him to fly off quickly in search of the hammer.

He flew to Jotunheim, where he found that Thor's hammer

was in the possession of a giant called Thrym, 'King of the realm of the Jotnar', who had crept up and stolen it from Thor while he was asleep. Thrym told Loki that he would only return the hammer if he was given permission to marry Freya.

An assembly of the gods was convened to decide how to respond. One of their number, a god called Heimdall suggested that Thor disguised himself as Freya, to trick Thrym into giving up the hammer. Thor was not keen to take on the appearance of a woman, but Loki persuaded him that it was necessary to get the hammer back.

Loki, disguised as a maidservant, accompanied Thor, masquerading as Freya, to the great hall of Thrym, where the great wedding feast was to take place. The giant plied them with food and drink. Thor, in his disguise ate a whole ox and eight salmon and drank copious amounts of mead. When Thrym questioned the 'bride's' unladylike behaviour, Loki, made excuses, saying that 'she' had fasted for eight days prior to her marriage, because she longed so much to be wed to Thrym. Again, when Thrym approached 'her' for a kiss, and saw hatefulness in 'her' eyes he remarked on 'the indelicacy of his bride to be' (Apel) and for this Loki made further excuses, saying that this was simply due to lack of sleep as she waited restlessly to marry the Giant King.

Because of these excuses made by Loki, Thrym did not doubt that 'the bride' was Freya herself. When Thrym retrieved the hammer from its hiding place, Thor snatched it from him and kills Thrym and his entire entourage.

But Loki demonstrated his mischievous behaviour again in a story in the Poetic Edda where he quarreled with the gods at a banquet they were attending, given by the sea god Aegir. The assembled company thanked Aegir's servants Fimafeng and Egdir for the work they had done in preparing the feast, but Loki was far from satisfied and took revenge by murdering

Fimafeng. The gods took up arms against Loki and chased him out of the building. Loki later returned for what was known to the Norse as a 'flyting', meaning an exchange of insults. Loki made wild accusations of incest and adultery against most of the gods who were present, calling 'Thor a coward and Odin a heretic' (Apel). When he was done with insults, he transformed himself into a salmon and slipped away to safety in the river.

The patience of the gods with Loki's mischief finally snapped when Loki brought about the death of another god, called Baldur.

Baldur was known as 'the fair one' and was loved by all the gods and humans alike. Both he and his mother Frigg had dreams that he would come to an untimely death. He contacted a seer from the underworld who confirmed that this was true but would not tell him the circumstance in which this would come about. His mother meanwhile made all things that existed promise they would do no harm to Baldur, and all agreed, except the mistletoe. Frigg decided that this omission was not important, as mistletoe was unlikely to bring about the death of her son.

Loki, meanwhile, hatched a plot to get Baldur killed, using his usual trickery. He organised an event where the gods jokingly pretended to harm Baldur by throwing spears at him, which because of his mother's intervention, could do him no harm. Seeing as the other missiles were having no effect, Loki persuaded Baldur's blind brother Hodr to throw a spear at Baldur, which was made with mistletoe and since he was blind, Loki directed his aim.

The spear mortally wounded Baldur, by striking him in the chest. Despite the fact that Hodr was not to blame, Odin, who was Baldur's father, vowed to take revenge. He did this by fathering a son with a giant named Rindr. The boy, named Vali, according to Apel, 'grew to manhood in a single day and killed

Hodr for his crime'. But for Loki, a much crueller fate was devised. He was pinned to a rock by his fellow gods with a venomous snake suspended above him, which continually dripped venom into his face.

Loki's wife Sigyn captured most of the poison in a bowl which she held under the serpent's head, so that Loki was only troubled by the poison while she was away emptying the bowl. When the venom did afflict him, it made him 'tremble so much that the Earth quaked' (Groeneveld), which was the Norse explanation for this phenomenon. Loki continued to suffer this punishment until he was eventually released to fight in the final battle of Ragnarok, which would be the end of all things, but followed by a new beginning.

In this battle, Loki, now clearly distinguished as the adversary of the gods, fought on the side of the Jotnar. Two of Loki's sons would fight alongside him. The former was the great sea serpent of Midgard who was Thor's nemesis, and the latter was the giant wolf Fenrir, who was fated to kill Odin in the battle. Almost all the combatants in this battle were destined to die in the conflict, including Loki and the god Heimdall who fought each other as the battle came to an end.

O d i n

Described by Daniel McCoy as 'One of the most complex and enigmatic characters in Norse mythology', Odin was their chief god, known as the 'All Father', who nonetheless, like Loki, was something of a trickster. He was a wise old god, who as well as being a war deity and a benefactor of the elite, was also a patron of verse, the runes, magic and even of outlaws. As a war deity, the reasons for armed conflict did not concern him, but he gloried in war for its own sake. Surprisingly for a god of war, he was somewhat effeminate in nature, which as Georg von Rosen (McCoy) puts it, is 'a quality which would have brought great shame to a Viking warrior'. Odin himself was not immune to criticism.

While Odin was above all other things a god of war, he is not depicted as a warrior in any Viking era illustrations, unlike Thor who was always battle-ready. But he did give advice to those preparing for war. In southern and western Germanic texts, he was described as an arbiter of victory in war or whatever consequences resulted from a war. In warfare Odin, like Loki, used trickery and cunning rather than brute strength, a quality which was instead conferred on the god Thor.

'The eleventh century chronicler, Adam of Bremen translates

the name Odin as "The Furious"' (Rosen). But this is disputed with some historians calling him, as Thomas Apel describes, "" the passionate" the "inspired" or more appropriately "the inspiring"', since he was the inspiration for warriors going to war. He was known in Old English as Woden, and in Germanic regions he was referred to as Wutan or Woutan. The day 'Wednesday' was called 'wodensday' in Old English, meaning 'day of Woden'.

He was often in the company of female warriors called the Valkyries and took the souls of half of the most valiant warriors killed in battle to Valhalla, a paradise exclusively for warriors who had died in combat. Freya looked after the other half, yet the two deities showed no interest in the souls of ordinary soldiers.

For this reason, Odin was worshipped by warriors, while his other followers were mainly the nobility and the upper echelons of society, which included kings, warlords and poets, who were held in high regard. But as McCoy puts it, 'as well as being a benefactor to people of high status, he was paradoxically a patron of outlaws as well; people who, like himself, showed no respect for social norms and the rule of law'. According to the 12-13th century Danish historian Saxo Grammaticus (Rosen) Odin was expelled from Asgard, the realm of the Gods, by his fellow deities, for ten years because he gave the gods a bad name with humanity.

Yet, together with his brothers Vili and Ve, Odin was one of the creators of the world. The forefather of the gods, Buri, was born out of the primordial ice. He had a son whom he named Borr who together with 'the frost giant Bestla' sired Odin. Bestla was also the mother of Odin's brothers. Emma Groeneveld relates that: 'The brothers slew the proto-giant Ymir (and) created the world with his flesh, the sun with his skull, the mountains with his bones and the sea with his blood'. Once they had done this, they created the first human couple, Ask and Emba who went on to populate the world.

Odin was married to Frigg, a goddess of 'wisdom, foresight and divination' (Thomas Apel), who was indistinguishable from the goddess Freya. They had a son whom they named Baldur, described by Apel as being known as 'the fairest of the Norse gods. Legend has it that like Zeus, Odin fathered many more children by his infidelities. These included Thor, whose mother was Jord, one of a race of giants known as the Jotnar. Another of his sons was Vali, whom he fathered with the giant Rindir. Vali's destiny in life was to avenge the death of his half-brother, Baldur.

Despite returning from his temporary banishment, he spent much of his time, as Apel puts it: 'wandering, in the guise of a traveller'. Odin was often depicted riding an eight-legged stallion named Sleipnir. Habitually dressed in a hat and cloak, he was one-eyed with a long beard, brandishing his spear Gungnir which was especially significant, and is represented by a multitude of miniature spearheads found in much of Sweden. He wore a ring, Draupnir, which had magical powers, and as Groeneveld describes 'dripped to form eight new rings every nine nights'.

He is depicted on many rune stones preceding 800 CE, accompanied by two ravens, Hugginn and Muninn, which represented thought and wisdom. These two birds flew around the world spying on people and eavesdropping on their conversations and returned to Odin, whereupon they uttered the information they had gathered into his ear. For this reason, Odin was known as 'the raven god' (Groeneveld). Additionally, ravens as well as crows were associated with death on the battlefield. By 500 CE, his image appears on ornaments where he is accompanied by warriors and birds. It also appears on stone carvings dating from the Viking era (793-1066 CE).

The Valkyries often appear alongside him in illustrations of the god and often take the form of 'small female figurines, sometimes holding a drinking horn' (Groeneveld). He is also accompanied by a pair of wolves, Geri and Fleki as well as a band of bloodthirsty warriors known as the 'berserkers.

As well as being the leader of the Aesir tribe of gods, Odin was defined as being indistinguishable from Odr, the leader of the Vanir tribe. But in pre-Christian times Odin was not seen as the 'all father' of the gods, more as one of a family of gods. Instead, he acquired this title during the Christian era, influenced by the concept of the Christian god.

Yet he was a well-known practitioner of the magic arts, more so than his fellow deities, and he used this power to foretell the future. This was one reason why his advice was sought by those preparing for battle.

Despite lacking such values 'as justice, fairness and respect for the rule of law' (Rosen), he was a god of great knowledge, either because he cast his eye into Mimir's well or because he was in possession of Mimir's head. (Mimir was renowned for his knowledge and insight.) Legend has it that this was chopped off by a group of fertility spirits belonging to the Vanir who sent it to Odin, so that he could make use of its magical powers, in return for him giving up one of his eyes to them. Odin embalmed the head with herbs and used magic to bring it back to life.

It passed on secret messages to him from the realm of the dead. There are other, contradictory accounts of how Odin came by his phenomenal knowledge, recorded in the 'Poetic Edda'. In one story he does this by winning a battle of wits against the giant Vafpruonir. According to one particular account, Odin is captured and tortured by the Norse king Geirrod to make him reveal the secret of his wisdom.

On one occasion Odin challenged the wisest of the giants

(McCoy) to a contest to see which of the two of them was the most learned. The prize for the winner was his opponent's head. Odin slyly won this by asking the giant a question that no one could answer but himself.

Snori Sturluson relates the story in which Odin acquired his great gift for poetry by stealing 'the mead of the skalds' (poetry).

Odin's first attempt to do this was by deception. He appeared in the guise of an agricultural worker called Bolverk, curiously meaning 'bad worker', offering to help Suttungr, the giant who owned the mead, bring in the harvest. The labourer did his work, but Suttungr 'refused him even a sip of mead' (Apel). Next Odin tried to obtain the mead by sleeping with Suttungr's daughter, Gunnlod, who as Groeneveld describes was 'guardian of the mead', for three nights. When she allowed him to take a sip of the mead, he drank it dry, transformed himself into an eagle and flew away, leaving Gunnlod, as Apel puts it 'to suffer her father's wrath'.

Once he had stolen the mead, Odin spoke only in verse. He shared his talent for poetry with gods and humans alike, if he thought they were befitting of this gift.

In his relentless search for knowledge, he also went to great lengths to gain an understanding of the runes. He underwent trials such as suspending himself from a tree for five nights. This was no ordinary tree but Yggdrasill, which was known as the 'world tree'. He also inflicted wounds on himself to near death. Having done this, knowledge of the mysteries of the runes were revealed to him.

In the battle known as Ragnarök, which literally means 'Fate of the Gods', Odin's powers of magic and wisdom are tested to the limit. As the battle begins, menacing events such as an especially cruel winter afflict the Earth, and the Sun is devoured by the monstrous wolf, Fenrir, signalling the arrival of the powers of darkness. The gods consult Mimir's head which can foretell the future, on how best to combat these dark forces. This warns them that both sides will be wiped out.

When the battle takes place, Odin is killed in the jaws of Fenrir as he battles bravely against the creature. Most of the other celestial combatants perish combating various monstrosities but slay many of them before meeting their own demise.

According to Groeneveld: 'Belief in Odin was widespread in Germanic regions during the pre-Christian era'. That said, there is little evidence that he had a major cult following. Places named after him, which are a good indication of his standing with the people, do not exist in Iceland at all in the pre-Christian era. There are very few of them in southern Norway, but they are a little more prevalent in Sweden and Denmark.

There is much more evidence of a cult following for Odin's son, Thor, who was a champion of the people, unlike Odin who was predominantly a patron of the elite.

The chronicler Adam of Bremen (Groeneveld) described a statue of Thor in the temple of Old Uppsala in 1070 CE. By his side stood two figures representing Odin and Freya. Despite the differences in their status, sacrifices were made to all three. As Groeneveld explains, this was: 'Thor in times of famine, Odin in times of war and Freya for wedding related activities', all events which the Norse people believed were in the hands of these gods.

As well as being a god of war, Odin was a gifted poet. But he came by his literary ability by stealing 'the mead of poetry' from its Jotnar guardian. As a patron of the leaders of society, he was worshipped by the great and the good. But as a benefactor of outlaws, and anyone who did not respect laws and conventions, he was worshipped by many at the bottom of the social hierarchy as well.

Thor

As a cult hero, Thor was possibly the most popular of all the Norse deities and one of the earliest and greatest additions to the Norse pantheon. Archaeological evidence suggests that the worship of Thor in northern Europe dates back as early as the Bronze Age.

As a god of thunder and lightning, Thor was the fiercest of all the Norse gods, always ready to do battle. According to Daniel McCoy: His 'courage and sense of duty were unshakable'. He defended Asgard, the abode of the gods, and Midgard, where the humans lived. Using his mighty hammer, Mjolnir, he habitually slaughtered monsters and giants. Like most of the other Norse gods, and their adversaries, he was destined to die in the final battle of Ragnarok.

The word 'thor' in old Norse language means 'thunder'. When the northern Europeans adapted the Roman calendar, the day of the week known as 'Dies Jovis' (Day of Jupiter) became what translates as 'Thor's Day' now referred to in English as 'Thursday'.

Thor was known by many titles, including 'Atti' (the Terrible), 'Bjorn' (the Bear) and 'Einherjar' (the One Who Rides Alone). He would often go on his travels throughout the nine realms of the universe which is why he was known as a lone rider. He was also referred to as a brave warrior and one who would strike thunder over the world.

Thor was believed to be a son of Odin, the half-giant Aesir god, and Jord, a female giant. However, other sources suggest his mother was Hlodyn or Fjorgyn. He had many half-brothers by Odin. These included Baldur, Heimdall and Hodr. His wife was the golden-haired Sif, patron goddess of 'faith, family and fertility' (Thomas Apel). With her he had a daughter, Thrud, who may well have become a Valkyrie. Thor was unfaithful to Sif with the giant Jarnsaxa, and they had a son together, called Magni, meaning strength. As well as various extra-marital relationships he had many casual encounters which led to the birth of other children.

His patronages included bringing storms and generally controlling the weather as well as being responsible for crop harvests, good or bad. When threatened by hunger and disease, the people called on Thor to help them and made sacrifice to him, including human ones. People would petition him to bring about a bountiful harvest, protect sailors at sea and bring victory in battle. In fact, there is evidence, in the form of many surviving inscriptions, that the god was invoked in all manner of situations, including the drawing up of contracts and the consecration of marriages (Joshua J Mark).

Thor resided in his palace, Bilskirnir, in Asgard, which was reputed to contain 540 rooms. Thought to be red-haired and bearded, Thor was known for his qualities of bravery, strength and ferocity. He was always keen to engage in battle, whenever the opportunity occurred. He wore a belt known as his 'power belt' which as Apel describes 'doubled his already massive strength'. He was always ready with his trademark hammer Mjolnir which had unstoppable power and he used it to kill and occasionally to restore life. When wielding his all-powerful hammer, Thor wore Iron gloves called Jarngreipr (iron grippers). He also carried a staff, Gridarvolr, but used it in only a few instances. When he failed to win a battle, he was still the hero, because his mistakes were not of his own making. He did better than any human could have done in the challenges set for him by the giant Utgard Loki in Jotunheim, a story described in the chapter 'Thor and Loki's Contest with the Giants'.

He was usually accompanied by his servants, two brothers called Thjalfi and Roskva and rode through the skies as Mark states 'in a chariot drawn by two male goats'. When hungry he would eat these animals and then bring them back to life using the magic powers of his hammer.

As McCoy explains, Thor offered unwavering protection to the humans and the gods, against the forces of chaos represented by the giants. It is somewhat ironic, therefore, that he was three quarters giant himself. Many of the gods, were related to the giants, which goes to show that there was much more to the relationship between the giants and the gods than simply enmity.

He was not only the protector of his fellow deities and valiant warriors, but would help anyone from all walks of life, including farmers, housewives and craftspeople. People would call upon him to help them out of tricky situations in their lives, despite his rashness and violent temper. Although he was renowned for his aggression, he was seen as a virtuous god, who meted out justice to his enemies.

What Thor had in physical strength was matched by a lack in intellectual ability and problem-solving skills. Unlike Loki, who used his shrewd powers of deception to win his battles, 'Thor faced his problems with a hammer in hand and violence in his heart' (Apel). The other deities depended on him to protect them from their enemies the Jotnar, comprised of monsters and giants. As Mark recounts: 'Of all the gods, it is

Thor who seems the characteristic hero of the stormy world of the Vikings'.

Thor had a confrontation with a giant called Hrungnir in which he showed his hatred of the Jotnar. Whilst Thor was away on a troll slaying expedition, which one of his favourite pastimes, Odin ventured into Jotunheim where he came across the giant Hrungnir whom he challenged to a race.

The two of them rode their steeds all the way from Jotunheim to Asgard. When they arrived at the hall of the gods, Odin invited Hrungnir to join him for a drink. The giant drank heavily and boasted that he would destroy Valhalla, the resting place of noble warriors, and all of Asgard too. He ranted that he would kill all the gods and take Freya for his wife. The gods understandably lost patience with their guest and called on Thor to assist them.

Thor duly arrived wielding his mighty hammer which he raised to slaughter Hrungnir, but just as he was about to do so, the giant taunted him for attacking an unarmed man. Seeing that this seemed to be a fair point, Thor allowed Hrungnir to return to Jotunheim to fetch a weapon. The giant soon returned with a giant whetstone. Thor hurled Mjolnir at him but the giant threw the whetstone into the path of the hammer, shattering it to pieces. Yet with its magical powers, the invincible weapon re-formed itself and struck the giant dead. However, the stone thrown by the giant had hit Thor on the head and became trapped in his skull. Unable to dislodge it, the gods called a healer named Groa, wife of Aurvandill (the Valiant). While she was tending to his wounds, Thor recounted a story concerning her husband, which he thought would please her. But instead, she was saddened by the tale and was unable to finish her task. This meant that Hrungnir's stone was lodged in Thor's skull forever more.

The Serpent of Midgard, Jormungangandr, was one of Thor's

most significant adversaries. It was a monstrous son of the devious Loki and the giantess Angrboda. The couple had another beastly offspring, the great wolf Fenrir and possibly Hel, who ruled over the eponymously named underworld, although this creature may have been a later addition to the story.

Once the serpent had been born, Odin quickly cast it into the sea around Midgard, realm of the humans, hoping to get rid of it. But it grew in size so great that it held the entirety of Midgard in its clutches. Thor clashed with the serpent a number of times, but one particular encounter is recorded in the 'Poetic Edda'.

On this occasion Thor suggested to the giant Hymir that the two of them go on a fishing expedition, to which Hymir grudgingly agreed. They put to sea and Hymir caught several whales. But Thor's catch was much bigger than a whale; it was as he had intended, the serpent of Midgard. He gleefully started to chop up the serpent with his hammer, but the serpent survived. According to one version of events it escaped back into the sea before Thor could destroy it. Another story goes that Hymir released it back into the sea. In any case the story ended with Thor and Hymir coming to blows and Thor slaying the giant.

It was fated that Thor would meet the serpent Jormungangandr again at the battle of the end of the world known as the Battle of Ragnarok. As Apel states, according to the 'volva' (seers) 'the battle would come about when the serpent came out of the sea on to dry land, where its brother, the great wolf Fenrir would come to its aid'. The serpent was destined to poison the air with toxic fumes while Fenrir would turn the world into a blazing inferno. It was foretold that in the ensuing battle almost all the gods and their enemies the Jotnar would perish. Thor himself died from the venom of the serpent, but only after he had killed it.

The stories of the Norse legends were popular throughout northern Europe, especially during the Viking era (800-1100 CE). They were carried down by word of mouth rather than written down.

Still a popular figure in Norse mythology today, Thor was most famous in northern Europe during the Viking era. Images of Thor and his hammer are depicted on Norse jewellery and coins and other artefacts, such as amulets. These are among the most abundant relics that exist today.

At first the introduction of Christianity had little effect on the popularity of Thor, who was worshipped well into the Viking Era. Although there are no surviving accounts of Norse liturgy, evidence of the worship of Thor can be found in the stories told about him and in the amulets and other images of him which survive today. For centuries images of Thor's hammer such as amulets vied for popularity with Christian crosses.

The character of Thor, which made him the most popular Norse deity, were completely at odds with Christianity, which as Mark puts it, 'at least in theory', promoted the peaceful resolution of disputes. When the pagans found their religion under threat, there was no one better to turn to than Thor himself.

Christianity spread not so much by conversion as coercion, carried out by Kings such as Olaf Tryggvason. This newly established monotheistic religion could not tolerate the worship of gods such as Thor, and eventually those who worshipped him were either martyred or gave up on him. By the twelfth century CE all the temples dedicated to the Norse gods had been demolished and replaced by churches. Since worship was more of a part of everyday life rather than an organised religion, there were not many of these, but of those that did exist, the most important one was, according to

Mark, 'at Uppsala in Sweden, dedicated to Thor, Freya and Odin'.

During the twelfth century the worship of Thor and his fellow Norse deities disappeared altogether, although the stories about them were written down by Christian scholars, from their own rather biased point of view, for example in the Prose Edda and the Poetic Edda.

Thor and Loki's Contest with the Giants

Although Thor was admired for his physical prowess he was often portrayed as intellectually lacking and gullible.

Much of the mythology concerning Thor was a humorous take on the inadequacies of brute strength. Loki who features alongside him in many of the Norse legends, although physically weaker, won his battles using his cleverness and trickery. Yet according to the Mythology Book he was regarded as 'cowardly, malicious and deceitful'.

Although Thor and Loki were not the best of friends, they worked together to make use of Thor's strength and Loki's cunning. This brought them success in many of their adventures, but not all of them.

On one occasion Thor, Loki and a human companion Thilafi made a foray into Jotunheim and to the great hall of the giant king, here known as Utgard Loki, where they sought him out. When the giant saw the diminutive figures, he roared with laughter and declared 'This must be Thor of whom I have often heard' but added 'perhaps you are bigger than you look' (Mary Litchfield). The king told the visitors that all their guests must show their strength before being invited to drink with them.

Loki, who was feeling hungry, wagered that no one present could eat faster than he. He laughed to himself at the prospect of competing with as Litchfield puts it, 'the slow, lumbering giants'. The King beckoned a man of diminutive stature, especially for a giant, who was more agile than his larger counterparts, and called for a contest between the two to see who could eat the fastest. A trough of food was brought forward, and they each began to eat at either end of it. Loki ate ravenously, according to Litchfield out of 'pride as much as hunger'. He was dismayed to find that his rival had not only eaten all the meat from his side of the trough but had consumed the bones and even the trough itself. Loki had to concede that the giant, named Logi had triumphed.

The two gods' human companion, Thilafi then offered to prove that he could win any race by travelling as swiftly as an eagle. The giant king called forth an agile little man, supposedly a giant despite his diminutive stature, to race against Thilafi. The dwarf-like giant was faster than him and was on the home straight while Thilafi was still only halfway along the course. Thor cried out that it was enough, the dwarf had won (Litchfield), but then made a challenge of his own. This was a contest to see who could drink the most. The drinking horn was presented to Thor, who found that was seemingly of endless length.

He drank copiously only to find that the level of the ale had not reduced at all. Try as he might he could only make a small difference to it. The giant king urged Thor to try once more and as he drank the sound of ocean waves could be heard, but still the cup was almost overflowing. Thor, who was ashamed and embarrassed, admitted defeat, but he insisted there must be something he could do better than the giants.

The Giant King suggested a feat that was child's play to the giants, the ability to lift a giant's cat. He said that this was because Thor had shown himself to be weaker than he imagined. He tried to lift the cat but only succeeded in making it arch its back and raising one paw off the ground. This angered Thor who with fire in his eyes asked which of the giants could defeat him in a fight now that his bad temper had been aroused. The king told him that he would be defeated by any of his men, but instead called forth a bent old woman called Elli, who had been his nurse. He said that she had defeated many men of equal strength to Thor, in hand- to-hand combat. Thor was no match for her and was soon defeated.

The giant king told the visitors that although they were unable to win out against a race of giants, he was impressed by the powers that they had shown and invited them to dine with him. The now humbled visitors accepted the invitation. The feast was long, and much food and drink were consumed. Afterwards the two gods and their human companion slept to dawn. When they awoke the king accompanied them to the castle gate. Thor conceded that he could not match the strength of even small giants and expressed his shame at losing the contest.

Once outside his castle gates, the king told Thor he would be truthful with him. He told him never to return, but that it might console him to know that he had been deceptive in the contests, and that Thor and his companions had actually done very well. He explained how he had used deception to win the challenges.

Loki's eating competition with Logi was a battle against fire itself, 'which consumes everything' Mythology Book). The gods' human companion, Thilafi, had raced against thought, which travels faster than any human. The contents of the drinking horn which Thor was challenged by the giant king to drink dry, was connected to the sea so Thor had performed a great feat by reducing the level of it at all. The cat which Thor tried to lift was in fact the monstrous Midgard Serpent, which was so large that it encompassed the whole world. The old nursemaid that

Thor had fought with was old age itself, which no mortal can overcome, but she 'had only managed to force Thor down on one knee' (Mythology Book).

On hearing of how the giants had cheated him and his companions, Thor wielded his hammer ready to strike the giant king. But as he did so the giant disappeared. Turning to glance at the castle, Thor found that it too had disappeared, and he now saw nothing but a green open plain stretching into the distance. This myth demonstrates that there are some forces in creation which not even the gods can overcome.

Once back home in Asgard, Thor was still troubled by his encounter with the giants and vowed to take revenge, next time on the monstrous Midgard Serpent. This story is addressed in the chapter on Thor.

Loki shows the favourable side of his personality in the story of how Thor's hammer, stolen by a giant, was returned to him. This tale is narrated in the chapter on Loki.

Polynesian and Australian Deities

Maui

Maui is best known for using his skills in deception and trickery, often in the interests of the human population.

In Polynesian religion, particularly in Hawaii, Māui is a demi-god and ancient chief who appears in several different genealogies. In one of these he is the son of Akalanama and his wife Hina, whilst in another, his father's name is Ru. Maui's parents had five sons of which he was the youngest and one daughter also named Hina. In some accounts Hina is his daughter rather than his sister. He also had two sons.

His name is synonymous with the Hawaiian island Maui, although according to native tradition it is not named after him directly. It is instead named after the son of the discoverer of Hawaii, whose name was Maui, in honour of the trickster demi-god, who was believed to have created the Hawaiian Islands in the first place.

In the Māori tradition of New Zealand, he acquired a magical jawbone which he is believed to have fashioned into a powerful fishhook and used to scrape up the seabed to create the Hawaiian Islands.

Maui's fame as a hero of humanity spread from Hawaii to other cultures across Polynesia. He proved himself cunning enough to outwit any of the gods, which benefited the human population in many ways (Mythology Book). According to traditional stories he was a trickster with superhuman powers. Although he is recognised as a deity throughout Polynesia, the stories about him differ from one civilization to another.

According to Polynesian mythological tales, Maui was born prematurely, and his mother thought he was dead. Heartbroken, she cut off the topknot of her hair and wrapped the baby in it. She then put him out to sea. But Maui was alive, and the god Tangaroa is said to have ensured his safety, by asking a jellyfish to float him safely ashore.

It was here that an elderly man named Tame-Nui-Ke-ti-Rangi discovered him, while walking on the beach. The old man brought up Maui and educated him before he reached adulthood. He named him Maui Tiki-Tiki, meaning 'Maui formed in the top knot'. Once he was fully grown the old man told Maui to venture forth in search of his family.

He eventually found his mother and four brothers, of which he was the youngest, but his siblings treated him with envy and distrust, because they feared that he had the powers to go on and do greater things than themselves.

Despite his superhuman capabilities, he was human-like in nature, and chose to live in a thatched cottage where he looked after his mother, Hina. He is also known for playing tricks on his siblings, drawing them into all manner of escapades.

According to Hilo Hattie Maui Creation Story, with his giant fishhook, Maui is reputed to have tricked his brothers into helping him to create the world. While they were all out fishing, he deliberately caught his hook in the seabed, telling his brothers he had made a big catch. He persuaded his brothers to pedal the boat vigorously to help him reel it in. He did this repeatedly, and on each occasion, he fashioned one of the islands of Hawaii, by dragging up the seabed. What he created was 'a beautiful place', featuring lakes, mountains, valleys and cliff walls shrouded in 'mists and rainbows' (Legend of Maui).

There is another tale in Hawaiian mythology that describes how Maui stopped the sun travelling so fast. He did this to help his mother who found that the day was not long enough for her washing to dry out.

Maui ascended the Haleakala volcano, known as 'The House of the Sun'. When he reached the top, he captured the sun with a lasso as it rose one morning. The sun appealed to him to release it, which he did in return for longer hours of daylight during summer, albeit shorter ones in winter.

Another tale about the demi-god is related by the Mythology Book. According to this story, although he lived in the land of the living, Maui's mother was often to be found in the underworld. According to the Mythology Book, she always brought her son cold food, but the food she ate herself was cooked.

The ability to make fire was not known in the upper world, so the whole of humanity was in the same predicament as Maui, in that their food was always cold. Fire-making was a secret known only to the underworld which his mother Hina visited habitually.

Maui was not happy with the uncooked meals his mother brought him and stole his mother's hot meal while she was sleeping. Enjoying this food so much more, he became determined to find out how his mother cooked it. Maui realised that it would be necessary for him to enter the underworld and hatched a plan for him to visit it and return unscathed.

When his mother returned there, he secretly followed her back to her underworld abode. He saw her stop in front of a black rock, where she recited a verse and the entrance to the underworld opened up. Maui memorised this verse to allow him access. But he knew he would have to use his trickery to get in unnoticed. Before he went through the entrance, he visited an old friend by the name of Tane, God of the Forests, who owned a flock of pigeons. Maui asked Tane to loan him the best of these, which was an especially obedient bird. Tane agreed on condition he promised to return the bird unharmed.

Maui then made his way back to the rock that marked the entrance to the underworld, carrying the pigeon as he went. When he got there, he recited the verse his mother had used to gain entry. As the orifice opened Maui magically subsumed himself into the pigeon, which flew through the aperture.

Here the demons that inhabited the underworld tried in vain to catch the bird, but it flew too fast for them and all they managed to do was to grab a few feathers from its tail.

In the form of the pigeon, Maui flew through the underworld to find his mother. When she saw it, her suspicions were aroused because she had never seen a bird like it in the underworld. She suspected her son the trickster must be involved. Just at this moment Maui returned himself to his usual human form and the bird flew away on to a tree. Maui explained to his mother that he had come to ask her to reveal the secret of how to make fire. His mother told him she knew no better than him how it was done, since she always visited the fire deity Mauike, who gave her lighted sticks. She warned Maui not to approach this god because of his fearsome reputation.

Maui was not deterred and went directly to Mauike's abode and asked him for a lighted stick. The fire deity obliged but Maui threw the lighted stick into a nearby river. Maui then asked him for another firebrand and again Mauike was forthcoming, but Maui responded in the same way. On the third occasion Mauike gave him not only a firebrand but also some burning coals for good measure, which the trickster extinguished in the same way as he had done on the previous occasions. Maui was secretly plotting to provoke the fire deity and when he made his request a fourth time, Mauike's patience finally snapped.

He told Maui to go, or risk being thrown into the air with the god's great strength. But Maui's confidence did not falter, and he even invited Mauike to a contest of strength. While the Fire-God was limbering up, he noticed that his adversary had grown greatly in size. Mauike was still able to hurl Maui into a coconut tree, but as he fell, he transformed himself into a much lighter form, so that he was not injured when he hit the ground. This time Mauike cast Maui further into the sky, but he performed the same trick to remain unharmed. As the deity stopped for breath, Maui took hold of him and threw him twice, high into the air, causing many injuries. As Maui got ready to throw him for a third time Mauike pleaded with him to relent.

Maui offered to do so on condition that the Fire-God showed him how to make fire, instead of providing burning sticks or coals. Mauike conceded and took Maui to his collection of sticks. Maui gathered some sticks together in a bundle and following his adversary's instructions, and rubbed two smaller sticks together over the pile. The ensuing fire turned into a huge blaze which went on to engulf the entire underworld.

Maui rushed back to his mother's underworld abode, where he found the pigeon waiting. After using magic to repair the bird's tail, Maui used his powers to return himself into the bird. He flew back to the land of the living with the two sticks clasped in each claw and returned the pigeon to Tane.

Meanwhile the great fire that had started in the underworld had spread to the land of the living, where the people used it to cook food which they preferred to the cold meals they were used to. But Maui was the only person in the upper world who knew how to kindle fire. This meant when the flames abated no one except Maui could make a hot meal. Representatives of the people approached Maui and asked him to impart the secret, which he did, giving them the ability to use fire for whatever they chose.

In another tale told in the Mythology Book, it is said that after the creation of the world, the sky was approximately 2m (6 ½ feet) high which made humans feel rather boxed in. One day Maui's father, here named Ru, decided to prop the sky up with stakes in the ground to lift the sky a little further.

While he was doing so Maui impudently asked him what he was up to, but his father told him to stop his insolence, or he would, as the Mythology Book puts it 'throw him into oblivion'. When Maui persisted with his truculence, Ru hurled him into the sky. Maui saved himself by mutating into a bird, so that he was able to fly away. When Maui returned to his father he came in the form of a giant, much greater in size than Ru. The giant Maui lifted his father over his shoulders which caused the sky to reach the height that it is to this day. Ru's head and shoulders were elevated into the firmament and came to rest amongst the stars. Unable to move, the life was sapped out of him, and, according to the Mythology Book: 'His bones fell to the earth as the pumice stones that litter the volcanic landscape of Polynesia'.

In a tale from New Zealand, after tricking his way out of many difficult situations and defeating many enemies all the while, Maui embarked on the hopeless path of seeking immortality. His father (Akalanama) warned him that death was inevitable, but Maui was not put off. He sought eternal life both for himself and for humanity. His father told him that he would be killed by Hine Nui Te Po, 'the Guardian of Life'. This was a goddess described in the article 'Maui the Demi-God' as having flashing green eyes, teeth made from volcanic glass, a large fish-like mouth and hair that looked like seaweed.

Maui sought to enter the mouth of the goddess, with the intention of stealing her heart, which represented immortality.

He planned to give the gift of immortality to humanity as well as to himself. Maui retrieved the goddess's heart but as he was exiting her mouth, one of his brothers began to laugh and woke the goddess, who snapped shut 'her obsidian teeth' (Maui the Demi-God), killing Maui by breaking him into two pieces. Maui entered the realm of the dead, from which he could never come back.

Maui's deceptive personality was often deployed to come to the aid of humanity, creating the world, stealing the gift of fire to give to the people, and eventually trying to win them eternal life, against the wishes of the other deities. In the end, his mischief inevitably brought about his undoing, and he lost his life in the service of humankind.

Pele

The goddess is known variously as 'Madame Pele', Tutu (grandmother) Pele, Ka Wahine ai Honua (Earth Eating Woman) or is sometimes referred to as Pelehonuamea, meaning 'She Who Shapes the Sacred Land'. According to some sources she created the Hawaiian volcanic island chain. She continues to spew molten lava over the Big Island, the largest in the Hawaiian chain, yet this leads to the creation of new life.

According to Patti Wigington, 'There are 1000s of divine spirits in Hawaiian religion', but Pele is by far the most significant, despite attempts by European settlers to extinguish the indigenous faith.

Although it is today a state of the USA, Hawaii has a long history of conflict with Europeans and American settlers.

The first European to make landfall in Hawaii was Captain James Cook, in 1793. He was soon followed by traders and settlers keen to, as Wigington puts it: 'take advantage of the islands' resources' Missionaries were keen to replace indigenous beliefs with Christianity.

The settlers tried to coerce the islanders into agreeing to a constitutional monarchy in the European model, but one which would accede to their wishes rather than being truly independent.

In 1893, a century after Cook's arrival, Hawaii's Queen Liliuokalani was removed from office by settlers who staged a political coup. This led to unrest amongst the indigenous population and the Queen's arrest for treason. Five years later, the USA annexed Hawaii, but did not achieve the status of America's fiftieth state until 1959.

Even today, according to Wigington, Pele is much feared as 'a goddess of fire, lightning and volcanoes in Hawaiian indigenous religion'. In such a volcanic set of islands, it is not surprising that she is the most worshipped of all the local gods, although she is by no means the most powerful deity and had no role in the creation of the world. As Wigington explains, her parents, the Sky Father and creator god Kane Milohai and the Earth Mother and fertility goddess Haumea wished for her to become a water goddess, but her fascination with fire led her down a different path. As a goddess of fire, she is the personification of this natural element.

She set her home island of Tahiti ablaze, and her elder sister Namaka threatened to deluge the entire island. An alternative story is that Namaka did this in retribution for Pele having an affair with her husband. Some say Pele's father exiled her from Tahiti as a result.

In any case Pele's parents sent her and her other siblings to sea in a canoe to save them from the floods and take them to the safety of another island. After some time, they reached the Hawaiian Islands which are 2,625 miles (4226 KM) from Tahiti, a long way especially for those travelling in a canoe. This is also the way in which the Tahitian people reached Hawaii, which is why they assumed that Pele and her siblings travelled in the same manner.

But soon after they had come ashore on the island of Kauai, Pele's sister Namaka arrived, attacked her, and left her for dead. Pele recovered sufficiently to escape to the neighbouring island of Oahu where she started to dig fire pits, suitable for a deity of volcanoes to live in. But as soon as she dug the pits, her sister filled them up with water.

Namaka chased her to the island of Maui, where she is reputed to have created the Hawaiian volcano, Haleakala. But it was here that Namaka brought about her sister's demise by cutting her to pieces. Yet in death, Pele became a goddess and took up residence in the Kilauea volcano in 'Big Island', where she is reputed to reside to this day.

She had seven brothers with Shark God Kamohoali'I among them. Of her many other sisters, 13 of them shared the same name of Hi'iaka.

One of these was Pele's favourite sibling, but even she could not escape Pele's wrath. According to Liz Turnbull this sister of Pele's spent most of her time singing and dancing and tending to the trees of the sacred grove, with her poet friend Hopoe.

Pele trusted her seemingly innocent sister to bring back one of her erstwhile lovers, a chieftain called Lohi'au, whom she sorely missed. Hi 'iaka agreed to search for the young warrior and bring him back to her sister but as time went by it seemed to become a fruitless task. On her journey she encountered and defeated many demons, who stood in her way. When she eventually found her sister's lover, he lay dying of a broken heart because he thought Pele had abandoned him. Hi'iaka took her magical powers to the limit in trying to restore the young man to life. Despite their developing a strong mutual attraction she obediently returned him to the care of her sister.

But Hi'iaka was gone such a long time that Pele became suspicious and fantasied about the two of them making love. She was so convinced of her sister's infidelity that she burned her sacred groves to a cinder, accidentally killing her sister's friend Hopoe in the process.

When Hi'iaka saw what Pele had done, she made love to the

soldier in front of her, on the edge of the volcanic crater where Pele made her home. Pele responded by bringing forth a lava flow killing them both. When Pele realised how much she loved the man, she ventured into the underworld to seek his return. This is a theme of which there are many examples concerning mythological gods, across the world. But unusually for such stories, Pele's quest was successful, and the couple went on to have a happy marriage.

According to various sources Pele also had a short and tempestuous marriage to the Water God Kamapua'a. It was not long before she wrathfully pursued him with lava flows into the Pacific Ocean. This story represents hydrous volcanic eruptions, where the lava flows into the sea, although in Hawaii such eruptions were rare. Her present-day followers believe that continued volcanic eruptions are a sign that she still resides there.

Volcanic activity in Hawaii is often seen as a sign of her longing for her favourite lover. She is said to have had many of these and her many infidelities and passionate nature are symbolised by volcanic activity.

Pele was well known for her jealousy. She fell for a mortal man named Ohi'a but when he rejected her advances, she became furious and killed him and his chosen lover, Lehua. Pele later came to regret her actions and transformed Ohi'a into a shrub with eternal life and made Lehua into its ever-blooming flowers. Plants of this type, known as the Ohi'a Lehua tree, are the first to spring forth from the volcanic magma that Pele has created, bringing new life out of destruction.

Pele continues to be worshipped today as a sacred symbol of the persistence and resilience of indigenous culture in the face of the settlers' attempts to wipe it out. Pele represents not only the physical features of the Hawaiian Islands, but also the fiery nature of its population (Wigington).

Activities which provoke her fiery wrath include collecting and taking away volcanic rocks and eating certain berries without her permission. Although some locals believe it is a myth, pieces of lava rock taken by tourists are, according to Yordan Zhelyazkov, continually 'mailed back to the islands', in the belief that their removal has brought them bad luck. All of the islanders were at the mercy of Pele's fiery rages.

The Kilauea volcano, where Pele is reputed to continue to reside is as Wigington describes, one of the most active in the world and has erupted from time to time over the last few decades. It usually poses no threat to human habitation, but when it is especially active homes and lives are at risk. With the most serious eruptions, 'entire towns and forests are engulfed' (Young Yamanaka). When this happens, Hawaiians put it down to the displeasure of Pele, and leave out offerings of flowers and leaves in the cracks that form in the local roads, to placate the deity.

It has been reported that Pele often appears in the guise of a good-looking young woman, but on other occasions she appears in the form of an old woman with a white dog. It is believed that she sometimes makes an appearance as a beggar woman. Those who give alms are rewarded, while those who refuse to help are cursed with bad luck.

Apparent sightings of the goddess have been reported in the Hawaiian Islands for centuries, most often in Kilauea with its fearsome volcanic reputation where she made her home. She has also been spotted from time to time at other volcanic sites.

Although she had a fierce temper, Pele did not usually bear grudges. She regretted some of her violent actions such as distrusting her sister and the fury she visited on her as a result, and the deaths of Ohi'a and Lehua. Her fiery temper, like the volcanic magma that represents it, brings renewal in its wake.

Tangaroa

Tangaroa is worshipped across Polynesia as one of the original creator gods. Yet he is worshipped primarily as a god of the sea. His full name is Tangaroa—Whakamau-tai, meaning that he is controller of the tides and the ocean. Other names include Tangaroa – u-timu, which has the same meaning, and on some islands, he is called Tar'aroa, but is seen here as more of a destructive force than a creator.

According to some versions of events, Tangaroa, Kiwa and Kaukau are the three deities appointed at the dawn of time by the primordial couple, Rangi and Papa to be guardians of the sea. Tangarora in particular is the god of all the fish and other sea creatures that swim in the ocean.

As a Polynesian Sea God, he took his responsibilities very seriously not least because the ocean was seen as, as Rose Mulu puts it, the 'foundation of life'. He was also believed to personify the ocean. According to the Taranaki tribe of New Zealand, the ocean has 'four different energies' which represent different aspects of Tangaroa's personality. While it can sometimes be calm and peaceful at other times it is violent and destructive. This is why Tangaroa is particularly venerated by seafarers.

While the names given to the gods are the same throughout

the Pacific Islands, individual tribes have their own mythologies about them at a local level. Nonetheless, Tangaroa was seen by most Polynesians as a major god, and he had a cult status among many tribes.

According to the Māori creation story his parents Rangi and Papa, were, before the creation of the world, locked in a seemingly endless embrace, with their offspring trapped within it. Frustrated with their confinement their children hatched a plan to break free. They pushed against their parents to separate them and escape from their clutches. This caused Rangi to ascend to the sky, where he became the Sky God while Papa descended to the Earth, where she became the Earth Goddess.

Their offspring provided the world with vegetation which symbolically clothed Papa's body. Longing for the return of his wife, Rangi shed tears which rained down from the sky and created the lakes, rivers and seas on the surface of the Earth. A story from North Island states that Tangaroa was one of 70 sons born to this primordial couple including Tane and Rongo.

In Tongan tradition Tangaroa is the Sky God, and founder of the Tongan royal family, who were believed to be his descendants. For this reason, Tongan kings claimed the divine right to rule.

The Ngati-Awa tribe of the Bay of Plenty (North Island, New Zealand) believe he is the husband of Marama, Goddess of the Moon. Tangaroa is linked with the moon in many Polynesian myths. But the mythology of the Pacific islands in general states that he married a woman called Hina.

Some traditions state that he had a son called Punga, who in turn produced two sons of his own named Ikatere and Tutewehiwehi. The children of Ikatere entered the sea and morphed into fish while the children of his brother were transformed into reptiles.

In the Cook Islands Tangaroa is the twin brother of Rongo, born of the primeval parents described as Papa and Vatea. A mythological tale from the islands states that Tangaroa was the creator of fire. According to these stories he visited his brother Maui and pleaded with him to divulge the secret of fire so that he could show humanity how to make it. Tangaroa was warned to go to Maui's home by the straightforward route, but instead took what the University of Wellington website describes as 'the forbidden way of death'.

When the two encountered each other, Maui refused to divulge the secret. This enraged Tangaroa so much that he tried to execute his brother Maui, who managed to fend him off. Tangaroa then again asked Maui for the secret of fire, who again refused his request. This infuriated Maui to the point that he killed Tangaroa. The brothers' parents were so angry that a fearful Maui recited a sacred verse to bring Tangaroa back to life. Tangaroa's life was restored, and he made off with the knowledge of how to make fire.

Some communities including the Tahitians worship Tangaroa as the original creator god, again married to Hina. According to these traditions, he is the creator of the world and everything in it. He first created land, then humans, followed by the heart, the will and the thought which make humanity intelligent beings. He brought the Sun into existence and created night and day. To the Tahitian population he is recognised as the creator of the 'nine heavens' and took up residence in the greatest of these.

But Captain Cook noted of the Tahitians 'their prayers are more generally addressed to Tane', who represented forests and humanity, since this god was believed to play a greater role in people's lives.

Contrastingly, for Hawaiians, he is an evil deity of the underworld. In the Marquesan Islands he is seen as a similar character and is believed to have gone into battle against Atea, the God of Light and Order.

In one story, Tangaroa is said to dwell in the ocean depths with the other beings of the sea. He came into conflict with Manuhau-turuki, son of the god Rua, and killed him. Having done so he set his victim's body up on the roof of his house as a form of decoration. Rua responded by going to the ocean and killing its inhabitants by exposing them to sunlight, which was fatal to such creatures (Uni of Wellington).

An alternative version of events states that Tangaroa had originally been a land-based god but was banished to the sea along with his followers, by Rua, as a punishment for placing Manuhau–turuki's body on the roof of his home, which in this case was on land, after he had killed him.

There is a myth concerning Tangaroa that describes a feud between him and his brother Tane. Tangaroa was angered by the enforced separation of his parents which had been masterminded by Tane. This feud is said to be the reason why humans, supposedly descended from Tane, go out fishing to do battle with Tangaroa's progeny, the fish. All the same they invoke Tangaroa with chanting to secure a better catch.

The offspring of the primordial couple, often assumed to be Rangi and Papa, had their origins as human beings who had been elevated to godly status. Their sons, Tangaroa, Tu, Tane and Rongo were known as 'departmental gods', unlike their parents who were supreme beings. Departmental gods have dominion over specific aspects of nature. These deities, along with the tribal ancestors comprised the pantheon of early Polynesian mythology and were worshipped in various island groups, although stories about them differed from one tribe to another.

Although he is not one of the trio of the most senior departmental gods, which comprises Tane, Tu and Rongo, Tangaroa is the next in order of seniority after these.

Thus, the seniority of Tangaroa varies from one community to another. He is an important god to all of these but to some he is much more significant than he is to others.

Once European settlers arrived, stories that had been passed on by word of mouth were written down for the first time, usually by Christian missionaries, which would obviously be biased against indigenous religion.

In some cases, the most reliable information available about what islanders believed takes the form of traditional chants which islanders continue to sing today. Even if they do not understand the religious significance of what they are saying, the chants do convey the outlines of the mythological tales on which they are based.

The arrival of European settlers and in particular missionaries led to the erosion of indigenous religion. But while most of the gods have faded into obscurity Tangaroa has not been forgotten. This is primarily because as a Guardian of the Sea, islanders still want to keep on the right side of him. Tangaroa persists as a part of Polynesian culture in the present day. As well as the chants that are recited in his name across the region, Tangaroa is also represented on t-shirts and tattoos throughout Polynesia.

Rainbow Serpent

To many Aboriginal peoples of Australia today, the Rainbow Serpent 'is the Great Father and Mother of all forms of life '(AW Reed). Many tribes believe that without the Rainbow Serpent there would be no rainfall, the Earth would dry up and there would be no more life on it. As its name describes, it takes the form of a rainbow-coloured serpent.

The role of the Rainbow Serpent as a giver of life is based on its responsibility for providing rain and oceans and it is also associated with fertility rites.

It is known by countless different names by different Aboriginal tribes, along with a wide variety of stories about how it created the world. What all these myths have in common is that the Rainbow Serpent is regarded as the creator of the world. Goorila and Julunggul are two of its best-known names, while some members of the Yolngu people call it Witiji Witijii and in Queensland it is known as Kanmare.

The gender of the deity also differs from one place to another and the name Julunggul refers to its female manifestation, associated with good health, symbolised by rainbows and colourful flowers. She brings those who are faithful to her both children and healing. As the creator of the world and all that lives in it, Julunuggul is given the epithet 'Giver of Life'.

The Rainbow Serpent brings life-giving rains, but it can also visit deluges of destruction to drown people who offend against it. In its role as a bringer of rains, it is responsible for the fertility of the land and the animals that graze upon it. Additionally, the deity is known as a keeper of the peace. The Rainbow Serpent is not just the creator of plants and animals, but of humans as well, bringing water to the billabongs, rivers, creeks and lagoons.

As well as being a water deity the creature is the protector of life on Earth. According to 'Artlandish', it is venerated as the source of regeneration and reproduction in humanity and nature generally, which makes it the most important deity to the Aboriginal peoples of Australia.

Crucially, when enraged it turns from protection to destruction causing storms and floods by way of retribution. In parts of Australia where monsoons occur, this phenomenon is particularly significant.

When this happens, the serpent swallows people, 'spitting out their bones which turn to stone' (Artlandish). The serpent also kills people by impregnating them with 'little rainbows' which are its progeny.

It is understood to be a huge creature which inhabits deep, permanent waterholes and controls the supply of water. In some traditions it is regarded as the creator of the universe which inhabits the skies.

Archaeologists date the first rock paintings of the serpent to 4000-600 BCE, at the time of the end of the Ice Age when the seas rose. The images are based on the appearance of the Ribboned Pipefish, which would have been washed inland as the seas rose, due to the melting of the ice. The flooding brought warfare amongst the Aboriginal tribes, but eventually this made way for co-operation and the sharing of resources.

Later, the serpent came to be depicted as an elongated

creature with the head of a kangaroo and a crocodile's tail, or sometimes with the head of a bat or even of a human. It was often portrayed with a crest or tresses on its head. While it is illustrated as being single headed it is sometimes shown with a double body in Arnhem Land. Unlike regular serpents, this one is often illustrated with legs and feet and sometimes a tail. It was variously depicted as male, female or hermaphroditic, according to different tribal traditions.

As well as the bat, known to the Australians as a flying fox, the serpent is associated with other animals such as birds, crocodiles, dingoes and lizards.

It is believed by some tribes to be based on the 'Rock Python', while others link it with the 'Water Python', a notably colourful creature.

The Rainbow Serpent is connected with the menstruation of women and their ability to bring life into the world.

The name 'Rainbow Serpent' was coined by anthropologists who brought it to the attention of the wider world, and was used in common to represent the multitude of different tribal names. Although there are different religious traditions, it is believed that the Rainbow Serpent created the landscape by descending from the sky and sliding through the desert on its belly causing hills and valleys to arise, and creating gullies and channels along which water flowed.

The most widely believed story about the Rainbow Serpent is that before it arose the world was a flat, frozen wasteland not suitable for habitation. This was a time known as 'the dreaming' when the deity slumbered with all types of animals in its belly, waiting to give birth to them.

When it was ready, the serpent rose up and called out to the animals to awaken. As it did so it created fire, including that of the Sun. The first animals to appear were the frogs whose bellies were full of water. The creator tickled their bellies and brought forth the water which filled the gouges in the land, making the streams and rivers we see today.

As the water spread across the land, grass sprang up and trees started to grow. With food and drink available, the world was now ready for the animal population. While some lived in the sea, others lived in freshwater or on land while others flew through the sky.

The Rainbow Serpent introduced a set of rules for all animals to follow. If they complied, they would be transformed into humans, but if they disobeyed, they risked being turned into stone.

As Devon Allen explains, for humans, it is generally agreed by different Aboriginal traditions that the Rainbow Serpent was responsible for teaching the laws of 'civil society, morals and ethics.

According to one mythological tale, there came a time when it rained like it never had before, for a long time, and the Earth was flooded. Two young men, known as the Bil Bil or Rainbow Lorikeet brothers, lacking any shelter from the rains, went forward and asked the Rainbow Serpent for help.

The hungry creature tricked the men by saying that the only shelter he could provide was in his mouth. The pair duly entered its mouth and its jaws snapped shut.

But the Rainbow Serpent became increasingly worried that other men would seek out those he had eaten, following their tracks to the creature's mouth. The serpent decided to hide from them in the sky where they would be unable to find it.

Yet when he saw how sad the people were at the loss of their two fellows, he was sorry, and transformed his body into a beautiful multi-coloured ark, to make them cheerful again.

To this day, indigenous peoples believe that when a rainbow appears, the Rainbow Serpent is apologising for taking the two brothers.

Another tale describes how two women, known as the Wawalag sisters, were travelling through the wilderness with their mother, Kunappi, but the Rainbow Serpent was angry with them because they knew ancient secrets. It traced their scent back to the hut in which they were sleeping, symbolising the way a snake enters a hole, and ate them all. But, bitten by an ant, the serpent vomited them up and in so doing created Arnhem Land.

The Rainbow Serpent represents one of the oldest continuing religious beliefs in the world, since it dates back as far as 4000-600 BCE. To this day, indigenous peoples believe that when a rainbow appears, the Rainbow Serpent is 'sharing its beautiful colours' (Dreamtime) with them as an apology for taking the two brothers. Some aboriginals who follow the Christian faith resent its continuing relevance.

As well as its other propensities, such as providing life giving waters and being associated with the menstruation of women, the Rainbow Serpent plays a role in the rituals concerning the transformation of males from youth into manhood.

Today the serpent is especially popular in Queensland where an annual carnival takes place in its honour. There is also a yearly festival in Victoria where the deity is celebrated with 'trance music and abstract art' (Allen). It has also been adopted by groups such as the New Age movement and its colourful symbolism is utilised by the LGBT+ community.

Acknowledgements

Access Genealogy

Adofo, Spencer, Verona 'Folklore Thursday'

Allen, Devon 'Girl Museum'

Apel, Thomas & Kapach, Avi 'Mythopedia'

Artlandish

Auerbach, Patrick 'Greek Gods – the Gods and Goddesses of Greek Mythology'

Bremer, Jan N 'Encyclopedia.com'

Cartwright, Mark 'World History Encyclopedia'

Dashu, Max (feminist historian)

'Dictionary of Greek & Roman Biography & Mythology'

enacademic.com

Gieseke, Annette 'Classical Mythology: AZ'

Goddess of the Month

Gray, David 'Sons of the Vikings'

greekmythology.com

Greenberg, Mike 'Mythology Source'

Groeneveld, Emma 'World History Encyclopedia'

Hamilton, Mae 'Mythopedia'

Hill, J 'Ancient Egypt Online'

Hilohattie Creation Story

Jackson, Jake 'Polynesian Island Myths'

Kapach, Avi 'Mythopedia'

Kyak Tours

Larrington, Caroline 'Norse Myths: A Guide to the Gods & Heroes'

Litchfield, Mary 'Tales of the Gods, Sagas & Heroes'

Maestri, Nicoletta 'Thought Co'

Mark, Joshua J 'World History Encyclopedia'

Marinopoulos College 'Nontaboo and the Algonquin Story of the Creation of the World'

McColman, Carl & Hinds 'The Spirit of the Celtic Gods & Goddesses'

McCoy, Daniel 'Norse Mythology for Smart People'

Meehan, Evan 'Mythopedia'

'Mexicolore'

Mulu, Rose 'Symbolsage'

'Mythology Book (The)'

'New World Encyclopedia'

'The Collector'

Reed, AW 'Aboriginal Myths, Legends and Fables'

Rhys, Dani 'Symbolsage'

Stewart RJ 'Celtic Gods Celtic Goddesses'

'theoi.com'

Turnbull, Liz 'Goddess Gift'

'Valley Isle Excursions'

Von Rosen, Georg

Wellington, University of

White, James 'Handbook of the Indians of Canada'

Wigington, Patti 'Learn Religions'

Wikipedia

Wilkinson, Richard H 'The Complete Gods & Goddesses of Ancient Egypt'

World History Edu

Wright, Gregory 'Mythopedia'

Young Yamanaka, Katie 'hawaii.com'
Zhelyazkov, Yordan 'Symbolsage'
Zimmermann-Holt, Julie

www.ingramcontent.com/pod-product-compliance
Lightning Source LLC
Chambersburg PA
CBHW031121030726
47496CB00002BA/626